THE HOURS OF THE VIRGIN

BY LOREN D. ESTLEMAN

THE AMOS WALKER NOVELS
The Hours of the Virgin
The Witchfinder
Never Street
Sweet Women Lie
Silent Thunder
Downriver
Lady Yesterday
Every Brilliant Eye
Sugartown
The Glass Highway
The Midnight Man
Angel Eyes
Motor City Blue

THE DETROIT NOVELS
Jitterbug
Stress
Edsel
King of the Corner
Motown
Whiskey River

THE PETER MACKLIN NOVELS
Any Man's Death
Roses Are Dead
Kill Zone

OTHER CRIME NOVELS
Peeper
Dr. Jekyll and Mr. Holmes
Sherlock Holmes vs. Dracula
The Oklahoma Punk

WESTERN NOVELS
City of Widows
Sudden Country
Bloody Season
Gun Man
The Stranglers
This Old Bill
Mister St. John
Murdock's Law
The Wolfer
Aces & Eights
Stamping Ground
The High Rocks
The Hider
Billy Gashade
Journey of the Dead
The Rocky Mountain Moving Picture Association

NONFICTION
*The Wister Trace: Classic Novels of the
American Frontier*

SHORT STORY COLLECTIONS
General Murders
The Best Western Stories of Loren D. Estleman (edited by Bill Pronzini and Ed Gorman)
People Who Kill

LOREN D. ESTLEMAN

THE HOURS OF THE VIRGIN

THE MYSTERIOUS PRESS

Published by Warner Books

A Time Warner Company

Mysterious Press books are published by Warner
Books, Inc., 1271 Avenue of the Americas, New
York, NY 10020.

Visit our Web site at www.warnerbooks.com

  A Time Warner Company

The Mysterious Press name and logo are registered
trademarks of Warner Books, Inc.

Printed in the United States of America

First printing: August 1999

10 9 8 7 6 5 4 3 2 1

Library of Congress Cataloging-in-Publication Data
Estleman, Loren D.
    The hours of the virgin / Loren D. Estleman.
      p.   cm.
    ISBN 0-89296-683-1
    I. Title.
PS3555.S84H68   1999
813'.54—dc21   98-48001
                                                    CIP

THE HOURS OF THE VIRGIN

Part One

The Hours of the Paladin

1

I spotted Merlin Gilly standing against the empty space where the Hotel LaSalle had stood two minutes earlier. It was a bum trade.

The hotel had been a going concern in July 1930, when Jerry Buckley signed off his radio broadcast at midnight, went down to the lobby to meet a woman, and was met instead by three men in silk suits who shot him eleven times. They never identified the woman and they never found the shooters, but the memorial service on Belle Isle lit up the sky on both sides of the Canadian border. That was when Detroit was run by the Irish, who thought a wake was better than a trial any day.

In the decades since, the LaSalle had hit all the land-

ings on the slippery back stairs of modern history: resi-
dential hotel, home for the aged, crack house, and black-
ened shell in the biggest ghost town this side of Sarajevo.
Pigeons sailed in through the missing windowpanes and
cartwheeled back out on a contact high from the angel
dust blowing about inside. The time had come to end its
suffering.

The new mayor, dapper in a borsalino hat, tan
Chesterfield with gray suede patches on the lapels, and
gray kid gloves, said a few words on the order of Detroit
rising from its ashes, then squashed down the red button
on a remote control the size of a pocket Webster's.
Following a shuddery pause, the joints of the scabby old
girders blew out, starting at the cigar stand and walking
up toward the presidential suite. Beneath the concus-
sions there was a long, silvery tinkle of several tons of
rose-tinted mirrors collapsing inside, but for a moment
after the final charge went off everything was silent. It
appeared as if the construction methods of the turn of
the last century were more than a match for the high-
tech demolitions of the millennium. But it was just mortal shock. All eighteen stories slid into the foundation in
a single sheet, like a magician's velvet cloth. Dust—marble and mahogany, gold leaf and leaded glass, horsehair
plaster and cut crystal, and worm-eaten Florentine tes-
sellate—rolled out from the bottom and settled over the
galoshes of the TV reporters, car-crash buffs, police officers, and pickpockets watching from outside the yellow
tape.

When it was over, they applauded, whistled, and
cheered as if the relic were making way for a school or
a free clinic. A casino was going in next year, or the year
after that if the Japanese held out. Until then it would be

just another vacant lot in a city with more empty spaces in its skyline than a goal-tender's grin.

Snow covered the ground. The old mayor was in Intensive Care once again, corrupted finally to his vital organs; the spot in front of Henry Ford Hospital where the local news crews shot their stand-ups was beginning to look like a buzzard aviary. His legacy was everywhere. New York and Orlando had placed campaign contributions as carefully as the dynamite men had laid their charges, clearing space in the moral landscape for legalized gambling. The police were beefing up the Domestic Violence Unit for the statistical upsurge once the rent money started disappearing into slot machines. Two new stadiums we didn't need were going in downtown, J. L. Hudson's department store was next in line for destruction, and a couple of dozen long-established businesses were packing their inventories to make room for the chains.

They called it Renaissance. I called it opportunity; but then no one comes to me with work when he's happy.

"Walker! Amos Walker!"

Merlin was shouting and waving, in case I missed the overcoat. I'd have been nobody's idea of a detective if I had. It was a shaggy gray-brown tent that reached to his ankles, heavy enough for a Siberian sleigh ride. The species it belonged to wouldn't have any use for it in the Smithsonian. What it was doing wrapped around somebody like Merlin Gilly went with some story I was probably going to hear.

Pretending I hadn't noticed him wasn't an option. The mayor's white stretch limousine was sliding away through the slush and the crowd was breaking up, off in search of something else to watch fall down. Merlin was heading my way across the flow, dipping in and out among the Carhartts and London Fogs like furry flotsam. Very soon he was standing in front of me, adjusting the big coat and patting down the hairs that had managed to work their way loose from the mousse, as black and shiny as fresh asphalt. He was black Irish, swarthy and small-boned, and taller than he appeared from a distance, although he had the jerky nervous mannerisms and bantam bounce of a born runt.

"Best show in town, am I right?" he said by way of greeting. "Boom! Whoosh! The city's missing a bet. They ought to sell tickets."

"I was just waiting to cross the street."

"You can do that anytime. Motor City, phooey. The Wings ought to practice on Woodward at rush hour."

"Hello, Merlin. What'd you do, skin every rat in your building?"

"Rat? Oh, this?" He shrugged the coat up and down across his shoulders, as if that would improve the fit. He could have turned around inside it and brought a friend. "Pine marten, the genuine article. Go ahead, feel it." He held up a sleeve with manicured fingers sticking out of it. His hands were pink and shiny, like a doll's. He never bent them except to grab a glass or a buck.

I kept mine in my pockets. "I better not. I might startle it."

He felt it himself with his other hand. "It's warm, all right. I wish I could pull it up over my ears." They were as red as banker's dye.

"You should have had them kill the cub too. Then you'd have a hat."

"Aw. You ain't one of them. I seen you eat steak blood

rare. You ever see a picture of one of these in the woods? They're better off on my back."

"I bet you're going to tell me how it got there."

"Over drinks, boy, over drinks. A little premium's what I need to cuddle up with. You know a pump near here? I'm kind of off my lot." He almost never got above Corktown.

"If you mean a bar, there's one around the corner."

"There always is." He beamed. "And this town's got more corners than the country's got Kennedys. Let's go bob for olives."

We went around the corner. I didn't have an appointment with anything but the magazines in my office, and they'd been waiting since Desert Storm. Anyway, Merlin was a man with a mission. This was an accidental meeting the way the Hotel LaSalle had fallen down without help.

The bar was a cigar lounge now. Before that it had been a brew pub, and before that just a bar. They'd torn up six strata of linoleum to find the original oak planks—oiled golden yellow and no more than an inch and a half wide—replaced the slippery red vinyl with brown imitation leather, installed a backbar, paneled the walls, and hung them with rusty advertising signs. Then they'd gone over everything with steel wool and paint remover to make it look old. A cloud of blue Havana smoke hung just under the pressed tin ceiling, but it was last night's exhaust. That time of the morning was reserved for veteran drinkers. Later the young legal sharks from downtown would glide in wearing their Armanis and Donna Karans, firing up Montecristos with gold lighters, talking too loud and slurping Arctic gin from glass funnels, like William Powell and Myrna Loy. By then the reinforcements would be out. Just now the bar was under the sole command of a heavily made-up blonde in tuxedo pants and a man's white dress shirt with a red bow tie, who came over to our booth and took my order for a screwdriver. I was fighting the flu and thought the vitamin C would help. The vodka was just there to help me forget I was drinking orange juice. She turned to Merlin, and the glitter in his eye told me to sit back and shake a smoke out of the pack. He was experimenting again.

"I got something new," he told her. "How's your game?"

She glanced back at the clock, ringed in green neon with a picture of the Rat Pack on the face, and let out some air. "Good enough, I guess. It's early yet."

"You might want to write it down."

"Just jump right in. I'll holler if I get lost."

"Start out with a rocks glass. Mix two ounces Gordon's gin, two ounces creme de cacao"—he pronounced it *cocoa*—"two ounces black coffee. Everything's two ounces, got that?"

She nodded. "*Hot* coffee?"

"Cold if you got it. Throw in ice if you ain't, but don't do a *Titanic* on the son of a bitch. One thing more. A teaspoon of blackstrap molasses."

"Molasses?"

"Most important part. Well, except for the gin." He sat back, beaming. "I call it the Bubonic Plague."

She rolled her eyes and left.

"Still searching for the perfect drink?" I lit a Winston.

"Not no more. I come up with it ten days ago at the Erin, fifteen minutes before closing. That's how I got this coat. Tommy McCarty bet me I couldn't invent a drink before the lights come up that wouldn't send everyone in the joint running to the crapper. He went home wearing that moldy old Harris tweed I bought in Ecorse."

"Congratulations. You shafted your best friend and made the *Bartender's Guide* all in one shot."

"Tommy stopped being my best friend when he voted for Bush."

The barmaid returned and set down my screwdriver and a rocks glass containing a dead black liquid. "Can I interest either of you in a cigar?"

I shook my head. Merlin produced a slim box from an inside breast pocket and stripped off the cellophane. "I got my own, angel cake. Why send thirty bucks to Castro when I can burn ten boxes of Grenadiers for the same price?" He speared a slim green cigar between his lips and leaned over while she lit it with a wooden match as long as a swizzle stick. The stench reminded me I needed to get my brakes relined. When we were alone, he blew a ring at the ceiling and slid his glass my way. "Go ahead, take a hit."

I put out my cigarette in a glass ashtray with a picture of General Grant in the base and sipped. "Not bad." I pushed the drink back across the table. "A little sweet."

"That's the molasses." He looked at the cigar in profile. It was an excuse to admire the half-carat diamond on his pinky. You never knew when Merlin was eating catfood or hauling his wallet around on a hand truck; his suits always fit, even if the coat didn't, and the shine on his cordovans would attract low-flying aircraft. I'd inherited him from Dale Leopold, my late partner. A long time ago, when the Irish were in charge, he had run interference between Mayor Cavanagh and the local building trade. These days he hung around the Erin Go Bar in Corktown, peddling dirt in election years, swapping war stories, and living off a succession of women who thought he could do with a little reforming.

I drank some of my screwdriver and put it down. It tasted like a Bubonic Plague. "Whatever it is, Merlin, it better not cost too much. I haven't had a client in a week."

He stuck a hurt look on his face. It was all skull, bad skin plastered over the cheekstraps and eyesockets. "Dale should of taught you respect. The two of us was like that." The pair of fingers he held up were exactly the same length.

"His dying words? 'Don't give Merlin Gilly the time of day if you expect to get it back.'"

"Dying words my ass. He was dead on arrival at the pavement."

I shrugged out of my belted coat. The sight of him in all that fur overheated me, but he hadn't broken a sweat. If he ever did it would come out pure Gordon's gin. "Paper says snow," I said. "I've got a throbbing rib says the same thing. A bullet splintered it eighteen years ago last November."

"Who cares? I got something will cost you an easy fifty."

"I don't have any easy fifties. What can I get for a sweaty sawbuck?"

He filled his mouth with smoke and let it roll out. A complacent Merlin Gilly is harder to look at than a C-section. I folded two twenties and a ten into a tight rectangle and walked it across the back of my hand. That fascinated and irritated him. Parlor tricks weren't in his repertoire.

"Guy downtown needs a good detective. They're all busy so I thought of you."

"Jail or Holding?"

"DIA."

I walked the bills back the other way. "DIA to me stands for the Detroit Institute of Arts. What's it stand for to you?"

"Same thing. You think I ain't got no culture? I gaped at a Van Gogh there once." He pronounced both *g*'s.

"Forget it, Merl. Where would you fence it?"

He thought about getting mad, then let it blow. "This is about missing property. There's a ten percent finder's fee, might run ten grand."

"Stolen painting?"

"A book, if you can believe it. I mean, with the liberry right across the street, where you can borrow one free gratis and nobody chases you. Crime's gone to hell in this town."

"When did you ever borrow a book?"

He pushed back his chair. "I come up here to do you a turn, you insult me. I guess I'm leaving."

"You're still sitting." But I stood the fifty on its end within his reach. He scooted up his chair and stuck the rectangle in the pocket with the cigars.

"His name's Harold Boyette. He's got him a private line." He gave me a number from memory. I pulled out my notebook and scribbled. "Some kind of old book expert," he said. "I guess there's a living in it. I'm a people person myself."

"Uh-huh. All dead presidents." I put away the notebook.

"Hey, if I started paying taxes now, Uncle Sam would have a stroke."

"Who's your source?"

"Cost you another fifty."

I moved a shoulder and drank orange juice and vodka. "I never knew you to take the short money when there was more than a hundred to be made."

"Aw, you know my contacts. All they know about books is the point spread in Cincinnati." He glanced at the clock, pressed out his Grenadier, and picked up his drink. "I'm due at the Erin. Get this?" He cocked an elbow toward the check the barmaid had left.

"Why should today be any different? Got a date?"

He grinned. His teeth were his only good feature and he took care of them. "Auto money. She thinks I look like Johnny Depp."

I played with my glass.

"I never figured you for screwdrivers," he said.

"I'm fighting a bug."

"That ain't the way to do it. You need hot Vernor's and Smirnoff's, half and half."

"What do you call it?"

He finished his Bubonic Plague and set it down, gently and with pity. "You only get to name one drink. Everybody knows that."

2

My building had changed hands from a corporation based in Phoenix to a doctors' syndicate with a P.O. box in Toronto. The immediate difference to me was I had to put on an extra stamp when I mailed my rent check. The next involved workers in radiation suits punching holes in the hallway ceiling outside my office and scooping out asbestos insulation by the bushel. I'd been offered the chance to relocate until they'd finished replacing the carcinogens with blown-in fiberglass, but I bought an extra carton of cigarettes instead, on the same theory that snake venom was used to treat snakebite. My clients' thinking was less advanced. I hadn't had a walk-in since before the new year.

One glance at the waiting room told me my record was intact. I shut both doors to muffle the whining of power tools and dialed the number Merlin Gilly had given me. The line purred several times before Harold Boyette came to the telephone. He didn't sound anything at all like George Arliss in an old movie set in a museum. He was surprised to hear from me, wouldn't discuss his situation or admit that he had one over the wire, but asked for references. I gave them to him and we banged out an appointment for that afternoon. I hung up with the prospect of earning half a year's income before Easter. Some mornings are like that. About one in ten thousand.

On my way downstairs later I excused myself to get around one of the asbestos workers, who had shed his hood to light up an unfiltered Camel. I had a convert.

The car radio was all talk, no music. WJR was interviewing an environmental scientist in California about global warming. They broke for a weather bulletin about a winter storm watch and record cold temperatures, then returned to the subject. I punched up an old-time radio drama on WXYT. G-men Charles McGraw and Frank Lovejoy were closing in on a counterfeiting ring when I pulled behind the DIA. I was five minutes early, so I left the motor running with the heater on until they shot the leader and arrested the others. There was no mention of the ozone.

I walked around the dead gray granite walls of the 1966 addition, leaning into the wind, and let myself in the white marble front. In the lobby, the Ford line workers in the Rivera mural went on assembling Model A's and paid me no more attention than they had the artist.

Henry had solved the problem of showboating for visitors by scheduling daily public tours for fifty years.

The woman behind the admissions desk, silver-haired and immaculate in a navy blazer and blue silk blouse, took my donation and handed me a map to the galleries. On my way through the American wing a security guard with an African tribal insignia tattooed on the back of one hand looked me over quickly and nodded a greeting. I was wearing a new suit.

"Amos Walker? Pleased to meet you. Sorry about the venue. My office is being renovated."

Harold Boyette looked even less like George Arliss than he sounded over the telephone. He was just in the shade of thirty, soft-looking but not fat in a medium-gray suit with a light violet stripe, tailored to blend into walls. His sandy hair was thinning, his eyes were too small, and his ears too flat to his head. He had strawberry lips, fascinatingly moist, red, and ready to pick. It was a little boy's mouth, untouched by the cynical years. His grip was firm enough, and dry; all that contact with old parchment would leech the water out of a rice paddy. In his left hand, he was carrying a burgundy leather briefcase with a brass combination lock.

The venue was one of the larger galleries open to visitors. The ceiling was high and the indirectly lit walls were painted an unobtrusive shade of white. We were surrounded by bold slashes of color on old canvas: reclining duchesses, simian-faced royal families, and sundry atrocities involving scythes and sabers and French soldiers in uniform, still vibrant under layers of varnish ancient and modern. The Goya exhibit was in its second week.

"I thought the DIA was in a money crunch," I said.

"A chronic condition. I'm paying for the renovation out of my own pocket. You see, I'm a collector as well as a consultant. Books and antiquities are one market that never goes down, and I've done well by keeping track of what happens at auction. I spend a great deal of time in that office and I don't share my predecessor's infatuation with sisal and bleached oak."

"I'm stuck with an avocado-green stove and refrigerator myself." We were alone in the room with a guard, this one female. "Lonely work."

Boyette rearranged his ripe lips into a scowl. "There's an auto show going on at Cobo Hall and the Red Wings are in the running for the playoffs. That's stiff cultural competition for a simple Spaniard whose paintings changed the course of empire in Europe. It wasn't always this way, not even in a blue-collar town like Detroit. Society's gone into a tailspin with God knows what waiting at the bottom."

"Probably a private detective. You want to go somewhere, or do you plan on yodeling later?"

"Sound does travel here. I've converted a storeroom in the south wing into a workspace, if you have no objection to clutter."

"Clutter is my business."

We passed down a series of carpeted corridors and through a couple of thousand years of Roman emperors, South American fertility gods, gaunt mummies, and fat prosperous Flemish silk merchants done in slick marble; up a shallow flight of stairs, through a fire door marked AUTHORIZED PERSONNEL ONLY, and along a dusty linoleum-paved hallway with splotches of gray spackle on the unpainted walls. Here the hum of an industrial-grade humidifier—or maybe it was a dehumidifier, I never get

that straight—clicked on and off like the respirator for a
culture on the critical list. Near the end he fished out a
black leather key case, unlocked a blank door, and
switched light into a room that was a kind of charnel-
house of dead civilizations.

"Be it ever so ugly," he said, stepping aside for me to
enter ahead of him, "it's home to me. At least for the time
being."

It was a big space, whitewashed and windowless, with
a bare plywood floor and exposed ceiling joists. A large
worktable like the kind tailors used to cut out patterns
on took up most of the room, piled high with rolled documents, empty plaster frames, and miles of bubble wrap.
A network of narrow aisles wound among odd items of
statuary, leaning canvases, porcelains in crates, and
chunks of classical architecture, some of it sheeted, the
rest naked under a skin of chalky dust. It looked like
Charles Foster Kane's basement.

I brushed a plaster bust off a pedestal with my elbow
and rescued it in a diving catch. The subject was a bald
geezer in a toga, with a seriously hooked nose and that
skeejawed expression you see on the face of an antiques
dealer when you've traded a hundred dollars for a rusty
Coleman lantern you could buy new in an Ace Hardware
for less than fifteen. I set the bust back up without shaking or wetting myself.

"Reproduction of a Victorian attempt at neoclassicism."
Boyette closed the door. "Thirty-eight bucks plus tax in
the gift shop. Did it give you a turn?"

"No, green is my natural color. Is all of this stuff fake?"

"No, much of it's genuine, either awaiting exhibition or
in transition to better storage. Trivia, for the most part;
students of students and one-time great masters forgot-

ten by history and the fickle antiquities market. We keep
the really valuable stuff in a vault." He stood looking
around, like a visitor. "I come here often to order my
thoughts. There's so much hope in these objects, so
many grand plans untainted by reality. The authentic ge-
niuses burned themselves out young. Rembrandt became
prosperous and dull, then just dull. Rodin grew as cold
as his stone. In their prime they never approached the
kind of wide-eyed, pathetic hope you find in these fel-
lows. Too rich a diet can make you just as miserable as
plain bread and water."

"I thought your specialty was books."

"Sorry. It's the building. You can't pass someone in the
hall without some of his obsession rubbing off on you. I
know quite a bit about early American rugs as well, and
far too much about Chinese bottles."

We were standing on opposite sides of the big table.
He cleared a corner and laid down his briefcase while I
hung my coat on a convenient centaur.

"I checked your references," he said. "I hope you don't
consider those people your friends."

"I don't work for friends. Did they say anything ac-
tionable?"

"That's between you and your counsel. They did say
you're honest, in a slippery sort of way. They also said
you get results. I was given to understand those results
might not be what I requested."

"They almost never are."

"You haven't said yet who told you I needed a private
investigator."

"I wouldn't wait."

After a moment he nodded, as if that were the right

answer. "I assume you have a badge, or something else that will prove you're who you say you are."

I got out the folder and flipped it onto his side of the table. "You won't find that badge number on the active list in Wayne County," I said. "The sheriff's department called them all in years ago, but they forgot that one. It scares away kids on Devil's Night. The ID's current."

He looked at it carefully, then slid the folder back toward me. "You take a lousy picture."

I put it away without comment.

"I suppose I was foolish to think a secret can survive in the Age of Information. That's the reason I didn't go to the police. However, you're here, and if what I learned about you is the worst of it, I'm satisfied." The strawberry lips formed a smile. "All this is an academic's long-winded way of saying the job is yours if you want it. You may not, once you've heard the details."

"I heard there's a finder's fee involved."

"The missing item is worth at least a hundred thousand dollars. It could sell at auction for as high as a million, but I'll guarantee to pay ten thousand based on the original estimate, when the item is in my hands and I have determined it to be genuine."

"I'd like that in writing."

"You'll have it."

"So far I'm okay with the details."

"I'm not an employee of the DIA," he said. "I'm an independent consultant, currently under contract here as an authority on the illuminated manuscripts of the fifteenth century. Are you familiar with the subject?"

"Monks, right?"

"That's the popular conception: hooded ascetics hunched over desks in drafty cloisters, laboriously copying out devotional passages letter by elaborate letter. But they had competition in the secular world. For four hundred years, a handful of monasteries and commercial workshops were the sole producers of books in Europe. In many cases they enhanced the beauty of their work by creating illustrated borders and further decorating, or illuminating, the ornamental first letter of each page with precious metals and semiprecious stones.

"My area of study involves the manuscripts of the late period," he went on. "They reached their exquisite peak just before Gutenberg and the invention of movable type; but I'm pontificating. We're here to discuss the Plymouth Book of Hours."

"That's what's missing?"

"Have just a little more patience with me. The *Horae*, or Books of Hours, were commissioned from workshops as manuals of private devotions. They contained a calendar of saints' days and feast days, lessons of the gospel, specific hours of services, and assorted prayers. The Plymouth book is a masterpiece, executed on vellum in letters of gold and lapis lazuli for the wedding of a royal duke. It's in the British Museum in London."

"So it isn't missing."

"Only part of it. One section, devoted to Mary, the Holy Mother, disappeared at the end of World War Two. I found it."

"Congratulations." I wanted a cigarette, but the air in the room was dry and I didn't want to burn any history.

"Thank you. More precisely, I supervised its acquisition for the DIA. During the Blitz, the various sections were divided and removed for safekeeping to the country homes of certain trusted museum employees. All of them were returned after the war, except the Hours of the Virgin.

"I was approached last fall by a prelate with the local Catholic archdiocese, who informed me that upon the death of a parishioner, certain of the man's personal possessions were donated to the church in accordance with the terms of his will. It seems the deceased was an American infantryman billeted in the English countryside during the war. He brought home a number of souvenirs. At the end of his life he had a change of heart and made arrangements to return the most religious of these items to God's house. Of course I'm talking about the long-missing section of the Plymouth Book of Hours."

"The church decided to give it to the DIA?"

"To keep it would have been illegal," he said. "It's a British national treasure. Let's just say the prelate's honesty was rewarded by a generous contribution to the archdiocese. It would have been cheap at many times the price. The Hours is a major find."

"I'm surprised I didn't read about it."

"We were keeping it quiet until we could negotiate with the U.K. for the Hours' return. I have my eye on some incunabula the British Museum is sitting on; an exclusive U.S. exhibition would be the envy of every library in the country." He rested a hand on his briefcase. I was beginning to wonder about that case. "Only a few here were let in on the secret. But it's a large, echoing building. People hear things. You heard."

"When did you notice it was missing?"

"Christmas Day. I came in to remove some things from my office before the carpenters came. The manuscript was gone from the cabinet where I'd put it the day before. I should have placed it in the vault, but I wanted to finish translating it while it was in our hands. The cabinet was locked. It just never occurred to me there was any real danger. It's not the sort of theft one associates with Detroit."

"Don't underestimate the place. Who do you suspect?"

"A former employee. We'll go into that later. The office was locked, but there are any number of keys floating around. I planned to have the lock changed when I remodeled. So far as I know, I have the only key to the cabinet."

"Cabinets are easy. How does one go about fencing a thing like that?"

"One doesn't. One sells it back to the people he stole it from."

"Uh-huh," I said; and I meant it. "What's in the case?"

He tapped his fingers on it, lips pursed. Then he stood it up facing him and used his thumbs on the combination wheels.

3

"This arrived Friday," Boyette said. "Priority mail, not even registered."

When the lock clicked, he unlatched the briefcase and drew out a scuffed leather portfolio tied with a cord. He set the case on the floor, moved aside a Chinese dog with one ear broken off, and laid the portfolio on the table. He paused with his fingers on the cord, looking at me.

"An old Celtic legend maintains that only the clean in spirit may read the words of the Lord. All others are struck blind."

"Fortunately, I flunked Latin." I waited.

He slipped the knot and spread open the portfolio.

There was a fold of something inside, unbleached flannel or thin fleece, followed by a sheet of gauzy paper, and he peeled that away like a silken undergarment. When he finally got down to it, it was smaller than I thought, no larger than a leaf of ordinary drugstore bond, buff-colored and wrinkled all over like very old skin, which is what it was, the membrane of unborn lamb or something like that. The fetus it belonged to had died nearly six hundred years ago without ever seeing the light.

The first letter of the text was an *L.* It was hard to miss because it covered most of the page, raised slightly and chased with gold and the purplish blue that Boyette had identified as lapis lazuli, ground with a stone pestle into a fine dust and sprinkled over animal adhesive or whatever else passed for glue in the days when Columbus was still floating ships in his bathtub. A bordered background depicted biblical scenes in fine lines of brown ink, colored in with vegetable dye, faded but still vivid long after the illustrator had returned to the soil. The writing itself, done in Gothic pointed letters, was Latin, which as I said was all Greek to me.

"Nice," I said, straightening.

"Is that all you have to say?"

"It's a little gaudy. Is there any more to it?"

"There are nine pages in all. This is the only one that was returned."

"Sure it's genuine?"

"Of course," He rummaged among the clutter on the table, found a Sherlock Holmes magnifying glass with a fat wooden handle, and held it above the bottom left corner of the page. "Take a look."

I bent over the glass. What looked at first like an old bubble in a blob of ink turned out to be horseshoe-shaped and serrated inside, like a tiny pincer. It was smaller than the head of a pin. "Is that what I think it is?"

"Pthirius inguinalis," he said. "The common crab louse. This is one fellow who preferred not to spend all his time at his desk. I'd noticed it the first time this page was in my possession. I seriously doubt anyone could duplicate it."

"Nor want to. Was there a note?"

"No." He put down the glass, recovered the page, closed and tied the portfolio, and returned it to the brief-case. "Yesterday he called with his demand."

"He?"

"The suspect is a man. He didn't even try to disguise his voice. He wants a hundred thousand dollars for the safe return of the remaining pages. He knows they're worth at least that, and that we'll pay it to keep him from destroying the Hours of the Virgin. A loss like that can't be calculated in dollars and cents. As well try to write a fire insurance policy on the great library at Alexandria."

"Then you're going to pay it."

"I jeopardized an irreplaceable treasure once. I won't repeat the mistake."

"Who's coming through with the cash, you or the shop?"

"I can't ask this institution to foot the bill for my mis-take." He locked the briefcase. "The instructions for the exchange were explicit. It's an enormous responsibility, particularly on the way back, as we'll be in actual pos-session of the manuscript. That's why I'm willing to pay you ten thousand dollars for your protection. I assume you own a gun."

I said I might have one lying around. "We might need it on the way in too. There are still a few unenlightened mugs who would rather put their mitts on a hundred grand than an old picture book. You don't have to go along," I added. "I'm bonded up to a million."

"That's not the point. This person knows me, and I've been told to come alone. I can't accept the risk of a clumsy substitution."

"The alone part's a poser too. I won't fit in your brief-case."

"Oh, but it's a public place. We could go in sepa-rately." He produced a fold of paper from an inside breast pocket and snapped it open. "I'm to bring the money to a place called the Tomcat Theater on Tele-graph Road at seven o'clock tomorrow evening. Do you know it?"

"By reputation. Lobby, auditorium, or toilet? Pardon the redundancy. The Tomcat isn't the Fox. The Detroit Vice Squad has season passes."

"Auditorium. I'm to put the money in a large mailer in hundred-dollar bills, seal it with tape, and sit in the front row, putting the package on the floor beside my seat. The feature begins at seven. If I turn my head or leave before it ends—"

"Standard. He must be planning to jump town or he'd ask for smaller bills. They're easier to pass, but they're less portable. Can you get the money together on such short notice?"

"I have it already." He read my face. "I told you I'm a collector. Sometimes collections that have been out of circulation for many years suddenly become available on terms of a rapid sale. I maintain a liquid operating fund for just such a contingency."

"I do the same thing with cigarettes. You probably

could have bought more time. If he thinks you're too eager he might bump up the price at the last minute."

"Time isn't on my side. Apart from the threat of deliberate destruction, every minute the manuscript is exposed to oxygen and modern pollutants contributes to its decay. He knows that as well as I."

I sucked a cheek. I shouldn't have mentioned cigarettes. "Museum theft is FBI jurisdiction now. Those spooks in the federal building can hang on to a secret in a hurricane. You might have tried them."

"I'm not satisfied the Justice Department would approve of any of the actions that have been taken in this affair," he said. "An American GI succumbs to the common temptation to smuggle a souvenir home, his priest comes to me in confidence and with the thought of helping his parish, I take steps to restore a native document to its rightful owner and incidentally contribute to the prestige of the institution for which I work. Then Washington steps in and it all becomes perverted. If I honestly thought federal involvement would improve my chances of recovering the Hours of the Virgin, I'd take my chances and we wouldn't be having this conversation. My loyalty belongs to something bigger than any one government."

"You sound like a one-man militia. Okay, no feds. I don't like them either." I sneezed.

"Bless you. That's a nasty cold. Are you doing anything for it?"

"Just what you heard."

"You ought to take zinc tablets. How shall we manage the exchange?"

I used my handkerchief. "I'll be parked out front at six. You can't miss my crate: blue Olds Cutlass, white vinyl top, battered fenders. You've probably got one just like it on display in the Mesopotamian Wing."

"We don't have a Mesopotamian Wing."

"It's an old car, Mr. Boyette. You wouldn't look at it twice in this town. But it's got a big Cadillac engine and burns regular gas like the Armored Cavalry. What kind of car do you drive?"

"Yellow Toyota. This year's model."

"Shame on you."

He smiled as dryly as one can with lips like his. "That's not the first time I've heard that. I had my tires slashed three times before I caught on and started parking in a guarded lot."

"Next time buy an Expedition. I'll follow in my car and go in and catch the show a couple of minutes behind you. I'll be seated a few rows back where I can see everything. For obvious reasons they never turn the lights down at the Tomcat."

"I thought you only knew the place by reputation."

"That was a joke, like the one about my car. I don't get to go to many book auctions in my work." I gave him a moment to feel worse about that than I did. "My day rate's five hundred, nights too. I normally charge three days up front, but since this one promises to wrap up before Ted Koppel I'll let it slide."

"I offered you ten thousand."

"And I'll take it, minus the five hundred, if we get the Virgin back in the vault where she belongs with her virtue intact. Until then I need to maintain a liquid operating fund."

He scribbled with a fat gold pen in a leather folder, tore out a check, and stuck it at me. "I'll write up our agreement tonight and send it around to your office in the morning by messenger."

I put the check in my wallet. "Does your suspect have a name?"

He fumbled getting the checkbook and pen back into his pocket, missing it the first time. The die was cast, he was going out to make a ransom drop.

"He does. Accounts Payable fired him last month for embezzlement. It was a simple scheme, and ingenious: He opened accounts in several banks using the names of various companies the DIA does business with, drew the checks himself, and deposited them, withdrawing the money later. There was no telling how much longer he might have gone on if one of his own office-mates hadn't happened to turn over one of the canceled checks and seen his signature on the endorsement."

"Is the DIA prosecuting?"

"Individual cash contributions are important to the institution's survival. That source would dry up rapidly if it got out a thief was employed here. The board of directors thought it wiser to just let him go. He cleaned out his desk Christmas Eve. Would that that were all he decided to clean out."

"Cheer up. He could have come back with an AK-47. I take it no one knows where he's living."

"I doubt very much his last action was unpremeditated. I'm one historian who doesn't believe in coincidence." He considered my question. "He rented a house on Kercheval. I called his landlady. She said he moved out some time ago, naturally without leaving a forwarding address. He didn't work here long, perhaps a year. His name is Earl North."

I hesitated, then went ahead and plucked a Winston

out of the pack. I rolled it along my lips until I found the groove, but I didn't light it. "Is there a picture?"

"They may still have one in Personnel, but the fewer people who know about this the better. Anyway, it's not necessary. I'm engaging you to help me get back the manuscript, not bring the man who stole it to justice."

"Describe him."

"Why? I just said—"

"He might come in late. If I know what he looks like I'll be more alert when he shows up. Maybe I'm getting old, but skinflicks just put me to sleep."

"I barely knew him well enough to say hello to. Your height, I think, slighter build. Red hair fading at the temples. I think he had a bald spot on the back of his head. Middle forties."

"Blue eyes?"

"I think"—he screwed up his soft pale face, looking at the ceiling joists for inspiration—"yes. Sort of washed out, almost gray. How did you guess that? Do you know him?"

"Well enough to say hello to. A long time ago he killed my partner."

4

I cranked up the Cutlass and joined the rest of the statistics on their way home. I'd been feeling hungry, not having eaten since breakfast, and I never eat breakfast; but I'd left my appetite in that windowless room behind the green-faced Madonnas and bearded-lady Christs at the Detroit Institute of Arts. I passed the handful of restaurants that had managed to survive twenty years of local government-by-Swiss bank account like a eunuch in the locker room at the WNBA.

Woodward was quiet at that hour, as it had been at most hours since plastic; the population had dipped below a million in the last census, prompting the old mayor to demand a recount and bus in enough of humanity's loose change to keep the gravy flowing. The scraped gray of January without snow had the Motor City's main street in its bony grip. Old sports sections and empty Styrofoam cups slid and capered along the pavement, rattling like loose teeth. The Detroit Public Library, my voting address when I wasn't eating stale cheese sandwiches behind the wheel waiting for a door to open or a car to pull out of a lot, looked as bleak and uninspired as the spray-painted obscenity drizzling down the stone steps in front. I read it aloud and with feeling.

I know you like the old movies, kid, Dale Leopold had said the day I joined the agency, doubling its size. *Go ahead and watch, but don't buy into 'em. They're not liars, just selective. For every hour you spend pumping hard-asses down by the docks for leads, you'll spend a week polishing a chair with your pants in the library or schmoozing with some gassy records clerk in the basement of the City-County Building; some mook you wouldn't stop to throw a rope to if he was drowning in the Rouge. It ain't so bad. You might even get to like it. That's when you'll know your edge is gone. You forget you're still doing cop work, and that eye in the back of your head heals over. Then you might as well throw yourself down a stairwell, because you're through.*

Good advice, and he proved just how good it was when he forgot it himself. Routine tail job: track the bored-to-the-balls-of-his-feet middle executive through the extramarital jungle, note where he stops and for how long, and report back to his wife, a slam-dunk. The infidelity was the only colored thread in the monochromatic skein of Earl North's life. The scenario, chiseled in granite by Piltdown Woman's divorce attorney and never revised, called for the wandering spouse to come across with a fat settlement when confronted with the evidence of his unimaginative little affair. North, a gray super- numerary chiefly engaged in taking up space for thirty years or so in a rabbit-warren of corporate cubicles—not counting two weeks each August in a time-share condo on Lake Michigan—was no challenge for any investiga- tor with half Dale's experience. He only took the job to cover a quarterly tax payment. The best he had to look forward to in the way of entertainment was an attempt to buy him off, and even that was way out of character for this particular pigeon.

That the pigeon would suddenly turn into a cornered rat, swing around with a gun in his hand, and pump three bullets into his shadow was a scene from another movie slipped in between reels. Dale had once claimed that nothing had surprised him since the day his mother parked him at the Michigan Central station and stepped off the center span of the Ambassador Bridge, but he'd have been the first to laugh at the look on his face when a sleepy attendant pulled out his drawer for me at the Wayne County Morgue. He was fifty-one.

The funeral was as bland and respectable as a covered dish. He'd have preferred the tragic poetry of Willie Loman's, but he'd made too many connections in twenty-five years at the same stand. In addition to his es- tranged wife and grown daughter, the procession had in- cluded friends from the police department and the county prosecutor's office, from which he'd been bounced as an investigator when the city administration changed color along with most of the area bureaucracies; the sheriff's chief of detectives, who had partnered him on the old Detroit racket squad; and a couple of Jackson prison alumni whose kids had clothes because Dale had pretended the information they gave him was worth an occasional twenty, although he'd have broken your nose if you called him on it. There was a number of old girl-friends as well, tough-faced redheads with nicotine stains between their fingers, who bawled all through the eu-logy, delivered by a former Detroit police chaplain, who closed with a reading of the epigraph from John O'Hara's *Appointment in Samarra*.

Instructions for the disposal of the remains, written in Dale's thick scrawl and locked in a box in his desk, were specific. He was cremated, and the ashes were placed in the care of his surprised sister, who he'd once said was fond of complaining that he never gave her anything.

The new county prosecutor didn't like the case against Earl North. The gun used in the murder never surfaced, no eyewitnesses came forward, and thanks to Dale's lone-saddle methods and refusal to maintain a formal log, there was nothing to place the accused at the scene. But he took it to the grand jury, possibly because he re-gretted canning his best investigator to make way for a Wayne State University graduate with a law degree and no practical experience, but more likely because Dale had left a partner to make sure he didn't forget to regret it. The jury heard the case, deliberated for forty minutes, nol-prossed, and went to look for their umbrellas. North was headed home on the John Lodge before the judge left the Old County Building.

Dale would have appreciated especially the role played by North's wife, the woman who had hired Dale to tail him. Called to testify, she told the jury her husband was home with her in Redford Township at the time of the shooting, asleep in bed.

*People suck, kid. Thank Christ for it, or we'd both be
calling folks at home trying to sell them storm windows.*

It could have been somebody else, of course. Had he
bothered to keep one, the Leopold Enemies List would
have run as long as *Cats,* and several of them were out
on parole. But his eyes and reflexes were better than
those of most detectives half his age, and his memory
was a mug file of all the faces he'd seen since age ten;
none of his anti-fans would have gotten that close. All
three of the bullet wounds were in front and delivered at
close range. If it was robbery, the thief had overlooked
his Chronograph watch and his wallet with the five hundred dollars he carried for emergencies folded in the
change compartment.

The North case was the only thing Dale had had on at
the time, and Mullett Street at 3:00 A.M. Tuesday, a street
where it's always Tuesday at 3:00 A.M., even at seven on
a Saturday evening, wasn't the kind of place he'd go jog-
ging even if he lived within three miles of the place and
didn't think joggers had Ben-Gay for brains to begin
with. There was nothing in the neighborhood to draw a
middle-aged detective that far from his house to walk off
a case of insomnia.

What was there was a joint named the American Eagle
Motor Lodge, frequented by a hooker who called herself
Star LaJoie. It was a tinselly kind of name with a little bit
of originality, rare among the breed, and you tended to
remember it. Particularly when it appeared several times
in Dale's barely legible notes on the case. Particularly
when the woman who went by it never returned from
her annual convention migration to Miami Beach. That
was as much as the night clerk at the Eagle, a needle
hound with his own drawer at Detroit Narcotics, knew

about his regular guest. He couldn't even describe her, and if she had a record with Vice it was under some other name.

The other coin on North's side of the scale wasn't evidence, even if I weren't the only one who seemed to have witnessed it. It was the way his wife looked at him when the prosecutor was asking the big question, and the way North's hands gripped the edge of the defense table during the long pause before she answered. And it was the way the smile bagged on his face immediately afterward.

Three weeks later, husband and wife were back in court, agreeing on a divorce settlement whose terms were sealed. But I didn't need the details. I'd seen the negotiation.

The first street sign I was aware of since I'd pulled away from the DIA belonged to my street a block west of Hamtramck, and I had to jam on the brakes to make the turn. I might have driven through an artillery barrage for all I remember of the trip. Driving's like that sometimes; the same as smoking and shaving and not blowing your skull through your scalp because you've got a dentist's appointment Friday. Habit.

The house isn't much, like all the others on the block except for those with a new brick facade or a windmill on the lawn, two of the dozen or so things you can do to a 1946 tract job to express your uniqueness short of violating the anti-blight ordinance or putting up a Republican poster in a town still mired in the New Deal. Attached garage, shared driveway, white aluminum siding gone chalky like the paint on a junked Studebaker, an asphalt roof with a leak that was as easy to track down as Jimmy Hoffa. A home, when you're in a good mood. Three rooms and a Michigan basement between you and the Perpetual Mission when you aren't. I cranked up the thermostat, checked the cupboard above the sink for the bottle I knew damn well I'd put out with Tuesday's trash, found a third of a six-pack in the refrigerator, and worked on that at the kitchen table until I felt warm enough to climb out of the overcoat. Coughing, I wandered into the living room and stood looking at the one good easy chair, the rows of records in their sleeves in the cabinet, the little bookcase containing Dale's collection of first-edition John O'Haras; my inheritance. Looked at it all like the furnishings in someone else's house. Someone I didn't know too well. The antique clock said *tick* and then Russia fell and apartheid went out of favor and CD's replaced LP's and Carl Perkins died and eleven guys with medals of valor got the sack for using the *F* word to a female staffer and then the clock said *tock*. It needed cleaning and winding, so did I. The rest of the world was running on quartz.

Into the bedroom and the scorched-metal smell of stale cigarettes and nobody lying on the west side of the mattress to nudge me and say I shouldn't smoke in bed. A dresser drawer I opened only once a month contained a sprinkling of old curled snapshots and a box. I did a quick inventory: a couple of wedding pictures someone had taken with a Polaroid, the old kind you had to peel apart, because there's not enough room for a professional photographer and all his equipment in a judge's chambers; a formal posed shot before an American flag of a youthful roughneck in dress khakis, the edges of the picture still creased from the frame; the same youth in civvies, hair grown out, grinning and clasping the hand of a shortish square-built man twice his age with a crisp crewcut that would never go gray and a thicket of creases around his eyes from squinting at bad handwriting in old plat books and peering through binoculars. Behind them hung a pebbled-glass door lettered:

APOLLO CONFIDENTIAL INVESTIGATIONS
D. Leopold, Pres.   A. Walker, Vice Pres.

The black paint of the last four words still glistened, fresh as a second chance.

The box that shared the drawer with the pictures had held White Owl cigars until the day Dale gave his word to his doctor he'd smoked his last one. The doctor didn't believe it, but from that day to his death he kept his promise, depositing the precise amount that he would have spent on smokes at the end of each month in a college fund under his daughter's name. He'd kept the passbooks there, but they had gone to her after the funeral. Now the box contained his obituary from the *Free Press*, gone as brown as the cigars that had preceded it, and a Colt .45 Army semiautomatic pistol. He'd carried it ever since Monte Cassino, but since V-E Day he had only fired it on the police range. The cops who investigated his shooting had found it in the glove compartment of his battered black Plymouth Fury, parked around the corner from where he'd fallen. *It's your wife and your best buddy, kid; are the top kicks still teaching that? If they ain't, the hell with them and today's army too. Friends and wives ain't much good if you don't keep 'em to hand.* You can always tell authentic wisdom from idle blather. It's the one most often ignored by the people who care enough about you to share it.

I picked up the pistol. The heft of the M-1911 surprised people who were accustomed to modern nine-
millimeters built on aluminum frames with plastic grips,
half-loads in the magazines. The friction of handling had
rubbed most of the hand-chiseled checking off the black
walnut grips and the bluing had worn down to the bare
metal in places; but the action moved noiselessly and
without effort. When I worked the slide, the vanilla smell
of fresh oil filled my nostrils. The reason I bothered to
open the drawer once a month was to clean and oil the
weapon. The pictures and obituary I knew by heart.

The room was growing dark. Dusk silvered the window looking out on the house next door, making a
smoky reflection on my side of the glass, vaguely
human. It made as good a target as any. I turned sideways to it, extending the pistol at arm's length at shoulder height, my left arm straight down at my side with the
thumb parallel to the seam of my trousers; Dale's old-
fashioned stance. *If a gun was meant to be held in two
hands it would come with two handles, like a grass whip.*
I sighted down the barrel with both eyes open, the way
they still teach downtown, focusing on the vaguely
human shape in the window, and pressed the trigger.
The hammer fell on nothing, deafening in the silence of
the house.

5

Another dusk.

This one guttered out of the low overcast, brimming over as if the clouds had become saturated with darkness and couldn't hold any more, spilling down the sides of the gaunt, boarded-up buildings on Woodward and into a creeping pool on the pavement. Harold Boyette's Toyota, a canary-colored thumb on a Japanese nose there in the middle of General Motors country, crept out of the driveway in front of the DIA building behind pale daytime running lights, hesitated even though there was no traffic coming from either direction, and swung north. I flirted the big 455 out of hibernation and followed. The same ten snowflakes jitterbugged in front of my head-lamps all the way up to Seven Mile Road.

The Tomcat Theater was one of those historical relics no one would miss when they finally went the way of all brick. Fifteen years ago it had been one of a hundred places around town where a lonely man in a raincoat could go when all the impressionable young ladies were unavailable for flashing; those throbbing hot-pink wombs smelling of bleach and mildewed plush and chewed Spearmint, lit chiefly by the dusty beams of out-of-date projectors and the grainy flesh onscreen. The erosion of city fines, committees of decency, and—most important—stiff competition from chain video stores had ground them down to this one cinderblock building, painted celery green and set back from Telegraph Road under a stuttering marquee whose weight seemed to be pressing the structure into its own foundation. At that hour, with the yellow bulbs just making headway against the last exhausted glow of a sun that had squandered it-self meaninglessly above the cloud cover, Boyette's car and mine doubled the number parked in the little lot. The advertised feature was *Psycho Night Nurses in Chains,* or some shopping list of appropriately prurient nouns and adjectives like that. The bottom half of the double bill, *Horny and the Bandit,* was in the eighteenth year of a three-week run.

My client had gone inside, carrying a bulging mailer under one arm, when I pulled into a slot and got out and kicked all my tires just in case someone was watching. The two strange cars, a Pontiac station wagon with ter-minal Michigan cancer and a silver 1978 Firebird with its rear end jacked up on stilts, looked unoccupied, but you can only be so thorough without drawing fire.

In front of the building I stopped at a painted plywood booth and gave six singles and a Kennedy half-dollar to a debatably female attendant in purple leather with a hoop through her nose. She closed one black-shadowed eye and studied the fifty-cent piece closely with the other.

"He was a president," I said. "Nobody you'd know."

She moved a bare tattooed shoulder, flipped the coin into a tackle box, and tore a ticket off a roll the size of a bicycle wheel. I asked her if the feature had started.

"It don't matter." She took a bite out of her sandwich, liverwurst and something green. "They run back to back, twenty-four hours."

I thanked her and went in through a steel door with a buzz lock. That put me directly inside the auditorium; the building had begun life as a construction-materials wholesaler and had no lobby. On the screen, a woman in an old-fashioned white nurse's cap and a black garter belt was busy performing a variant kind of CPR upon a man with wide sideburns and three-alarm eczema. In the reflected glow, a couple seated near the door improvised on the scene with all the enthusiasm of two off-duty gravediggers excavating a basement. I figured it was their anniversary. The back of a motionless dark head in the center row and Boyette's fair one up front topped off the attendance. Good house for a weeknight.

The linoleum snatched nastily at the soles of my shoes on the way down the aisle. The seat I chose, three rows behind Boyette on the end, squawked when I tipped it down. It felt as if someone were already sitting in it. I squirmed around until I found some dales that fit my hills, unholstered the .38 Smith & Wesson I carried into street combat and movie theaters on Telegraph, and propped it on the cushion between the armrest and my thigh. Now I had everything the well-prepared cinema-goer needed, except popcorn and penicillin.

Psycho Night Nurses was painless as those things go, ten minutes of plot stretched over an hour and a half of orgasms spliced together from the outtakes of a dozen other films shot at the same time. Some of the actors' lines were dubbed by a ham-fisted German engineer with a Dutch-English dictionary and a hole in one eardrum; the rest were delivered with the amount of skill you expect from would-have-beens who had been rejected for one-line walk-ons in television commercials. This one boasted a celebrity appearance by Doug McClure, but coming in thirty seconds after the opening credits I must have missed it, because I never saw him. The sex was redundant, awkward, and dull. That part at least rang true. The back of Boyette's head was more interesting, and after the first half hour I focused on it exclusively. What he thought of the movie was anyone's guess. Probably wished he were home rereading *Beowulf.*

The place began to fill up. A flock of teenagers in Turkish pants and fatigue coats five sizes too big for them swooped in at the end of the first reel and took over the front row on either side of Boyette, loudly evaluating the performances during the grope scenes and offering advice. A man in his seventies wandered in a few minutes later holding his hernia and sat down next to a wall. A college-age couple took possession of the two seats directly in front of me and the young man spent the rest of the show trying to unbutton his date. Two tailored ladies with gold-rimmed glasses and silver-blue rinse jobs came in and sat across the aisle from me with their knees together and their hands folded in their laps. They were the only ones I couldn't figure out until the girl showed up.

She was a pale-skinned brunette of twenty or so who excused herself in a whisper when I stood to let her slide in past me. When she took the seat next to mine, black hose showed between the dark red hem of her dress and the fur tops of her ankle boots. The rest of her was wrapped in silver fox, and to hell with animal rights because no fox ever wore it like her. She fished a gold-tipped cigarette and a silver lighter out of a clamshell purse the size of a compact, failed to get a spark out of the flint after two tries, and said, "Damn!" in a way that made it sound as if it had never been said before. The girl seated in front of us disentangled herself from her escort long enough to turn her head and tell her to shush.

"I think smoking's off limits," I whispered.

"Foreplay too, apparently. At least onscreen." Smiling, the brunette turned my way and raised the cigarette to her lips.

It was one of those honey-over-grits accents, sweet and slightly scratchy. Below Kentucky, way below. I struck a match. Her hair was cut short and to the shape of her head, exposing her ears; reflections of the flame crawled on the surfaces of dangling earrings bent into open triangles. As she leaned forward I saw that her eyes didn't match. The right one was baby-blanket blue, the left that reddish brown with hints of green they call hazel so it will fit in the blank on a driver's license. Flaws in the features of good-looking women interest me. I was still looking at her eyes when they twitched past my shoulder.

That set off an alarm. I used my elbow, colliding with her cheekbone where it met the mastoid and following through with the rest of my arm, sweeping her out of the way while I snatched at the revolver next to my leg. The vague object was to get the gun and go to the floor. The floor was my friend.

For a flash I thought the Smith had gone off accidentally. A pistol report indoors at close range is louder than Krakatoa and more disorienting than a stroke. Voices raised, feet thudded, dully and without resonance in the echo of the blast. I glimpsed the sole of a fur-trimmed boot scrambling away. I felt the barrel of the .38. It hadn't fired. The sulfur stench freshly laid in over the normal ones said somebody else's had.

Someone was talking. I stayed on the floor and listened.

WOMAN: Alberto, stop!

MAN: What's wrong?

WOMAN: Your organ; I don't think it's big enough.

MAN: Sorry. I didn't know it would be playing in a cathedral.

The voices were loud and echoed around the edges as if they were being pushed through a P.A. system in a deserted terminal. They were coming from the theater's speakers, buzzing along the floor and vibrating through the hand I was using to support myself. The movie was still playing, just in case anyone was paying attention.

I leaned against the back of a seat, swung the cylinder out of the revolver from habit to make sure all the chambers were dressed, and snapped it back. My free hand was crusted with the things that collect on linoleum that hasn't been mopped since Boy George. I plucked a bit of shiny metal off the heel of my palm, looked at it, and stuck it in a pocket. I wiped the rest off on my pants, grabbed an armrest, and levered myself up onto a cushion. The couple onscreen had stopped fencing and were now coiled together in a chaise longue that looked like the same one a different couple had used for the same purpose in the living room of a high-rise apartment earlier. If so, I was the only one there to appreciate it. There is no alone quite like being alone in a movie house with the feature ratcheting away for one's own entertainment. I felt like a Hollywood mogul in a private screening room. A dumb Hollywood mogul. That got-a-match gag had rheumatism.

I thought of Boyette, got up, still holding the .38, and trotted to the front row, where the screen towered overhead and if I'd wanted to I could have looked up into all kinds of interesting orifices. Then I walked back the other way, checking all the rows. My client wasn't in any of them. The package he'd brought in with him was as gone as my good opinion of myself.

Both emergency exits were chained and padlocked, a violation of the fire ordinance the City of Detroit had managed to overlook during its many election-year efforts to close the theater permanently. I flattened myself against the main entrance door and eased it open. No one shot at me. Under the security lights an icy gust blew a purple advertising leaflet against the right rear tire of my car, then took the sheet across Telegraph. The Cutlass was the only car parked in the lot. The ticket clerk had been in too much of a hurry when she left the booth to close the door or finish her lunch; half a Twinkie lay on the greasy paper sack that had contained her liverwurst sandwich.

I went back inside and did some more detecting. One of the electric wall sconces was out. When I took a closer look, I found out where the bullet had gone that was meant for me. The slug had punched a hole in the tin fixture, parted a wire, and buried itself in the mortar between two cinderblocks. I couldn't reach it with my pocket knife.

The movie ended while I was still trying. The screen went white a minute later, accompanied by a distant flapping, like a moth hurling itself against a screen. I found the door to the projection-room stairs behind a seam in the carpeted wall opposite the one where the bullet had penetrated. I could see my breath in the well; no sense wasting heat on the help. At the top I grasped the knob of yet another steel door, tightened my grip on the revolver and went in fast, spinning on my heel to cover all the corners. A plastic dashboard troll with orange hair greeted me with the demented grin of a major-appliance salesman. It was glued to a lighting console studded with buttons and metal switches.

The room had a folding cot with a doubled-over pillow and a blanket as thick as a dishtowel, none of them in use at present. A plastic coffee mug with the South Park kids on it steamed on a folding card table next to a copy of *High Times* spread open to an article on Colombian papers. That old familiar smell of scorched grain clung to everything, but no half-finished joint smoldered in the molded-plastic ashtray. The projectionist hadn't left in such a panic he forgot the important things.

I almost wasted a bullet when the small electric space heater on the floor kicked in with a buzz and a whir. I returned the Smith to its clip on my belt.

The take-up reel on the big projector was still spinning, throwing a spoked shadow on the walls and ceiling. I located the switch and turned it off. There was no window, but that was okay. I had a feeling if I looked outside I'd see a world bombed into kibble, with me the sole survivor.

The first siren swooped and fell then. I should have known the cops would make it too.

6

When John Alderdyce saw me he hesitated a step and said shit.

I'd found the rest of the house lights on the console and turned them up. When he came in I was in the auditorium, sitting on one hip on the arm of one of the back-row seats, facing the entrance. He looked blacker than ever in the light of the recessed ceiling fixtures, a polished ebony carving in a camel's-hair overcoat and light gray double-breasted suit, tailored to his garage-door frame. Since reaching middle age he'd put on forty pounds and lost a lot of hair, but he had the bone structure to handle the extra weight, and his balding front just accentuated the angular configuration of a head that would have been at home on Easter Island. We've known each other most of our lives.

"I wish I'd shaved," I said. "I didn't think no tussle at the Tomcat rated no visit from no inspector." I'd only seen him a few times since the department promoted him out of my league.

"I was on the Southfield Freeway when the radio call came through. Any car in the vicinity. My luck." He swept his coattail aside and returned the nickel-plated snubnose he'd come in with to his kidney holster. He was the only cop in the city who hadn't gone to elephant calibers after the riots. "Where's the body?"

"Under this suit."

"What the hell happened to the suit?"

"All-night grindhouses and gas station toilets affect me the same way. I can't resist rolling around on the floors."

"You're slipping, Walker. Where you are there's usually a couple of hundred pounds of USDA Choice waiting for the wagon."

"I'm coming down with something. Well enough to be shot at, but too sick to shoot." I coughed.

"Do what I do, pump aspirins. Thinner blood kills germs." He held out his hand.

I squeaked out the .38 and gave it to him. He sniffed at the barrel, inspected the cylinder, and returned it. His nose kept working. "Somebody shot something."

I pointed toward the damaged sconce. "You'll find the slug behind there. The reason it doesn't have my brains on it is the reason my suit looks like this. How'd the cops get it?"

"Nine-one-one. A fight, she said."

"She?" I saw eyes that didn't match, a pair of triangle earrings.

"She said she sells tickets. Dispatch believed her. She couldn't put together a coherent sentence without a building permit."

"Oh. The girl in the booth. I'm surprised she took the time. She rabbited along with everyone else, including the projectionist."

"Who can blame them? The place has more priors than seats. The concession stand is a guy named Atticus in the parking lot. What's the story?" He leaned back against the block wall with his hands in his coat pockets. He looked as casual as the Kremlin.

I found an uncrushed Winston in the pack, lit up, and darkened my lungs another shade while I gave it to him from Chapter One. I edited out Earl North. That wasn't city property.

"You stepped on that old rake?" he said when I got to the girl with the cigarette.

"If I were smart I'd be two-thirds of the way to a pension."

"No wonder that bullet missed your brains." He looked at the empty screen, as if the story were playing there. "What's your take on this bird Boyette? You've only got his word for it that money's his. It wouldn't be the first time a courier took off with the pony."

"I thought about it. I don't like it. I initiated contact. He didn't search me out."

"Good con guys almost never do. Merlin Gilly would shill for the Prince of Lies."

"Pick him up."

"Are you filing a missing-persons report on Boyette?"

"My specialty's missing persons. I'd never live it down. Anyway, for all I know he's sitting in his living room right now, unrolling a Dead Sea Scroll."

"How about attempted murder on you? That's got to be a misdemeanor."

I shook my head.

"Then it's your scooter," he said. "All I've got is a shot fired inside city limits and maybe a property damage complaint, if anyone bothers to come down and swear one out. No one will. In a minute or so I won't even have the shot fired. My specialty's homicide."

He should have played the lottery. Exactly sixty seconds later a uniform came in, young, with the marks of the academy mold still on his shiny leather jacket and in the crease of his trousers. Alderdyce flashed his shield, then walked away with him a few yards, speaking low. The uniform nodded and went back out. The inspector stayed where he was with his hands in his pockets.

"Something?" I asked.

"Not likely. I just remembered I'm in no hurry. My daughter's using our living room for her divorced women's meeting."

In a little while the uniform returned and read something out of his notebook. "That's next door, isn't it?" Alderdyce asked.

"Yes, sir."

"Stay here and wait for the manager." The polished-ebony head turned my way. "Temperature's about twelve. Good for the lungs."

I crushed out my cigarette on the linoleum and buttoned my coat.

"Ticket clerk has an apartment next door," Alderdyce said as we headed across the parking lot. "She left the address when we called downtown. I had the kid get it from Dispatch. Maybe she knows your brunette."

I didn't say anything. The wind was full of razor blades.

It was another block building, this one the original gray, with a Laundromat on the ground floor, locked up and dark. The door to the stairs came open when he tugged on the handle. "No wonder I never run out of work," he said.

"Maybe she's from Iowa," I said.

"Nobody leaves Iowa."

We climbed a steep flight of gridded iron steps between walls three feet apart. The number he wanted belonged to a door just off the landing. He knocked, and when the lid slid away from the peephole inside, introduced himself, holding up the gold shield in its folder. The lid squeaked back into place. A series of clicks followed.

"Told you," Alderdyce said.

The door opened wide enough to show a black-shaded eye, a gold hoop in a pale nostril, and half of a pair of lips painted green. The chain wouldn't let it open any wider.

"You ought to lock the door downstairs too," said the inspector. "By the time they get up here they might be mad enough to break this one down."

"Lock's busted downstairs." She waited.

"You called the police about a disturbance at the Tomcat earlier. You work there, don't you?"

"There was a fight."

"Didn't you hear the shot?" I asked.

The eye flicked my way, then back to the inspector. "There was a fight."

I described the brunette, short hair, odd-lot eyes, fox coat, earrings, and all. I asked her who she came in with.

"Nobody came in looking like that."

"Think hard. You'd remember her, even without the eyes."

"Nobody came in looking like that." She started to close the door.

Alderdyce and I leaned against it at the same time. It was a wonder the chain held. I said, "What about a guy carrying a package? A big mailer under his arm."

"I saw him."

"The girl came in about forty-five minutes later. She was one of the last ones in."

"Last two people I sold tickets to was a couple of little old ladies." She spoke through her teeth.

"Do you remember me?"

"You gave me a funny coin."

"Thanks for your help." Alderdyce took his shoulder off the door. She pushed it shut then, in spite of my resistance. She was a strong girl.

"She wears green lipstick," I told the inspector.

"So does my son."

"She's a poster girl for rehab."

"Pupils look okay. At a guess I'd say she wouldn't be ordering police on anything stronger than grass. I can pull her downtown if you want to change your mind about that attempted murder complaint."

I shook my head. We started downstairs, but two steps down I went back and poked a business card under the door.

"What was that about?" Alderdyce asked when I rejoined him.

"Casting bread on the waters."

Back in the parking lot the uniform's scout car was bouncing blue light off the front of the theater. Alderdyce opened the door on the driver's side of his unmarked Chrysler and got in. "Jesus, I hope those women are gone. If there's a strange car in my driveway I'm going right on past."

"Thanks for the time, John."

"Thank my daughter." He started the engine. "So how was the picture?"

"The heroine gets it in the end."

I got my foot out of the way of his tire in time and walked to my car, digging in my pocket for the keys. I came up with the small open triangle I'd found stuck to my hand when I raised it from the floor of the theater. It looked like silver, but I was betting on platinum. As often as they lose them you wonder why women bother to wear them at all.

7

Rosecranz, the superintendent who held down the basement of my office building and occasionally fixed a pipe, had come in with Coolidge, seen the city burn down twice, and watched the rest of the country go to hell through the nine-inch window of the 1946 Admiral in his dank little office next to the water heater. Before that he had been passed through a hole in the wall of a house in Yaroslavl, a nine-pound bundle, to protect him from Cossacks, smuggled across an angry black ocean in the hold of a rusty steamer, and folded, stapled, and spindled by U.S. Immigration into a gray little man in bib overalls with tools in his pockets and a piece of silver duct tape holding his glasses together at the bridge of his nose. All of which should have made him colorful, but you could pass him a dozen times on the stairs and never realize you weren't alone. He was as much a part of the place as the cigarette burns on the runner outside the door of my office, only less inspiring. Topping the third-floor landing with my keys in my hand the morning after my visit to the Tomcat Theater, I didn't notice him until he spoke.

"You are still here?" he said. "I was afraid you'd gone like the others."

I looked at a blob of pink insulation bulging through the ceiling grid where a panel had been removed. The workers hadn't reported in yet.

"I can't afford the rent anywhere else," I said. "What about you?"

"I have nowhere else."

"What's your stand on asbestos?"

"For a hundred years it's okay. Then it isn't. I think I will live to see it's okay again. Or you will if I do not."

"Only if I hold my breath." I slid my key into the lock. It was already unlocked.

"I should not have, maybe." Between his spotted hands he was carrying what looked like the same stained rag he'd had in his pocket the day I came to work with Dale Leopold. They were oddly graceful hands despite the splotching, with slender spatulated fingers and fine knuckles. He was never without the filthy and tattered gloves he carried in his bib. "You said always to open the door for anyone who asks to go in and wait when you're gone."

"That hasn't changed," I said. "Who's the customer?"

"A young woman."

I spun the key ring around my finger. "Brunette, short hair, one blue eye, one hazel?"

He shook his head. "I stayed out here in case she steals furniture."

"I don't think we're talking about the same young woman." I gave him a couple of singles, which he folded into his old rag like part of a magic act. "If she bothers to carry it down the stairs she's earned more than I can get for it," I said. "She give a name?"

"Mrs. Dracula, maybe."

He shoved the rag into his hip pocket along with the responsibility and went for the stairs, dragging his left leg a little. He claimed the Pinkertons had broken it with truncheons during a protest rally for Sacco and Vanzetti.

I lingered a moment to center my headache before going in. On the way home from the theater the night before I'd stopped to buy a bottle of Scotch, then spent the rest of the evening with a glass in one hand and the telephone receiver in the other, trying to track down Harold Boyette. His number didn't answer and my source at Ameritech for unlisted patrons couldn't find him in the directory. My plant in the secretary of state's office in Lansing plugged into the company computer and reported that the license number of Boyette's Toyota was registered to a leasing company headquartered in Jackson. Of course there was no answer there at 10:30 P.M.

I should have asked my client for his home number when I still had him. I should have asked for his birth certificate and two references, but it was a one-night job, his agreement to pay ten thousand dollars upon recovering the Hours of the Virgin had arrived at my office on schedule, and his check for five hundred had cleared at his own bank without a belch. I drank the bottle down to the plumb line and went to bed.

Now the Battle of Bannockburn was going on inside my skull. I'd outgrown hangovers; the petri dish that was my bloodstream had launched a frontal attack on my nervous system with catapults and a battering ram. I was too sick to work and not sick enough to stay home. So I came to work.

The little waiting room smelled like leaf-burning season in Bogota. She was seated on the upholstered bench with her knees spread, getting all the good out of half an inch of roach on a toothpick clutched between fingers with black lacquered nails and dirty knuckles. I thought the nails and the seven-inch heels on her scuffed vinyl boots made her a she, but I hadn't tuned into MTV that morning for the latest. The rest of her was all ribs and Mother Death tattoos in a purple imitation leather jacket and a brief statement of a skirt, with a thatch of brown hair growing on top of her shaved head like moss on a rock. She was pushing twenty but not hard enough to dent it. The tattoo on her left shoulder was the spread wingfeathers of a bird of prey. The rest of the bird was under the jacket. It was quality needlework. There are some real artists waiting out their probations in the parlors along East Jefferson.

Today a gold chain linked the stud in her nose to a scimitar dangling from her right earlobe. She hadn't replaced the black shadow on the eye I'd last seen looking at me from behind the door of her apartment near the Tomcat; merely freshened it with a second coat.

"Good morning," I said. "If I'd known it was formal I'd have worn my snake."

She pinched out the end of the joint—flesh sizzled—

poked it into a slash pocket, and zipped the pocket shut. Her eyes, mud-colored with shrunken pupils, drifted from me to the framed *Casablanca* poster on the wall. "Who's the old dude in the hat?"

"Rutherford B. Hayes. He played center field for the Giants. Who's watching the booth?"

"I don't come on till four. You remember me, huh."

"I never forget a tattoo. Care to come inside? You clash with everything out here."

"What's inside?"

"Privacy."

She scratched her crotch. "What's that?"

"Let's find out." I unlocked the inner door and held it for her. She'd be used to that.

"This place is the bomb," she said, looking at the butterfly wallpaper, the desk and mismatched chairs and kicked-in file cabinets, Custer on the wall violating the civil rights of Native Americans at the Little Big Horn. "Like a picture we run once."

"*The Dark Corner?*"

"*My Gun Is Thick.* Tony Gonads and Cherry Yesterday. A classic." She plopped herself onto the chair on the customer's side and slid down until she was sitting on her spine, rucking her skirt up to her pelvis. She hadn't listened to her mother's advice about what you should do in case you get in an accident. "I'm Vyper. That's with a *y*."

"Why?"

"Huh?"

I shook my head and sat behind the desk. I milked the last four aspirins out of the office bottle, filled the pony glass from the pint I kept in the belly drawer, and washed them down all in a lump.

She watched me. "You sick?"

"You don't want to kiss me." I picked up the telephone and tried Boyette's number again. Still no answer. I worked the plunger and called the automobile leasing company in Jackson. When a woman came on I said I was Sergeant Albert Winder with the General Service division of the Detroit Police Department, checking for wants and warrants on the license number of a yellow Toyota, current year model, and needed the lessee's address and home telephone. While she was running it down I pointed my chin at Vyper-with-a-*y*. "Did you see the piece about Colombian papers in the new *High Times?*"

"I use toilet paper." She sat up and folded her arms on the desk. "You're like a private pig, right?"

"Right. I only wallow when I'm paid."

"How much they pay you?"

"If you're looking for a job, the hiring here is restricted to my own species."

A green lip curled. "Just 'cause I don't look like Betty and Veronica don't mean I'm crud."

"It does in this world." The receiver clicked in my ear. "Hello?"

"Sergeant?" A different woman this time. "We're not at liberty to give out the names and addresses of clients without written authorization. Could you fax us your request on department stationery?"

"What gave me away?"

Her tone grew thorns. "If I told you that, next time you might get away with it." The connection broke.

I cradled the receiver. The queen of chains and leather was starting to look good. "What are you selling?"

"A woman."

"No thanks. I just had one and it didn't agree with me."

"A woman in a fur coat."

"Blue eyes?"

"One was. I don't know what color you call the other one but it wasn't blue."

That was a step in the right direction, but I'd mentioned the mismatched eyes the night before. "Brooklyn accent?"

"More like Mississippi, only not quite. I used to live with a dude from Mississippi and he talked like that, only different. Someplace south, Atlanta maybe. Is Atlanta a state?"

The aspirins were beginning to kick in. I found the triangle earring in my pocket and dangled it over the desk. She squinted, cracking her eye shadow.

"Yeah. She was wearing them."

I put it away. There was still some liquor in the glass. I sipped at it, but it wasn't what I wanted and I dumped it out in the wastebasket. "I thought she didn't exist."

"That's what I said in front of that pig. I don't like pigs."

"I'm a pig."

"You don't bust people."

"Drugs?"

She showed her teeth. I guessed she thought she was smiling. "No thanks. I just had some."

Her arms were still folded on her side of the desk. I grasped a wrist at random and pulled the arm straight. The same Michelangelo who was responsible for the bird of prey had rendered the Yellow Brick Road in intricate detail inside her forearm. The Emerald City glimmered in the crease of her elbow. I couldn't see any marks that weren't artistic. I gave it back to her.

"I'm clean since I'm sixteen." She rubbed the wrist. "They didn't bust me for that. They said I put my baby in the snow."

"Did you?"

"I wrapped it in a towel first. You want the woman or not?"

"Depends on the price."

"Thousand. Cash."

I laughed in her face.

"Take it or leave it."

I reached for the telephone. She thought I was going back to work.

"You called it, pig." She got up and went to the door.

I lifted the receiver and dialed. "Thirteen hundred? C.I.D., please. Inspector Alderdyce."

She spun around. Her chain jingled. "Asshole!"

"Oink."

"Big bluff. I ain't done nothing to get busted for."

"There's an extortion attempt involved and a person missing, possibly kidnap or murder. The cops have a name for it. They call it withholding evidence."

She came back and sat down. "Hundred."

"Fifty."

She started to get up again.

"John?" I said. "Amos Walker. Guess who's in my office."

She reached out and slapped down the plunger. "Asshole," she said again.

I cradled the receiver. *Titanic* was playing downtown at 4:30, 8:00, and 11:40, if it matters.

She counted the tens and singles I placed in front of her, unzipped a pocket over her left breast, and made the deposit. "Strangeways is her name," she said. "Lauren Strangeways."

"Any relation to Gordon Strangeways?"

"Just by marriage."

"How do you know her?"

"Strangeways owns the Tomcat. They say he likes to make surprise visits to places he owns, peek at the books to make sure he ain't cheated. He come around last month in a limousine and the manager come out to talk to him. She was in the back. I heard Strangeways introduce her."

I waited until she was at the door again. "What happened to your baby?"

"Somebody adopted it, I guess."

"Was it a boy or a girl?"

"I don't know. I didn't check."

"Slither, Vyper."

She banged the door shut behind her. She was the only person I'd met in days who didn't have a cure for the flu.

I wrote the name Laurel Strangeways on the telephone pad. I don't know why. I wasn't likely to forget it. Her husband had a million dollars for every letter, with enough left over to buy the pad and the desk and the building that held them. I was still saving up for another pad.

8

A freezing mist was falling on Woodward when I parked down the block from the library, glass needles shattering when they struck the asphalt and the vinyl roof of the Cutlass. I noticed a new crack in the marble when I climbed the steps to the library entrance, and about a pound and a half less pressure in the pneumatic closer when I pulled open my favorite door. The tube needed replacing. Money for such things had gone into the old mayor's private investment firm, and the new administration was waiting for the casinos to make up the difference.

A security guard and one of the older librarians smiled and said hello on my way to the reference section. The vagrant who was sleeping his way through Shakespeare at the first reader's table had gotten as far as act two, scene three of *Troilus and Cressida,* then passed out again. I don't know what I'd do without free public access to information. Buy a book, I suppose.

I walked right past the customer computer terminal to the shelf containing the *Readers' Guide to Periodical Literature.* Ten minutes' congress with the big red-bound books sent me off in five directions, and when I had everything stacked on one of the partitioned tables near the windows, I set out my notebook and pen and killed the rest of the morning enlarging upon my education.

The subject of Gordon Strangeways presented a litmus test for the differing styles of the magazines and other sources. *People* was sly and slangy, *Time* dowdy and ponderous, *Newsweek* just dowdy. *U.S. News & World Report* had a serious case of hemorrhoids, *The Christian Science Monitor* needed a doctor. *Who's Who* asked, "Who?" Only *Forbes* and *Fortune* seemed to approve; you could hear the raspy dry-washing of miserly hands over the columns of figures on the black side. At a conservative estimate he was worth two and a half billion, and making two million a day.

There was some conflict. His age varied along with the place of his birth, and nobody seemed to be clear on whether he had served with the army or the coast guard or waited out the fall of Saigon in Quebec. The business of checking facts has tended to lag behind technology in the Age of Information.

The *Playboy* interview was the most informative and plausible, an in-depth personality profile based on many hours spent in conversation with its subject, and as many more divided between libraries like this one and dusty reading rooms in records bureaus strung out between Detroit and the Dark Continent, poring over old newspapers on microfilm and translating bureaucratic hieroglyphics in boxes of defunct files. It made up for the missing centerfold.

Born into a family of professional Linotypists in either Mossel Bay or Port St. Johns, South Africa, in either March or December of 1943 or maybe February 1945, Strangeways had through a series of intelligent suggestions on his part been removed from the print shop to the editorial staff of a Cape Town quarterly at age twenty (or eighteen), then emigrated to England and later to America just behind the Beatles as overseas correspondent for the London *Times*. Never a great hand at carrying out assignments dreamed up by other people, he had quit that post in favor of a partnership in a failing men's fashion magazine based in Birmingham, Michigan. There was plenty of room for photographs once he'd deep-sixed all the articles containing grooming tips and spirited discussions of plaids vs. pinstripes, so he hired a staff of lensmen out from under the even shakier girlie magazines in his market. When he was through tinkering, *After Six* resembled a four-color manual of gynecology. The first featured pictorial under Strangeways' editorship was headed "Snatch of the Day."

Despite an improved circulation, the revamped magazine might have passed unnoticed among the common lot of masturbation monthlies had not the Birmingham City Council and the United States Postal Service pressed separate and simultaneous actions to close it down for distributing obscene material. The federals gave up after a mistrial, as they always do when they're especially determined, but a ruling in the city's favor was appealed by

Strangeways' attorneys, overturned at the district level, then sought again by the city in Lansing. Eventually the case wound its way to the U.S. Supreme Court, which refused to hear it and let stand an earlier dismissal on Constitutional grounds. *After Six* had won; but that was only half the story.

The publicity, stoked by the continuing debate over how far the founding fathers had intended for the First Amendment to stretch, netted the magazine a national readership. The ACLU, NOW, and the Catholic Church weighed in on both sides of the issue. There were death threats and offers to help with legal expenses. Gordon Strangeways became a celebrity. All the major TV and radio talk shows had had him on, and the president, campaigning for reelection in Missouri, had referred to him as "a purveyor of public prurience." The purveyor had in the meantime become naturalized, acquired a wife and been divorced by her for desertion, and invested his balloon profits in a chain of "health spas" (quotation marks courtesy of *Newsweek*) and adult theaters throughout the Great Lakes region, concentrated most densely in metropolitan Detroit. He was the first distributor of X-rated material to open video outlets across the Midwest, then the United States. Wall Street lifted its head out of tickertape when he turned down an offer of two hundred million from a Japanese corporation to acquire his video stores.

After Six was still publishing, but the sexual revolution and its plague-ridden aftermath had fostered even raunchier fare that cut into its bottom line at the newsstands. A series of police raids on Strangeways' That Touch of Venus health spas had forced its prostitution activities underground, if they hadn't eliminated them entirely. But the video business was going strong. Young couples, randy singles, and lonely seniors who wouldn't risk being seen going into or coming out of a porno theater rented copies of *Texas Ta-Tas* and *E.T. The Extra Testicle* in handbaskets. Of late, the Strangeways empire had been selling off its theaters and investing heavily in the computer online video market. The Tomcat on Telegraph was one of the few old-time grindhouses still operating under the company banner.

It was one of those Streets of Gold stories told with a strong Detroit accent, but it carried a coda: Three years ago, while riding in a rented limousine to his hotel from the airport in Little Rock, where he had bought ten acres to construct a kind of sexual shopping mall (videos, sex toys, edible underwear, calendar photography studio, Starbuck's), the Horatio Alger of hormones was stopped by a mob of angry Pentecostals, pulled from the back seat, stomped, and beaten with picket signs and baseball bats. Although the police intervened before he was battered to death, he hadn't taken a step or stood on his own since. The few public appearances he had made in recent months were in a wheelchair, and these days he spent most of his time behind the walls of his estate on Grosse Ile. Not so the ringleaders of the mob that had crippled him; they'd made the round of all the afternoon talk shows after three Arkansas juries failed to convict them for assault and battery and attempted murder. Some audiences cheered when they came onstage.

Strangeways had posed for his latest picture last summer, on the occasion of his second wedding. The bride, the former Laurel Triste, originally of Baton Rouge, Louisiana, was a blur of double-exposed colorplate in the "Milestones" section of *Time*. Her general configuration,

leaning devotedly over the groom's wheelchair in a tailored ivory suit, could have belonged to the brunette
whose cigarette I'd lit in the Tomcat just before my own
flame flickered. If so, her hair was longer last summer.
It was impossible to tell the color of her eyes from the
photograph. Coming from Louisiana, her speech would
put one in mind of honey poured over grits.

The empire builder himself, turned out in a tux that fit
him as well as can be managed when the customer can't
rise to be measured, looked patient and dissipated. The
blade-straight, silver-haired entrepreneur to the American
male libido had lost weight and the loose skin of his
cheeks matched his starched dress collar.

There wasn't much on the new Mrs. Strangeways. She
was eighteen at the time of the troth, one-third her husband's age, and had modeled lingerie for an agency in
Baton Rouge. They had met when she came north to
shoot tests for a spread in *After Six*. It was plain from the
tenor of the brief piece in *Time* and one-paragraph items
appearing elsewhere that the reporters had grown bored
with the subject after the sensation of Little Rock. Now
that graphic sex had moved into the jurisdiction of polit-
ical pundits, it had lost most of its old salt. Gordon
Strangeways had become as respectable as a Norelco.

I left the material for the librarians to return to the
shelves, the way they like it, and used the pay telephone
to try Harold Boyette once more. When I hung up on the
dial tone and turned to face the glass doors, I was looking at the DIA directly across the street.

Waiting in the icy rain for a break in the traffic on
Woodward I didn't even know why I'd come this far, ex-
cept I was still living on Boyette's five hundred dollars.
That and Earl North.

Never tangle yourself in the case, kid. The client's all twisted around when he comes to you or he wouldn't come to you. You won't be any good to you or him if you get twisted around too. Words to go on Dale Leopold's tombstone, if he had a tombstone. Last I heard he was still staking out his sister's living room in a jar on the mantel, next to the Pekingese she'd had skinned and stuffed when it died. He'd hated that dog.

The Goya exhibit was still pulling them in. A kid in a Wayne State sweatshirt was sitting cross-legged on the floor sketching *The Clothed Maja* on a big pad in his lap. *The Naked Maja* had been too inhibited to make the crossing. I found a security guard who rubbed his nose when I asked him if Harold Boyette had been in lately. As noses go it was a keeper, as big around as bratwurst and shot through with red and blue veins. It belonged behind a zipper.

"Boyette? I think that's in another wing."

"He's a man, not an exhibit. I met him here day before yesterday."

"I just watch the paintings. You better talk to Mr. Ruddy, he runs things. He's in the gift shop this time of day."

"What's he look like?"

"You won't miss him. He won't be no more than an arm's length from the cash drawer."

The gift shop was doing better business than the rest of the establishment; there are people who shop those places weekly who have never gone to see the exhibits. A mixed-race couple couldn't decide whether the poster from the Empire Period tour or the photographic mural of the British Crown Jewels would go better with the Care Bears wallpaper in the nursery, and a gang of kids

in eight-ball jackets were trying to imitate the facial ex-
pressions of the souls in torment in Bosch's *Garden of
Earthly Delights* on a set of coffee mugs. The cashier, a
busy young thing just tall enough to reach the keys, rang
up a purchase directly under the thin pale nose of Mr.
Ruddy.

I figured the name on the tag pinned to the lapel of
his navy blazer was a celestial joke. He was six-two and
looked taller because you can only get a hundred and
thirty pounds to go so far, and he appeared to be completely bald at first glance. On closer inspection, his fine
smoothed-back hair was the same bled-out color as his
scalp and face. He hadn't much face, but he had a lot of
angular chin and a broad forehead the shape and color
of a plastic bleach bottle. At the moment I spotted him,
he turned away from the register and the fluorescent
light seemed to shine right through his skin and clothes,
showing the shadowy outlines of the bones beneath. He
was a walking Visible Man.

"Mr. Ruddy?"

A frosty blue eye fixed and card-catalogued me from
his inch and a quarter of superior height. "Yes?"

I showed him the ID. "I'm handling a little matter for
Harold Boyette. Is he around?"

He reached up and adjusted his name tag with a finger. It wasn't crooked. "Mr. Boyette is no longer associ-
ated with this institution."

"He quit? When?"

"This institution doesn't discuss matters of personnel
with the outside."

"That means he got canned."

"I repeat—"

"I heard. Thing is, Boyette seems to have dropped out

of sight. From here I go to Thirteen hundred, that's Detroit police headquarters, and file a missing persons complaint. There's extortion involved and maybe kidnapping. You won't mind cops coming around asking questions, strictly on the whisper. Open cases are public record, but unless it's a slow news day I wouldn't worry too much about the press. This has Section B written all over it."

"Please join me in the stock room."

I considered it a breakthrough; he'd stopped referring to himself as "this institution."

The room was smaller than the one where I'd spoken with Boyette, considerably neater, and a whole lot less interesting. Shrink-wrapped picture books were stacked horizontally on built-in shelves and there were boxes marked FRAGILE on the floor and packing material and a postage meter on a worktable. Ruddy drew the door shut and stood with his back to it, in case I tried to make a run for the cophouse.

"If you're working for Mr. Boyette's attorney, I advise you to inform him that legal action is unwise. We allowed him to resign without prejudice rather than take the matter to the police. I'm afraid there is no smoking allowed," he added.

I lit up anyway. Smoke kills viruses and clears muddled thinking. "What'd he do, fondle the Venus de Milo?"

This time he used both eyes, turning his head this way and that to focus one of them on me at a time, like a bird. "If you were employed by his attorney, you'd know the answer to that question."

"Probably. If I were working for Frankie Lymon I'd know why fools fall in love, but like I said I'm working for Boyette and right now I don't even know where the hell he is. A situation which if it goes on long enough and if I get tired enough of these here verbal gymnastics I will take to the cops. Hell, I'm tired enough now. Stand aside."

He took in air through his thin pale nose. When it came back out it made a noise like a teakettle.

"This institution contracted with Mr. Boyette for his services as a consultant on historical manuscripts," he said. "It came to our attention that he had authenticated certain items which he knew to be forgeries. The inference was that he had conspired with the forgers to defraud the museum."

"Came to your attention how?"

"Mr. Boyette was not the only expert we consulted. The number of counterfeit manuscripts was too great to be a coincidence. In two cases particularly they were too obvious—crude, really—not to have been identified as false by a scholar of his experience. The conclusion, that he was an accomplice in the fraud, was no less obvious."

"Was the Hours of the Virgin one of the fakes?"

A crease appeared in the bleach-bottle forehead. "Which one? There are many books of hours."

"Plymouth. The duke's wedding present."

The crease went away. "Balderdash."

"Did you say balderdash?"

"I did. Poppycock."

"Balderdash is plenty rich enough for me. What's wrong with Plymouth?"

"This institution has never been in possession of the Plymouth Virgin. If anyone were to offer it to us we should certainly denounce it and them. That manuscript was destroyed during the Reformation."

"Not the Blitz?"

"It hasn't existed for four hundred years."

"What I saw looked real."

"How much do you know about illuminated manuscripts?"

"My recent education has improved more than a hundred percent. Two days ago I didn't know one from Billy Graham." I told him about the crab louse stuck in the ink.

"That would be a matter for an entomologist to determine. As a layman I'd guess the species hasn't changed much in four centuries." He glowered at his wristwatch. He'd been away from the cash register ten minutes. "Is there anything else?"

"Just one thing. When did you can Boyette, yesterday or today?"

"Neither. He hasn't worked here for well over six months."

9

I smoked my cigarette down to the filter, regarding Mr. Ruddy's long pallid exterior. He was wearing one of those toy ties that are supposed to make wearing them fun, all primary colors and whimsical patterns. This one had Egyptian pyramids. I ground out the butt against the side of a steel wastebasket and dropped it inside. It hadn't done anything for my congestion.

"Harold Boyette," I said. "Thirty, middle height, about twenty pounds over. Receding hair. Kissable lips."

"That's an adequate description. I couldn't say about the lips."

"I met him here in one of the galleries forty-eight

hours ago. He said his office was being renovated and let us into a storeroom in the south wing. He had a key."

The institutional mouth bent down at the corners. It was as kissable as a paper cut. "That's distressing. He was forced to surrender his keys before he left. He must have made copies. Dr. Angelo has his office now, his area is Chinese porcelains. I believe he had the lock changed when he moved in. That office has not been renovated in years."

"Of course not. It was a dodge." I recited the telephone number Merlin Gilly had given me, and that I'd used to call Boyette.

"That's not a DIA line," he said. "It isn't even the right exchange. I should think a professional detective would have confirmed that."

"It's not the kind of thing clients generally lie about. I'm surprised security didn't throw him down the front steps the minute he showed his face."

"Guards come and go. I don't know half of them myself. In any case, he's at liberty to pay his admission and wander the areas that are open to the public like anyone else."

"Can you think of any reason why he'd pretend to be employed here?"

"Not unless he hoped to persuade you to invest in one of his forgeries." He took in my suit and overcoat with one eye, then with the other. "I'd say it's unlikely."

The walls were getting close and my head wanted to float free of my neck. It wasn't Saturday night, so the flu had to be gaining ground. I kept my sweat glands in check by sheer effort of will. "Was a man named Earl North fired from Accounts Payable last Christmas?"

He stiffened. That made him as brittle as a breadstick. "Yes. Is he involved?"

"Boyette said he was bounced for embezzling."

"He was dismissed, but not for embezzling. He was caught in my office rifling the files of wealthy DIA patrons. Only the board of directors and I are allowed access to that information."

"You're sure that was the reason?"

"I'm the one who caught him. I shouldn't be surprised he and Mr. Boyette knew each other. They were cut from the same crooked bolt."

"Thank you, Mr. Ruddy. You've been most adequate."

Heading out, I got a new angle on what it was I didn't like about museums. Every time I left one I knew less about the world than I had going in.

The freezing rain had glazed over my car and I had to get the horses out to tug open the door. That broke the dam; when I climbed under the wheel I was sweating freely and my head was taking on water. I hadn't the energy to get out and scrape the ice off the windshield. I started the engine, and while I was waiting for the defroster to kick in I leaned my forehead against the steering wheel. When I woke up ten minutes later the car was full of heat. I turned off the blower, mopped my face, and eased out into the glassy right lane.

Woodward was entertaining. I saw more spinouts by the time I got to Grand Circus Park than any three Grand Prix. I managed to avoid them because I was crawling along at fifteen miles per hour. By that time I was feeling good, too good. I was in a cocoon of shimmering euphoria spun by a fever that distorted the senses. It's a cheap drunk, but it wears off twice as fast. By the time I found a space across from the Erin Go Bar on Porter it

had worn off. My headache was back and I was starting
to shiver.

The Erin Go Bar, located a few doors down from Most
Holy Trinity Church, is just about all that's left of
Corktown. When the Irish ran Detroit, it was the seat of
government, and if you wanted to fix a ticket or submit
a bid to build something for the city, you passed up the
Old City Hall entirely, ordered a drink at the Erin, and
waited at the bar until you were called—if you were
called. If you were in good, you got to go upstairs to the
Shamrock Club, where good cigars were available and
corned beef was served around the clock and the
Bushmill's flowed until well past closing. If you weren't,
you finished your drink downstairs and went home and
either packed your things or put a bullet through your
head, because your chances of ever doing business in
this town were worse than the liquor they sold you at the
bar.

In those days the place was filled with chattering patrons and Irish music, sung around the piano and performed by live bands with national reputations. The St.
Patrick's Day parade stopped there to wet its collective
whistles before continuing uptown, and no locally
prominent Irish-American citizen went to his reward
without a wake in the Shamrock Club and one drink to
his memory served downstairs on the house. When
George M. Cohan stopped there on his way through
town, the entire building had closed its doors for a private celebration that lasted three days.

The 1967 riots put an end to all that. The O'Haras and
Rileys left office, the Washingtons and Kinshashas moved
in, and the corridors of power shifted from Corktown to
Twelfth Street. The Shamrock Club closed permanently

when the surviving members found flashier things to spend their dues on, like open-heart surgery and oxygen. After the death of the bar's longtime owner, his widow sold the building to a corporation based in Honduras, which rented out the second-floor facilities for Saturday night Bingo and meetings of Smoke-Enders, Mothers Against Drunk Drivers, and, sensitively, the Sons of Italy. Each day was a battle for supremacy between the fresh odors of tomato sauce and garlic and the old ones of cabbage and potatoes. But it was almost over. The Hondurans had submitted a plan to the city to tear down the building and erect a hotel and casino.

Today I shared the saloon with an old man drinking beer at the opposite end of the bar and a young Asian with a Mr. Moto moustache nursing a highball and clicking the keys on a laptop computer in a corner booth. The room was a dim grotto done in dark walnut and curly maple, with brass lamps over the bar and pool table, the last a massive slab of carved mahogany and slate with a felt top the color of Bob Cratchit's eyeshade. The wood was scratched and cracking, ropes of cobweb clung to the chains supporting the lamps where they were stapled to the ceiling. The boxers in the framed photographs behind the bar, smooth-muscled specimens with names like Dugan and Cooney and Dynamite Danny McGonigle, had long since faded into the scenery, like an eviction notice on the door of a building that had been condemned under Jimmy Carter.

"You can't be as sick as you look, or I'd be pounding your chest right now. What can I get to pick you up?"

I looked up at the man in the apron leaning on his hands on the bar, the only surface in the place that was still getting the attention it needed; spilled drinks and a million bar rags had polished it to a mirror finish. He had three inches and a hundred pounds on me and was as dark as Mr. Ruddy was pale. His head was shaved a shiny blue-black. Three gold rings glittered in one ear. He had as much Irish in him as a plate of pig's knuckles.

"I've got a bug," I said.

"Man, you got the whole colony. They say there's a Mediterranean thing going around. Looks like it done washed right over you."

"What've you got in the way of a cure?"

"There ain't no cure. You just got to sit it out."

"You're the first person who's told me that since I came down with this thing. Everybody's got a remedy."

"Folks don't like to admit there's anything can't be licked. That's why they build bomb shelters and bet against Jordan." He wiped his hands on the towel draped over his shoulder. He could have palmed a grapefruit with either one. "Now, what can I pour you to keep you busy while you're waiting?"

"A Bubonic Plague."

"Coming right up."

I jerked up out of the fog and watched as he took down a bottle of creme de cacao and a fifth of Gordon's gin and set them on his workspace. He poured coffee from the carafe on the burner into a small steel mixing bowl and left it to cool while he got a jar of Brer Rabbit molasses from a low cabinet and measured the rest of the ingredients into a glass. He used tongs to drop two ice cubes into the coffee, whisked them around with a glass rod, then scooped them out with a strainer and threw them into the sink. Finally he poured in the coffee, added the molasses with a long-handled teaspoon, and stirred vigorously until the liquid was a uniform black. He dealt me a plain cocktail napkin and plunked the glass down on top of it.

"One Plague," he said. "Friend of Merlin's?"

I turned the glass around, admiring. The drink had a gloss that had been missing the first time in the cigar bar. But that had not been a feat of alchemy.

"He told me he invented it," I said. "I didn't know whether to believe him."

"He invented it. Well, I suggested the creme de cacao. He wanted to use the molasses for a base, on account of he thought a drink called the Bubonic Plague ought to be black. I told him it'd take a half hour to pour, and then nobody but Mr. Ed would drink it."

I sipped. On top of the flu the drink made sense. "Merlin prescribed hot Vernor's and Smirnoff's for what I've got."

"I tried it last time I got sick. I heaved up my shoes. Seen him lately?" The muscles bulged under his white shirt as he wiped his hands with the towel.

"I was going to ask you the same thing."

"He was in day before yesterday. Not since."

"Ever known him to stay away this long?"

"Only every time I loan him money."

"How much does he owe you?"

"Not a cent. Matter of fact, last time he was in he paid me back everything he borrowed and bought a drink for the house besides. We had eight customers then. Busy day."

"He had fifty bucks burning a hole in his pocket."

"Had him a lot more than fifty. I seen three fifties on that roll he was flashing, inside of a couple of C-notes."

"Did he say where he got it?"

"You a cop?"

I gave him a card with a ten-spot folded around it. "He's helping me out with a case."

He read the card and stuck the bill in his apron pocket without looking at it. No one bothers to counterfeit anything less than twenties anymore. "One of his women, probably. Merl lives off women."

"Any names?"

He shook his big head. "He's kind of a gent when it comes to talking about women. I guess nobody's all asshole. He mentioned a sister once, but I think she's dead. I hope he's okay. The place don't seem right without him coming in and making up Irish holidays to get a free drink on the house."

"He'll come back when his money runs out. Do you know his current address? His last one was a booth in the City-County Building."

"Who knows that? Merl lives off women."

I put down five for the drink and laid another ten on top of it. "Ask him to call me when he comes in. Tell him there's another fifty in it."

"I'll give him the message." He watched me climb down off the stool. "How'd you like your Plague?"

"If you can make gin and molasses taste like that, I'm going to have to come back and see what you can do with a real drink."

"Better hurry. There might be a slot machine standing in this spot." He polished the bartop.

10

Whether it was the gin or some biological eye of the storm, I was having a power surge when I parked in the police zone at 1300 Beaubien. I found a coroner's sign among the little collection I keep in the glove compartment, clipped it to the sun visor, and climbed the steps, staying close to the railing in case I slipped. The blue ice crystals someone had scattered on the concrete were fresh and hadn't had a chance to begin working.

The sergeant at the desk, an old warrior with fingers of scar tissue on the pink scalp showing through his close-cropped white hair, was too busy directing accident complaints to the proper department to throw me out, so I got on the elevator and punched John

Alderdyce's floor. The motor whined a little under the weight of two street patrolmen who boarded when the car stopped at two. They were as big as trolleys and bathed in Aqua Velva. I disembarked at five and aired myself out in front of the wall directory.

I still wasn't used to the trip. Since making inspector, John had traded his glass cubicle amidst the typewriters and jabber of the Criminal Investigation Division for a quiet door at the end of a quiet hall on another floor with his name on the panel in platinum. The only thing that set the place apart from a thousand similar corridors in a hundred other buildings was the row of head shots framed in black metal on either side, a fraction of the Detroit police officers who had been killed in the line of duty since the department began keeping count. When I tapped on the door, the thick felt runner beneath my feet and the acoustical tiles above my head swallowed the sound, as if not to disturb the ghost gallery.

"Enter."

The room had a high ceiling, the way they were designed during the Art Deco period when the place was built, and white leather on the walls. He was sitting in a green leather chair behind a cherrywood desk with a red leather top, holding a telephone receiver the size and thickness of a cigarette case to his ear. There was a blue leather visitor's chair in front of the desk and three more like it lined up against the wall, waiting for the gathering of suspects. I don't know what's become of leather; it's been years since I've seen it in its natural brown. Family pictures in brass frames crowded the top of the credenza under a window with a first-class view of the Wayne County Morgue. There wasn't a file cabinet or a cigar burn in sight.

When I came in he said, "Oh," and pegged the re-ceiver. "Who's the new operator at your service? She sounds like Melanie Griffith."

"She looks like Andy."

"How come you still use one anyway? They went out when the answering machine came in."

"Once every three or four months, someone calls in scared. Some of those service girls could talk a suicide down off a ledge while they're doing their nails. When they invent a machine that can do that, I'll be first in line to buy it, just as soon as the price comes down." I sank into blue leather, shook out a Winston, and put it back. There wasn't an ashtray in sight either. After a dozen years of trying he'd gone from four packs a day to one of the lesser vices. "If it's about those sixty-three parking tickets," I said, "I never saw them. They must've blown off the windshield."

"Bullshit. You don't get tickets. I know all about those signs you carry in your car." He gave me the cop eye. "You're going to throw out your back walking around with one foot in the grave. How many places have you contaminated since you left home?"

"How's the bug going to get around if I don't give it a lift? What were you calling me about?"

"I wanted to ask you if that client of yours ever showed up."

"I'd swear I dreamed him up if I thought I could dream up a checking account for him too. His address wasn't on the check and his bank won't give out that kind of in-formation without a note from the pope."

"What about the girl in the fur coat, you dream her up too?"

I used my handkerchief. I don't know why I bothered

except to clear my head just long enough for a thought to come through. "What makes you still interested? Don't tell me your daughter's still holding that meeting."

He shook his monolithic head. "My name on the door, Walker. Up here I do all the angling."

"I haven't found her yet." I always try to tell cops the truth. "Merlin Gilly either, comes to that. He's the one who handed me Boyette to begin with, I told you that. I'm expecting all three of them to show up in Kalamazoo with Elvis."

"He won't. Gilly won't."

I had started to cross my legs. I lowered the other foot to the floor. The floor was a long way down even for a sick man. "Which river did you pull him out of?"

"There you go again, forgetting you're the fish. What makes it we pulled him out of anywhere?"

"That door with your name on it still belongs to police headquarters. So do you. You only go home to sleep and change horses. The last time you called me socially you had two World Series tickets to Tiger Stadium. Reagan was in office. Okay, no river. Trunk of a car parked in the long-term lot at Metro Airport. If Merlin had gone to high school, that's where he'd have been voted most likely to wind up."

"I was voted most artistic," Alderdyce said. "My first job in plainclothes was drawing the chalk lines around the corpses. Gilly died in bed this morning. He had fifteen holes in him."

"Why fifteen?"

"That's as many as a nine-millimeter Beretta holds. I guess she was too lazy to reload."

"She?"

"I think the word's still politically correct. I didn't see today's list so I could be wrong."

"Did her eyes match?"

"You can come see for yourself. We're interrogating her now."

He locked the office and we took the elevator to the CID. It was Deco there too, but seventy years of spent tobacco had stained the ceiling the color of green tea and a couple of thousand pairs of fallen arches had worn the floor as wavy as a warped phonograph record. Here and there a flowering plant in a pot splashed color against the institutional beige and green—female cops work a little harder on their feminine side than their white-collar sisters—but even the buds had a hardboiled look and probably ate meat. The inspector asked a woman with a Ruger in a holster snapped to a Pierre Cardin belt where the Blessing woman was being questioned, then led me down a short hall to a steel-core door with a gridded window.

"Viola Blessing," he said. "Her late father sat on the board at General Motors under Eisenhower. Trust fund's just about played out."

Two male detectives in shirtsleeves, one I knew slightly, the other a stranger, were sitting at a table across from a woman in a white blouse with ruffles and a gray wool skirt, both expensive and fitted well to her slightly overblown figure. Her high heels were too young for her, and so was her red dye job. She wore it pushed back from her ears, not a good idea. She had a flat pudding face, made up at some counter by someone who thought the Dragon Lady look was back. Maybe it was, but it hadn't come back for her. She was in her middle forties. Thirty extra pounds made her older. A big horse

of a girl the boys at Grosse Pointe Elementary could always count on to fill in for their absent tackle during re-
cess. The reels were turning on a tape machine the size
of a suitcase on the table. A white-haired party I didn't
know sat between captors and caught with a leather at-
tache case on his lap and a tragic face, watching them
turn. That would be the trusted family retainer.

"It's not her," I said.

Alderdyce nodded. "I was pretty sure it wasn't. Both
her eyes are brown, and she's the right age, only twice.
Did you ever meet?"

I said we hadn't. "Gilly told me about her. His latest
love."

"Last, too. He was staying in her apartment in East
Detroit—excuse me, East*pointe*. He slept in, so she went
out for breakfast at Bob Evans and brought some back
for him, only he never ate it. She took the gun, graduation present from the old man, out of a drawer in the
nightstand and gave him a break from all that cholesterol. Then she called nine-one-one. She was eating eggs
and sausages in the kitchen when the uniforms came.
Gun was on the table with the slide kicked all the way
back."

"How'd Detroit get it?"

"Eastpointe cops figured as long as all of Gilly's
records were here, we ought to have the rest of it. It
wouldn't be because her family kicked in to buy the city
its new name."

"She spill anything?"

"All the way downtown. The uniforms pulled over
twice to read her her rights. We're getting it down now.
On her way home from the restaurant she picked up her
mail and opened a letter forwarded to Gilly from his last

place of residence. It was from his wife asking if she could expect him home for Easter."

"Which one, the one in Corktown or the one in Rochester Hills?"

"Corktown. I didn't know about Rochester Hills."

"I think that one was common law. Her story check out?"

"She still had the letter in her purse. I just wanted you to get a look at her so we can deal you out of this one. One more domestic kill for the Eyewitness News maggots to munch on."

"He said she thought he looked like Johnny Depp."

"Love's blind. And as dumb as bottled water." He turned back toward the elevators.

I went with him. "Who gets the body, the wife in Corktown?"

"She might not want it. He was a lot more entertaining when his mouth was moving, that's how he reeled them in. There's a sister mentioned in his jacket, but it's old. The number's disconnected." He rang for the car.

"She's dead, I heard. Is there still a Potter's Field?"

"Developers snapped up the last of it years ago. We still get calls when some weekend gardener turns up a skull in his back yard. These days the county donates the unclaimed stiffs to the U of M medical college. I'd like to get a look at the med student's face when he cuts into Merlin and pure bullshit runs out."

"Poor dumb bastard."

"Yeah. They'll miss him in Stationary Traffic. He paid off a couple of hundred bucks in parking tickets a month just so he could go back to the Erin and tell the suckers who got them he'd put in the fix. Never could forget he was in Jerry Cavanagh's press corps, that was Merl's problem."

"He could barely write his own name."

"Sure. His job was pulling down the other guy's campaign posters." He rang again, then said shit, and headed for the stairs.

I put a hand on his arm at the door. He looked at the arm. John doesn't like anyone touching his tailoring. I let go, but he stayed put.

"Can you get a fix on Boyette for me from the company that leased him his car?" I asked. "They need it in ink on a police letterhead." I gave him the name of the place and the Toyota's license number.

"I got it." He left his notebook in his pocket. "Who owes who at this point? I lost track."

"Favor for a friend."

"Is that what we are? What's my son's name?"

"Alderdyce."

He pushed open the door. "I'll call you when I get around to it."

It was a cue line and I took it out of the building.

Part Two

The Hours of the Acquisitor

11

I'd been fighting the bug long enough. It was time to go ahead and have it.

I dumped a fast forty at Rite-Aid on Robitussin, two brands of antihistamine, the brothers Smith, a generic Nyquil, and a paperback novel about Navajo detectives investigating mysterious goings-on at an Indian burial ground in New Mexico; I hoped it wouldn't give me nightmares about suburbanites spading up skulls. I admired the nose sprays for a long minute, but the doctor who had undeviated my septum the second time had made me promise never to use them on pain of hemorrhage. I had never used them before, but there was an option closed forever; one more of the continuing benefits of sixty-two rounds of amateur boxing in college. I went home, took drugs, and slept. I didn't dream of skulls. Instead I was hunting polar bears at the South Pole and wild boar on a steaming island off the coast of Madagascar—depending upon whether I was chilled or feverish—and Earl North kept showing up. He put me off balance by wearing a fur parka in the tropics and a grass skirt in the Antarctic. The only thing that remained constant was every time I reached for Dale Leopold's .45, it turned into something ridiculous. Once it was a Bubonic Plague.

The last fever broke sometime around midnight. I woke up in a puddle of sweat in the dark and didn't know where I was. Then I recognized the luminous dial on the 1948 alarm clock on the nightstand and found the switch on the lamp. Other familiar things on the stand— cigarettes, water tumbler, the new paperback, the portable pharmacy, my revolver—grounded me in my little bedroom. I used the bathroom, washed my face, changed into dry pajamas, replaced the soaked sheets, and sat up smoking and reading the novel until the print blurred. Then I put out the cigarette and lay back with my eyes closed and the book on my chest. I woke up with the sun in my face. The lamp was still on and I was as hungry as a polar bear. My breathing passages were open.

I showered, shaved, and brushed my hair. My eyes were clear for the first time in days. I put on a robe and made a pot of coffee and threw half a pound of bacon and six eggs into the skillet. Wiping my plate with the last of my toast I thought there might be something to this breakfast fad after all.

I burned my morning cigarette over the *Free Press*.

Merlin Gilly got two columns in the first section under the headline LATE GM DIRECTOR'S DAUGHTER ARRESTED IN HOMICIDE, with a mug shot of Viola Blessing cropped from a ten-year-old file photo. I learned nothing new, aside from the fact she'd been married once, briefly, to a ski instructor at Mt. Brighton. Merlin was described as "a one-time Detroit politico with suspected ties to organized crime." He might have planted it himself if he weren't floating in formaldehyde downtown.

I thought about Merlin. There wasn't anything in it for the eulogy. If the son of a bitch had married anyone but a Catholic straight from Dublin he'd have had a clean divorce years ago and I'd still have him to bounce off the floor until he told me who'd set me up and why.

By that time it was 8:00 A.M., time to go to work. I got dressed and drove to the office, where I got out the reverse directory and looked for the Boyette number that I now knew didn't belong to the Detroit Institute of Arts. No listing. It was too soon after the last time to ask my contact at Ma Bell to look it up in the unlisted roster; getting caught by his supervisor meant instant dismissal and possible prosecution, and the favor he owed me didn't balance out the double risk. It wasn't worth burning a good source. Pending John Alderdyce's lukewarm promise to trace him through his leasing company, Boyette was as gone to me as the Hours of the Virgin.

At least through direct methods.

I found a number in the Birmingham directory and dialed it.

"*After Six*. This is Cynthia." She sounded as if they'd imported her from London's West End.

"Good morning, Cynthia. Boss in?"

"I have many superiors, sir. With which one did you wish to speak?"

"Gordon Strangeways."

"I'll transfer you to corporate."

I listened to Gilbert and Sullivan for thirty seconds.

"Strangeways, Priscilla." This one had an apartment in Windsor Castle.

"Hi, Priscilla. Can you put me through to Mr. Strangeways?"

"I'm sorry, sir."

"That's okay. You understand American better than I understand English." I repeated the request.

She waited in case I had anything else to say. Then, "I intended to explain that Mr. Strangeways isn't in. He seldom comes to the office."

"Is there a number where he can be reached?"

"Again, I'm sorry. I'm not at liberty to give out that information."

"Can you get a message to him?"

"One moment, please."

This time I got Victor Herbert. If Queen Elizabeth came on the line I was going to have to put on a clean shirt.

"Hi, this is Tamara. You've got a message for Mr. Strangeways?"

They'd thrown me a curve; an American one with a gritty twang, straight from the 'hood. I put away my McGuffey's.

"Amos Walker's the name. Spelled like it sounds." I gave her my number. "Tell him I'm about to swear out a complaint against his wife. Accessory to attempted murder and conspiracy in a kidnapping."

For half an hour after I hung up the office was quiet.

The environmental team hadn't reported to work for days and the pink carcinogenic mass hanging out of the ceiling in the hallway wasn't making any noise. My mail included two belated checks for old cases and a stack of bills that when they were paid would leave me with six cents over. I used eight cents' worth of ink to enter the figures in the ledger and since I was in the hole anyway I went ahead and brought the ledger up to date from Thanksgiving. Then I cranked down the Underwood from the top of the file cabinet and typed up my notes on the current mess. Everything I knew about it came to a page and a half double-spaced with wide margins.

The telephone rang while I was reading it over. I let the bell go twice more and picked up. The accent that greeted me, voice female, was American, but its owner wouldn't know Tamara socially. It sounded like it came from very high up in a building with sealed windows.

"Mr. Walker, please. This is Jillian Raider of Raider and Associates, Attorneys at Law."

"This is Amos Walker of Walker and Detroit Manufacturers Bank. What can I do for you, Ms. Raider?"

"It's Mrs. I honor my husband's memory. My firm represents Gordon Strangeways in personal legal matters. I'm in receipt of a message that states you've made an accusation against Mrs. Strangeways."

"You're misinformed."

"I am." It was neither a question nor a statement. She'd know her way around the witness box in a courtroom.

"I told Tamara I'm about to swear out a complaint against Mr. Strangeways' wife. Until I do that I haven't accused anybody of anything."

"I would advise against it. The penalties under Michigan law for filing a false police report are severe.

My firm would also file a suit against you on Mrs. Strangeways' behalf for libel and character defamation."

"So far that's the only argument I've found in favor of staying poor," I said. "Mrs. Strangeways would just end up owing eight thousand dollars on my mortgage."

"What do you want, Mr. Walker?"

"I'll answer that question in Mrs. Strangeways' presence."

"If it's money, this isn't the first extortion attempt that's been made. I should warn you this conversation is being recorded."

"Yeah, I heard the echo. A big firm like yours should be able to afford someone who knows how to hook up the equipment. I can interview the lady in the comfort of her own home or I can wait till the showup downtown. I'm offering her the freedom of choice. If I were her attorney I'd advise her to take it. It may be the last freedom she sees for a long time."

The reels on her end of the line took a couple of turns. "Who are you?"

"I'm a Michigan state licensed private investigator with a ringing in my ears with Laurel Strangeways' name on it. I got it when a friend of hers tried to put a bullet there instead. I also want to return one of her earrings. It's no good to me. I wear the clip-on kind."

"You're talking gibberish."

"I can't help it. It's my native tongue."

"I may call you back."

"If the line's busy I'm talking to the police."

"I will call you back." She left me.

I smoked and paid a couple of bills. Twice in two days I'd used the cops as a club. I was one taxpayer who was getting his money's worth. When the envelopes were sealed and stamped I got up and walked over to the window and looked out. The lunch counter down the street had been closed for two months; the sign on its boarded-up window informing customers where it had relocated flapped loose where a corner had torn away from its thumbtack. They were probably going to tear it down and build a casino, forty stories high and ten feet wide.

I went back to answer the telephone. "Police annex."

This time there was no echo. "Mr. and Mrs. Strangeways will see you at their home this evening at ten."

"Why so late?"

"Her plane doesn't get in until eight. She's been in Louisiana for a week, visiting friends."

"They must not have any matches there. She flew back three days ago just so I could light her cigarette."

Jillian Raider let two seconds go by. "Mrs. Strangeways doesn't smoke. Are you sure we're discussing the same person?"

"One blue eye, one hazel?"

"She has that condition."

"Tell her and Mr. Strangeways I'll see them at ten."

"Naturally I'll be present."

"Naturally." I got the address on Grosse Ile and we were through with each other for a while.

—What's the job, Dale?

Just another Dagwood Bumstead with a snake in his pants, kid. Don't worry your pretty little head about it. It's a one-man job.

—You're always telling me a P.I. who takes on a tail job solo is keeping company with an idiot. I'm not doing anything tonight.

Like hell you're not. You're being a husband. New wives got a thing about their men checking in once or twice a week for some reason. They grow out of it, and it's just too bad. Enjoy it while it's here. Go home. Make a kid. Where are all the new dicks going to come from otherwise?

—If you're sure.

Who said anything about sure? Your mother didn't send in the guarantee when she took you home. The only sure is dead sure.

—Okay, see you tomorrow.

Sure, kid.

Not a dream—I was wide awake, and my watch said less than two minutes had passed since I finished talking to Mrs. Jillian Raider—but as vivid as one, and I left it with a jolt and a chill in my back and shoulders as if I were suffering a relapse.

Sure, kid.

Last words aren't what they used to be; no far far better things or liberty-or-deaths or even Oscar Wilde's "Either that wallpaper goes or I do." Just an adjective and a noun, a noun he knew I hated. Kids always do. Not much spiritual fuel in it, but then Dale wasn't high on metaphysics, although he knew the word and what it meant. He bought only John O'Hara, but he read everything. After his death I returned fourteen overdue books I'd found lying around the office to the library, each with a page-corner turned down in a different place: some Robbinses and Ludlums, Freud's *Interpretation of Dreams*, a supernatural tract by Edgar Cayce, two volumes of Casanova's *Memoirs*, and a Viennese cookbook. He didn't cook and he lived on burgers and tacos and Pepsi-Cola by the case, but he said reading recipes was the only thing that wound him down after a heavy day or an overnight stakeout. "Winding down" being the closest thing to sleep he knew. He was a lifelong insomniac. But the reading and thousands of hours of solitary thinking couldn't soften his practical shell.

The next time I saw him, on a closed-circuit screen in the Wayne County Morgue, I was relieved at first, because that slack, pulp-colored face wasn't Dale's. Positive IDs often come second, the attendant said. The package looks different without its contents.

Echoes of words, a cigar-burn shaped like a caterpillar on the edge of the desk, an old felt hat worn shiny on the brim in the shape of two fingers that grasped it in the same spot every time he tugged it on or took it off. With the O'Haras and the savings account for the daughter and the Army .45, the sum total of the estate after the debts were cleared.

So why the dream/memory in the middle of a quiet Detroit morning?

It wasn't the big breakfast or the cigarettes I'd smoked. I didn't think it was the asbestos in the hallway; the surgeon general wouldn't have overlooked that. I had a clean bill of health from my head and a second opinion from my stomach, so hallucinations were out. A ghost message, maybe. They're always in code for some reason. Being stuck in limbo, ghosts got nothing better to do than sit around making them up.

Not a ghost. Dale always said there wasn't any point in dying if all you did was come back. If he did come back he would refuse to believe in himself.

Something forgotten. Important, probably. We only remember with absolute clarity the things that don't count. Vague but insistent, coming through as static, like an interfering signal from a pirate transmitter. The transmitter being A. Walker at twenty and change.

Okay, a ghost.

Just another Dagwood Bumstead with a snake in his pants.

Just another Dagwood Bumstead with a snake
Just another Dagwood Bumstead
Just another
Just

Nuts.

12

Grosse Ile is one of the two largest of some fifteen islands strung out along the Detroit River, the other being Belle Isle, which is a park where the Detroit Police Bomb Squad goes to detonate suspicious packages. Unlike Belle Isle, Grosse Ile supports a city-size community of its own, on the site of what was mostly farmland for three hundred years until the postwar housing boom wiped it out in less than twenty. Ten miles long and a mile wide, it noses into Lake Erie, with a canal called the Thoroughfare splitting it in two diagonally. Apart from its privately owned gardens and distinguished homes, it's best known as the place where Cadillac set ashore and said, "Here I shall build a city," then thought better of the decision and sailed upriver to say the same thing on the site of Detroit a day or two later. That's okay with most of the people who live on the island; if they could weigh anchor and drift out into the middle of the lake and away from the Motor City, they'd cast off tomorrow.

I drove out West Jefferson, crunching through slush that had thawed from yesterday's ice storm, then re-frozen, and took the free bridge to the island. It had been repaired recently after a boat had smashed into it, diverting traffic onto the toll bridge farther down. The company that operated the toll bridge had helped out during the emergency by pocketing the increased fare-load. By night, Macomb Street was lit by spindly lamps with long stretches of darkness in between, with here and there a lighted window suspended from the black like a Christmas ornament. Some of the houses the win-dows belonged to dated back to silk breeches and tri-corne hats.

My directions took me across the shining black waters of the Thoroughfare twice, flowing steady as a fat dog between bunches of elder and sumac overhanging its banks. At last I swerved to avoid hitting a possum that froze in the middle of the lane, eyes glowing turquoise in the glare of my headlamps, and there was the drive-way on the right. It wandered down from an artificial el-evation under a glistening coat of fresh asphalt, ending at an iron gate stretched between stone pillars. There a trailerload of gravel had been dumped onto the apron to discourage low-slung sports cars from turning around on it. As per instructions, I stopped before the gate and blinked my lamps off and on twice.

A pair of security lights slammed on, whiting out the entire block from twenty-foot towers hidden back in the trees. In a couple of minutes a Jeep Ranger came barreling down the winding incline and crunched to a stop on the other side of the gate. The springs were still rocking when two men in matching leather jackets and fur caps got out. One of them carried a shotgun. This one stood back behind the glare of the high beams, cradling his weapon, while his companion unlocked and opened one side of the gate and approached the car. I cranked down the window. Cold touched my face like an icy palm.

"Get out, please. Keep your hands in sight."

I did that. I had six inches on him and thirty-five pounds, but his were packed tight and squared off into a compact package around fifty, gray at the temples and battered about the face like a solid old piece of furniture. His voice was slightly wheezy. There's always work in the private security field for retired welterweights with damaged windpipes.

He asked me, not impolitely, to assume the position. I leaned on my hands on the roof of the Cutlass while he went over me from neck to heels, paying special attention to the hem of my topcoat and the insides of my thighs. It didn't hurt, it didn't tickle. Whoever had taught him had done his job and it had taken. Before leaving Detroit I'd unsnapped the Smith & Wesson from my belt and put it in the glove compartment.

He stepped back. When I turned around he was reading my ID in the beam of a Malice Green flashlight. I hadn't felt him sliding the folder out of my inside pocket. Facing him in the ring must have been like fighting a swarm of invisible hornets. A .44 magnum as big as a wrecking hammer rode in a half-holster at his waist with four inches of nickel-plated barrel poking out the bottom.

He handed me the folder. "Leave the car. Vernon'll drive it up."

Vernon, taller and more narrow, came forward then, lowering the shotgun. He was all shadow between cap and collar. It was one of those matte-finish black faces that don't reflect light. His partner answered for him when I mentioned the gun in the glove compartment.

"It'll still be there."

I followed the welterweight through the opening in the gate and we got into the front seat of the Ranger, where he adjusted his holster so the magnum wasn't poking him in the thigh. He swung the Jeep around in a tight *Y* and drove one-handed up the twisting private road. Pines and hardwoods flashed by in the wash of the lamps. A lot of arboreal work had been done to convince the odd visitor that he was a long way out in the country. As we rounded one sharp curve, an owl perched on a fresh kill swung its head 180 degrees, staring into the glare with eerily human eyes, then took off with a slow-motion flutter of broad dark wings, clutching its trophy in its talons. A strong acid whiff of skunk came through the air vents a moment later.

"How's the hunting around here?" I asked the welterweight.

"Don't ask me. I get mine at the counter."

We came around a bootjack and the house sprang out at us, ten thousand square feet anyway and all of it on one level, a sampler's plate of architectural styles ranging from early Georgian to *Star Trek*'s third season, with every window lit. The place had more roofs than *Vertigo*. Either it had been added on to many times by many different owners or the contractor had had the attention span of a fruit fly. I asked how long it had been there.

"The original part was built during the Civil War. Mr. and Mrs. Strangeways did the rest. There's still construction going on in the west wing."

"Don't you mean Reconstruction?"

He said nothing. Wrong audience.

We stopped in a rectangle of light from one of the windows. I didn't try counting them. You don't itemize stars. "Am I the first guest?"

"First and last. Go up and knock."

I barely got my hand off the door handle when the Jeep pulled away. It followed the driveway around the end of the house and disappeared. I mounted a Palladian front porch equipped with a non-period ramp for Strangeways' wheelchair, grasped the ring of a massive silver lion's-head knocker that had done most of its best knocking on some other door long before there was a New World, and used it. It drew a satisfying boom from the chased oak paneling. The date 1861 was chiseled into the stone lintel above the door.

It's a democracy, after all. There was no reason to expect anyone but Gordon Strangeways to answer his own door, except the act didn't go with the house or the physical condition of its owner. The inside handle was placed low enough for him to grip without reaching, and when I thought to look, I saw that a hydraulic contrivance mounted high on the frame did most of the pulling. At the moment, however, I was more interested in the contrivance that did the rest of it.

"Come in, then. I'll be damned if I'll pay to heat the whole island."

He was seated on one of those nifty motorized scooters, this one with racing lines and a patent-leather saddlebag on either side of the upholstered seat for carrying books and things. Deeply tanned and clad in rose-colored sweats and two-hundred-dollar track shoes, he looked healthier than he had in recent photographs. His dark eyes were bright behind the pink-tinted lenses of his aviator's glasses and his pewter-colored hair coiled back like crisp wire from a lush widow's peak to his collar. It was difficult to tell where the natural growth left off and the implants began. His face was lean and clean-shaven, not jowly. I stepped inside. He let the hydraulics suck the door into its frame and backed up the scooter for a better look.

"Gordon Strangeways." He didn't offer his hand. "I was expecting something in alpaca."

"They were out of stock, sorry. You get me in worsted."

"An observation, not a critique. Popular fiction to the contrary, blackmailers in general are men of taste. That's what motivates them."

His accent was British with a strong South African overlay, or so I guessed. I'd never been any closer than *Tarzan and the Lost City of Gold.*

"Met many of them, have you?" I asked.

"Price of wealth. You admit, then, that your business with me is extortion."

"I never admit anything in a doorway. And my business isn't with you." I looked around. "Where's the legal talent?"

"At the airport meeting Mrs. Strangeways. In addition to representing me at the bar, Mrs. Raider is my general factotum. My wife's flight was delayed an hour." He regarded me on a level; not an easy trick when the eyes you're looking into are two feet higher than yours. "What are you if not a highbinder?"

"Your guest. Do I put my coat here?" I climbed out of it and laid it across a filagreed bench that had been built back when sitting down was something you planned first. There wasn't a staircase in sight; if the original structure had included a second story, it had been eliminated during the improvements. The foyer, tiled in green-and-white checkerboard marble and hung with green silk, opened out in two directions through wide arches. A religious tapestry ten by twenty feet covered one wall—a Renaissance piece, I thought, until I looked again at St. Sebastian's pierced body and recognized Gordon Strangeways' head on top of it. Editors will editorialize.

"We'll wait in the library."

He backed the scooter around and led the way through the arch to the left. We passed a number of paintings in a hall, one or two of which might have been Picassos, and a couple of sculptures with holes in them. None of these bore the least resemblance to Strangeways. The place didn't have any more doors than it had stairs, just broad open entrances easily negotiated by a man without the use of his legs. I had to stride to keep up. Either he liked to make shakedown artists sweat for their take or he went through a battery a week.

"The house is a bit of a crazy quilt," he said, warming up a little. "The wish-fulfillment of a cripple with too much money. The old section, which we just left, is said to have been built by a spy for the Confederacy. When we took down a wall we discovered a secret passage that may have led to a hidden dock on the Thoroughfare, but that could just as easily have been added by the bootlegger who occupied the place during Prohibition. I'd admire to have installed a few such features myself, but today's construction codes call for too many inspections. I'd have had to have let half of Wayne County in on the secret."

There was nothing in that for me, so I let it float down the Thoroughfare.

At length we slowed down and entered a room the size of the Tomcat Theater. That was where the similarities ended. The twelve-foot ceiling was made entirely of stained glass, with ambient lighting installed above. This cast colors onto a mosaic floor designed to incorporate the patterns that resulted. Between them stood a hundred thousand books on shelves behind leaded panes. On three Eastlake easels rested loose yellow leaves of what I now knew to be vellum, each the size of a page from a world atlas and crusted over with elaborately wrought lettering in gold and tarnished silver and crushed semiprecious stones. A massive refectory table rested upon six seated lions carved from ivory, every square inch of its top stacked high with volumes bound in cracked calfskin, moldy buckram, and discolored silk. The room smelled of stale leather and genteel decay, like an old woman waiting patiently for the lover who had jilted her to return after sixty years. Somewhere a hidden air-recycler whirred, the white noise of the bibliomaniac.

Somewhere too, quieter than that, a dog-eared punch-card found its slot and dropped in. A tired brain turned over with a thud and started clicking.

"You collect?" I asked.

"An occupational inevitability, I'm afraid. Barbers pursue razors, farmers antique tractors. Publishers—well, you're not blind." He put his scooter into a spin on the

Biblical pastoral scene assembled at our feet and stopped on Cain's face, looking at me. "You know my history?"

"Some of it."

"Then you may understand my obsession. Hundreds—thousands of obscure men with dangerous ideas traded their lives for what's written in these books. They were burned, hanged, broken on the rack, drawn and quartered. Their eyes were gouged out and molten lead poured into the sockets to cauterize the profanity they had read and written. The only time I truly feel I'm not alone is the time I spend in this room."

"I get it. Thomas More gave up his head so you could publish pictures of naked ladies."

"The subject matter isn't important. Certainly it made no difference to the man who swung the axe. Or the inbred morons who incited the crowd that put me astride this machine. The man who buys the paper stock should be able to put what he wants on it without trading his life or his legs for the privilege."

He swept a hand about the room. "Obviously, I felt this way long before the attack. I assembled the core of my library when I was still living in rented rooms. Back then you could put together a world-class book collection for a fraction of what a Japanese CEO spent on one Raphael at Sotheby's. That was before Hollywood entered the market. Even a movie star can manage to appear literate by dumping half his gross points on a Shakespeare First Folio."

"Do you know the Plymouth Book of Hours?"

He lowered his hand. "I know *of* it. I've never seen it. Great Britain has it."

"Not all of it."

"The Hours of the Virgin." He nodded. "Lost, as I recall, at the time of the Civil War. England's, not America's."

"One expert told me it was lost during the Blitz. Another said the Reformation. All everyone seems to agree on is that it's lost."

"We can settle it with some bloody quick research." He laid rubber to the huge table, lifted a volume bound in green fabric off a stack, and spread it open on his handlebars. He spent a few minutes turning the brittle pages by their edges. He stopped and studied. The print was tiny, laid out in dense narrow columns four to a page, but he read without bifocals and without using a finger. Finally he boomed the book shut, returned it to the stack, and swung back my way. "My source, a primary one, says the complete folio was known to be in the possession of Charles the First when he met the headsman. It resurfaced late in Cromwell's reign, minus the Virgin. The question remains whether the Roundheads found something in that section to offend them and destroyed it or a Royalist spirited it away to prevent that from happening. Perhaps your expert confused the Restoration with the Reformation. So many high-sounding names for such lowlife acts. Nothing changes except the terminology."

"What would you say if I told you I saw the first page of the Hours of the Virgin three days ago?"

He didn't fall off the scooter. I don't know if I wanted him to. I didn't even know why I told him, except that sword was getting heavy and it was either swing it or forget it. What he did was smile. His teeth were white and even; they had probably been fashioned for him after his original set was kicked down his throat in Little Rock.

"A leech who moonlights in the false antiquities trade.

Your tastes are more expensive than I thought. And just where did you happen to stumble upon this El Dorado?"

"The last place you'd expect. The Detroit Institute of Arts."

"Indeed. I'm a patron member. I missed it on the last list of acquisitions."

"It didn't get that far. When I saw it, it came out of a briefcase in a storeroom at the DIA. The briefcase belonged to a man named Harold Boyette."

"Ah," he said.

13

The air recycler whirred through the little silence.

"'Ah' means what?" I asked.

"It means that the very same embarrassing details that the DIA directors would withhold from me as a patron are common gossip in the tiny village of private collectors. I'm aware of the reason for Mr. Boyette's dismissal."

"What reason is that?"

"He was in league with forgers to defraud the museum; but you know that as well as I. You claim to be a detective."

"I just wanted to make sure the reason you heard was the same one I did. A lot of stories keep changing.

Someone ought to write them down. Do you think the Hours is a fake?"

"It seems likely on several levels. How closely did you examine the manuscript?"

"I saw one page. What I don't know about fifteenth-century illuminata would fill—what's the name of a big empty space on Grosse Ile?"

"There isn't one."

"You get the idea. The page had a crab louse stuck in the ink. It looked convincing, but that might have been the intention. Boyette said the manuscript was stolen from his office, only he hasn't had an office at the DIA for more than six months. The thief sent him the first page, he said, and demanded a hundred grand for the return of the rest. I went with him to the drop to hold his hand. I made a mistake and let go. He's gone and so is the money. If there was money. All I saw was a big envelope."

"I suppose the page disappeared with him?"

"It's a theory. Anyway no one's seen it."

He sat back with his hands on his knees. "Are you always this incompetent?"

"This time I had help. That's what I want to see your wife about."

"My wife has been away for a week."

"Does she own a silver fox coat?"

"Yes, but she wouldn't have taken it with her to Louisiana."

"Could we take a look in her closet?"

"We will not."

I moved a shoulder. "I'll wait and ask her."

"Just who are you working for?"

"I told you. Harold Boyette."

"But he's missing."

"That's why I'm still working for him. He hired me to help him get back the Hours. I haven't done that, and he hasn't been around to tell me I'm fired. There's also the matter of a ten percent finder's fee on a hundred thousand."

"Now the fog lifts," he said. "Is ten thousand dollars a lot of money to you?"

"It's a lot of money to ninety percent of the population, Mr. Strangeways. I'm an unsuccessful man in a business that went out when Silicone Valley came in. If I get back the Hours I get to stay in business for another year, but only if I get Boyette back too. The manuscript was removed from England illegally. The British government won't pay me for returning something that shouldn't have been taken in the first place."

"There are private collectors who would pay more than ten thousand for it. You'd be surprised how many distinguished men and women don't care a jot about rightful ownership when it comes to something they want."

"Does that include you?"

"I'm not a distinguished man. I did not steal the Hours. If I did I certainly wouldn't offer to sell it back for a piddling hundred thousand."

"But you didn't sell it back. The thief didn't sell it back. It's still out there, if it hasn't been destroyed."

He rested his hands on the handlebars. "If the manuscript is genuine, chances are it's survived. That psalter on the easel nearest you dates back to the tenth century. It predates the invention of cheap self-oxiding ink and acid-content paper by nearly a thousand years. Barring fire or deliberate destruction, it will still exist in a state close to the original a century after all the reference books in which it appears have returned to corruption. Modern books are doomed at birth, their every line impregnated with the spores of its own death. Figure in a regard for venerable things that increases in direct proportion to their irrelevance, and you see before you the nearest thing there is to immortality. Something that was never alive can never die."

"You mentioned deliberate destruction."

"That would require the determination of a Henry the Eighth. We don't get many of those. Look at the detail work on that psalter, five hundred years before the technique reached perfection in the Plymouth Book of Hours. A hand that would cut the throat of an infant without quivering would be struck lifeless before the blade touched one leaf. Human life is worthless compared to that dead animal skin." He bit off the last three words.

"I thought you liked books."

"They happen to interest me at this point in my passage. When I was very much younger, I was interested in women, all women. That fixation didn't last, but it was strong enough to make me realize, when I was in a position to do something about it, that a very nice living could be made from those who still suffered from it. Being a crusader for the rights of a free press interested me right up until the moment I heard my spine snap. That's a sound you never forget." He smacked the side of the scooter. "This is my charger now, but I no longer ride to the sound of the guns, won't even be induced to sign a check for the cause. Life interests me, obviously, or I would have ended mine when they told me I would never walk again or even go to the bloody loo without help. The minute something ceases to hold my attention, I dispose of it."

That opened up several avenues of conversation. I was still choosing among them when a bell rang.

"That will be Mrs. Strangeways," he said. "I expected a call before this."

He executed a neat turn and lifted the receiver off a mahogany-colored telephone mounted on the molding between two sets of bookshelves four feet from the floor. "Laurel? Oh, hello, Jillian." He listened. "What about her luggage? I see. Did you call the airport in Baton Rouge? They didn't? No, you might as well come back here. There's nothing more you can do there."

He replaced the receiver, left his hand on it for a moment, then turned back. The scooter's electric motor whined softly.

"She wasn't on the plane?" I asked.

"No. But her bags were."

14

"How sure are you she was in Louisiana to begin with?"
I asked.

The question didn't take at first and he started to ask
me to repeat it. Then he decided to get mad.

"If you're suggesting something, put it into words. I'll
need the excuse to have Ben and Vernon take you out
and throw you down the hill."

"Two nights ago a woman sat down next to me in the
Tomcat Theater and let me light her cigarette. Let's call
her Laurel Strangeways, just in case there isn't a pack of
women who look like her running around with eyes of
two colors. Then someone sitting behind me tried to

light my head with a bullet. When I got up from the floor I was a detective without a client."

"Laurel wouldn't know what to do with a cigarette if you stuck one in her mouth."

"I doubt that. You don't have to prove you smoke before they sell you a pack. Say it was a coincidence. Say she decided to take up the habit, or had been indulging all along on the sly. She just dropped in to make sure the projectionist in a theater owned by her husband wasn't sneaking a Disney film in between *Leather Love* and *The Silence of the Mams*, and that she happened to pick on me as a likely candidate for a match just as the axe fell. When it did she got smart like everyone else in the joint and took the air. Now swallow all that and explain why she was in town when you and your lawyer thought she was down south burning shrimp."

"It wasn't she."

"There's a quick way to prove me a liar. Check and see if her fur coat is hanging in her closet."

He thought about that. Then he turned back to the telephone on the wall, took down the handset, and pushed a button.

"Is that Ben?" he asked. "Ben, do me a favor and go to Mrs. Strangeways' room and bring me her silver fox coat. I'm in the library." He hung up. "I'll expect an apology before I throw you out."

I said nothing. While we were waiting I took a walk and read the titles on some of the ancient spines under glass. I only learned how much I didn't know about old books.

The welterweight came in, making no noise at all on the tiles. He'd shed his coat and cap. He combed his graying hair forward over his creeping forehead and wore a navy turtleneck under a blue twill uniform shirt without patches or other insignia. His hands were empty.

"The coat isn't there, Mr. Strangeways."

"You checked her closet?"

"The coat isn't there."

"Very well. Thank you, Ben."

The guard left. He hadn't looked at me once.

"That doesn't mean anything," Strangeways said. "I didn't see her when she left the house. She might have worn it on the way to the airport. It certainly doesn't prove she was in the Tomcat the other night."

"She was recognized."

"By whom? You?"

I had my hands in my pockets. I felt the triangle of the platinum earring in the right, but it didn't come out. "I don't need to convince you. Let's concentrate on why her luggage came home from Cajun country without her."

"Don't you mean how? Who could have put it on the plane if not she?"

"We can fill in who later. How is easy: She ships the bags to a contact there, along with a ticket in her name. He or she checks them in at the curb using her ticket. That wouldn't work during terrorist season, but in heavy traffic a busy skycap might easily pass it on without asking to see identification. When the bags arrive in Detroit, everyone's convinced she intended to take the flight; what woman sends her clothes on without her? Now you're looking for her in Louisiana while her real trail grows colder by the minute."

"How do you know she never went down there?"

"How do you know she did? Who drove her to the airport on the way out, or did she drive herself?"

"She took a cab. The company will have a record."

"It might prove she went to the airport. It wouldn't tell whether she left it on a plane or in another cab. The passenger manifest would tell whether she made the flight, but you wouldn't be checking that right away because of the charade with the luggage. She still has her head start."

"Obviously you don't know Laurel. She isn't that devious."

I grinned. "For someone who made his pile undressing women, you don't know a lot about them."

"So bitter, so young," he said. "You must be divorced."

"I prefer to call myself a monodependent. Where did she tell you she was staying down south?"

"With friends. She called me from there twice. That's how I know you're mistaken."

"Do you have Caller ID?"

"Of course. I average two death threats a month."

"Then you should have a record of where she called from. Unless she used a cellular telephone."

"I'm afraid she did."

I dealt myself a Winston.

"Please don't smoke in here," he said. "It voids my insurance."

"Mine too." I put it away. "Let me know when I get too personal. If my wife's clothes showed up at Metro Airport without her in them, I'd have been on the horn before this, starting with the friends in Louisiana."

"You became too personal the moment you made me aware of your existence. It so happens I believe in my wife's ability to take care of herself."

"I hope you're right, for both your sakes. Whatever she's into, she's in it up to her eyes that don't match."

"That was the feature that first caught my attention." His watery smile was unconnected to the rest of his face, bloodless now under the tan. "When you've spent as much of your life as I have in the company of feminine perfection, it's the mistakes of nature that intrigue you. Laurel's soul is her perfection. You can't improve upon that with crowns and implants."

I waited. After a moment he threw the scooter into gear and circled the table, coming to rest half a foot from where he'd started. I couldn't see any sense in it, unless he was a born pacer; one of those cinched-in Tommies you see in old war movies, stalking up and down the command center smacking their boots with a leather crop.

"I'm a crippled lion, Walker. I roar and shake my mane, but I can't carry off the bluff. Something happens to a man when he acquires an attractive young wife whose needs he cannot fulfill. He becomes reasonable."

I took my hands out of my pants pockets and slid them into those of my jacket, leaving the thumbs out. That would be in the script. "You're afraid of who might answer if you call the number."

"God knows why I'm sharing this with a blackmailer."

"It's easier with a stranger. And you don't believe I'm a blackmailer."

"No," he said. "I don't know what you are, but I'm sure you're not that."

"Does your wife have a history of disappearing?"

"No."

"Does she have any boyfriends you know about?"

"No. She's either completely faithful or absolutely discreet. I'm grateful for the second. In my position I'm reluctant to hope for the first."

I let the ancient books around us age five seconds more. "What's your relationship with Earl North?"

It was a stab in the dark, and it drew blood. His pupils shrank a thirty-second of an inch. On him it was the equivalent of an epileptic seizure. "Why bring him up? Is he involved?"

"Where do you know him from?" I kept my hands in my pockets. I've done harder things, but not since Saigon fell.

"Here. This room. I employed him to catalogue and assess the library. I'd had dealings with Harold Boyette—nothing financial, just picking his brain on some acquisitions I was considering; it was before the scandal, and he was one of the leaders in his field. He recommended North to me. They were both working at the DIA then."

"When?"

"Last June. We'd only been in the house a month. The books were still in crates and I decided it was time I had someone in to develop a computer system. North was efficient. His familiarity with manuscripts and books was strictly general, but he was a wizard with a keyboard. He came in twice a week and remained for several hours, sorting the books into categories and sub-categories and cross-referencing them into the computer. He finished just before Thanksgiving. The machine's in the next room if you care to see his work. I wouldn't have it in here. The telephone is twentieth century enough."

"Seen him since?"

"No. I paid his fee and he left. Frankly, I'm surprised I haven't heard from him."

"Why?"

"I promised him a reference if he ever needed one. I heard he left the DIA last month." He smiled his watery smile. "Perhaps he thinks a letter of recommendation from a notorious sex merchant would bring him more harm than good. Perhaps he's right. What a world. Schools give out condoms to fifth graders, but a grown man has to whisper a request for one of my magazines to a clerk before he'll take it out from under the counter."

"Boyette said North was fired for stealing."

"If that's true, they did a better job keeping it secret than they did with Boyette. I never heard a thing."

"Ruddy at the DIA said he fired him for going through the files of patrons."

"Ruddy's a dry old bird and a penny-pinching Scot besides. But he doesn't spread false gossip. I'm inclined to believe him. All I can say is North behaved himself all the time he was here."

"The Boyette scandal broke while North was working here. He recommended North. That must have caused some concern."

"It did," he said. "I considered having him investigated."

"What stopped you?"

"What makes you think anything did?"

"If you'd had him investigated, you would have heard my name before your lawyer gave it to you and you'd have known I wasn't here to bleed you. Earl North and I are old acquaintances."

"I'm old school, Walker. In the absence of evidence of guilt I'd rather be betrayed by someone I trusted than betray myself by being too damn smart to trust someone I should. By the time I learned the circumstances of Boyette's dismissal, North had proven his worth to me. I asked him straight away if he was involved in any of the frauds. He said he wasn't. I chose to accept that."

"You're a liar, Mr. Strangeways. An old-school liar, but a liar just the same."

It was the first color his cheeks had shown in some time. I was impressed. Any man who still thinks being called a liar is an insult is worth getting to know.

He used the telephone again. "Ben, Mr. Walker is ready to leave. Please show him to his car."

"You don't trust Earl North," I said. "You don't even like him. You've spent more time at conference tables than Winston Churchill, and you're pretty good at keeping the lid on, but I'm just as good at prying them off. I saw your eyes when I mentioned North. I see the same thing in mine every time he comes into my head while I'm looking in a mirror. You'd like to knock him down and run your electric moped back and forth across his face. What made you decide not to have him investigated?"

Ben appeared, silently as before. This time he had on his leather jacket and cap. Strangeways looked at him. I'd made up my mind not to be so impressed with him if he went through with the bluff.

"Thank you, Ben. I've managed to talk Mr. Walker into staying a bit longer. I'm sorry I disturbed you."

The welterweight hesitated, then took himself away. He was as light on his feet as anyone in the ring or the ballet.

"It was Laurel," Strangeways said. "She made a joke of it. She said if I insisted on being a suspicious old spinster she'd knit me a shotgun. Didn't I tell her myself I'd still be setting type in Mossel Bay if some cynical old Tory hadn't taken a chance on me. It was most convincing."

"How long did it last?"

"I'm disabled, not blind. They were too formal with each other whenever I was in the room, and Laurel was spending entirely too much time at her vanity on days when he was expected. There were other things, too small and too many to go into now. But I didn't admit to myself that I knew what was taking place beneath my nose until the moment she spoke up for him. I backed off."

He spread his hands. He was eloquent with them; compensation for the loss of body language elsewhere. "Understand, Walker, I'm not a coward. I can't work up a fine melodramatic rage over the circumstances of my wife's orgasms when I'm incapable of giving her one myself."

"It's not something you give." I took my hands out of my pockets. "Offering your wife's lover a work reference is carrying self-sacrifice a long way."

"I was curious to see if he'd have the nerve to take me up on it."

"If he did, you'd have killed him."

"Worse. I would have destroyed him."

I looked at him, a man stuck on wheels in a big house on a wooded hill where predators swooped and slew twenty minutes from the heart of a great city. I wanted a cigarette. I took a walk. I stopped and turned my back on a row of crumbling Bibles.

"Where's North now?"

"I don't know," he said. "His office number was the only one I had for him." He adjusted his aviator's glasses.

"You haven't yet told me what his connection is with your quest."

"Boyette said he thought North stole the Hours and set up the ransom drop."

"Do you believe him?"

"I'd believe anything of North."

"Just how are you acquainted?"

"Not intimately. I only saw him once. That was the day the People of the State of Michigan decided not to prosecute him for my partner's murder."

"Ah."

"I'm disappointed," I said. "I was holding that back for the surprise."

"Murder is the easiest crime to commit. The only one that's almost always committed by amateurs. Anyone is capable of it." He breathed in and out. The sound was the same as the one the machine made changing the air in the room. "In a little while—after you leave—I shall find the courage to lift that telephone and call the number in Baton Rouge. If the person who answers is indeed an innocent friend of Laurel's, and if she doesn't know where she is, I may call you to request your professional services."

"Save your money for books, Mr. Strangeways. Finding your wife is part of finding Boyette and North."

He nodded. "If you should happen to discover something I'd just as soon not know, I hope I can count upon your discretion."

"If I do, you won't."

He offered his hand then. I took it.

As we broke contact, a woman entered the room in a scarlet slack suit and black all-weather coat tied around her waist. She was almost my height in flat heels, with red-gold hair combed straight back from an even line high on her forehead and chopped off square at the base of her neck. She had Scandinavian cheekbones and could pass for thirty, but not in this light. She stopped when she saw us. "Gordon."

"Amos Walker, Jillian Raider," Strangeways said. "I believe you met over the telephone."

"Your lawyer has a key to your house?"

"Why not? After fifteen years in litigation she's practically a partner. Nothing new, I suppose?"

She shook her head. Her chill gray eyes were on me. "You two appear to have become quite friendly. I hope you didn't discuss anything important in my absence."

"Oh, you know," I said. "Good books and travel."

15

The things you remember.

Dale drank his whiskey without water in bars that had no name, coffee you could float a shoe in, Pepsi with all his meals, and rusty water in smeared glasses with old exoskeletons bobbing on top. He sent back a steak if it showed signs of having passed within twelve feet of a stove, and when his bladder was full and his plate empty he picked fights with the biggest and ugliest thing in the room that didn't plug into the wall and play records. But the item he knew the most about after sleuthing was comic strips.

He knew Superman's childhood name and which color Kryptonite did what to him. He could rattle off the names and fixed ages of all the kids in the *Family Circus* and the date of the *Thimble Theater* strip that introduced Popeye the Sailor to Castor and Olive Oyl and the world, and once won fifty bucks off a precinct commander over the color of Beetle Bailey's eyes; or so he claimed. He was the only person I ever saw laugh at a cartoon in *The New Yorker.* I was still coming across buried booty he'd clipped and stashed in the desk in the office, fragile as sloughed skin but still funny. He'd killed two men as a foot patrolman and a third in private practice, defending himself against a missing person who objected to getting found, but he giggled like a troop of Brownies whenever Lucy jerked a football out from under Charlie Brown's foot.

I don't know why I thought of it. At Christmas I'd surprised myself with the gift of a VCR, the dividend from a credit check I'd given up on getting paid for until the mail came on December 23rd, and I started thinking about Dale and his comic strips while standing in the classics section of the video store two streets from my house, three minutes to closing on the way back from Grosse Ile. The movie I was thinking of renting was *The Harder They Fall,* which didn't belong to the same world as Nancy and Sluggo. I wound up renting *The Adventures of Rocky and Bullwinkle* and watched it straight through at home without taking off my coat. It didn't help, although Mr. Peabody reminded me a little of Gordon Strangeways.

Watching Boris and Natasha getting ready to roll a boulder onto Frostbite Falls, I wondered what Laurel Strangeways and Earl North had in common besides hot blood, and what it had to do with Harold Boyette and the Hours of the Virgin. This was no more successful than the boulder. While the tape rewound I mixed a drink and poured it into the vacuum, but that was no good either, so I poured another one on top of it and turned in. I dreamed I was married to a woman named Blondie and working for a man named Dithers, who was depending on me to do something important, but I was too busy making giant sandwiches and tripping over the mailman to hear what it was. Every time I opened my mouth to say something, Dudley Do-Right's tenor came piping out. When I woke up I was grateful I hadn't rented *Scream*.

The next morning was Saturday. The sky was the color of crude but there was no sign of snow or freezing rain. I stayed in and read the paper, sucking on a cough drop. You can't make bricks without clay and I was fresh out. There was nothing on any page about anyone I knew or anything I was connected with, unless it was in the comics section, and for once I skipped that.

In the afternoon I walked to the video store and returned the tape. I checked the classics section but it looked like a meat locker to a vegetarian. I knew everything there by heart. All the titles in New Releases either had Roman numerals or starred someone from *Saturday Night Live*. I walked home through the iron cold and watched a bowling tournament. That sparked the question of which was sadder, being a professional bowler or watching one on TV. Saturday, what a day.

Sunday I had coffee and half a grapefruit for breakfast. I hate grapefruit, but I wasn't sure when I'd have lunch and didn't want my blood supply messing around with a load of eggs and sausages in my stomach when I needed it in my brain. I had awakened with a mission.

I put on jeans, boots with felt liners, a heavy cable-knit

sweater from my hunting days, a navy peacoat, and a hat with not much shape in the crown but plenty of brim, big and soft enough to pull down over my ears if the wind came up. The Smith & Wesson fit in a coat pocket. I felt like Boris Badenov. Frost made white cobwebs of the cracks in the asphalt and crunched like tiny ribcages under the Cutlass' tires.

Mullett Street had changed in the years since I'd had any business there, but neither up nor down, only sideways. The city had knocked down some crack houses but put up nothing in their place, so the druggies had to do their dealing in empty lots with weeds tickling their ears. The adult theater had moved out of the truss building on the corner and a massage parlor and escort service had moved in. The sign in the window said OPEN but the front door was padlocked. The remains of a cease-and-desist order from Detroit Recorder's Court fluttered from the frame. The paper had outlived the body that had issued it. In a little while someone would smash the window and turn the building into a trysting place, with or without the consent of his companions. Progress. Across from it a municipal basketball court languished inside a chainlink fence with a locked gate, thistles growing through holes in the pavement. Shotgun pellets had punched morsels of daylight through the steel sign bearing the old mayor's name. Look on my works, ye mighty.

Before it was a basketball court it had been the Grand Marquis Hotel. Before that it had been the American Eagle Motor Lodge and before that, in a time of reduced circumspection, it had been the X-T-C Retreat, complete with parallel bars in every room and a costume rental shop in the lobby. It was the American Eagle the night Dale Leopold followed Earl North there from the offices of Paul Bunyan Mutual Life and Property in the National Bank Building downtown, where the subject earned his salary supervising the transfer of the company's files from cardboard folders in steel cabinets to its new mainframe computer.

Dale never wrote anything down for anyone but himself to read, but from the bits of paper covered with his crabbed common-law shorthand found on his body and in his desk, it wasn't the first trip there for either of them. Detroit Vice had nothing on the name "Star LaJoie" found among the notes, and a hooker sweep by Homicide drew only vague descriptions of a teenage female caucasian without outstanding physical characteristics. Whether she was the one North kept company with or just another source of information in the network of grifters, pushers, shopping-cart ladies, cigarette-smugglers, and concrete concubines Dale liked to call his Baker Street Irregulars, the notes didn't say. The Eagle night clerk, a methadone addict whose window faced a narrow lobby lit by a fifteen-watt bulb, told the city detectives that the only thing all of Star's gentleman friends had in common was a tendency to stand in the shadows while she paid for the room. She'd been in three times that night and he hadn't seen any of them well enough to furnish a description. He said. Forty-eight hours in holding without a needle to his name might have leeched a different story out of him, but it wouldn't have stood in court, and anyway he OD's a month later on an uncommonly rich heroin mixture that was floating around the city, and then he was doing his talking for ears that had heard it all.

Star wasn't around to ask either. The Detroit Major Crimes Division, then made up almost entirely of veterans of the late controversial STRESS crackdown unit, which included friends of Dale's, filed copies of all the prints and partials they'd managed to lift from the room she'd used that night, including three they couldn't match. None of the prostitutes they interviewed could recall having seen Star since the night of the shooting. Encouraged to guess, one or two remembered she usually caught a train that time of year to work the southbound convention trade, making back her fare in the sleepers on the way. Circulars went out to all the larger police organizations between Toledo and Key West. Sometime after that a sergeant named Richman drove down to Raleigh, North Carolina, matched one of the unknown Detroit prints to the body of an unidentified young woman found stuffed in a county storm drain with her throat slashed, and Star LaJoie's file was pulled from the drawer marked MISSING.

Evidence found at the scene helped convict a suspect in six rape-murders committed in three southern states over a period of a year and a half. Meanwhile North's wife alibied him for the night of the shooting and the case went away. In time even Dale's friends forgot.

All except one.

Mullett was quiet on a Sunday morning. It's generally quiet in that continent-without-boundaries that's called the Neighborhoods, regardless of the day or hour; not like Hollywood's idea of a ghetto with its teeming streets and squalling children. Each block is a separate country with its own laws and government, and since no passports are honored, a foot trip anywhere is made under penalty of death. There hadn't been any gang activity in that area in a while, but the longer that went on, the greater the risk. Everything that was there was necessary. Nothing that was there was beautiful. The cement fronts of the stores were as blank as the faces of convicts in lock step. The paint on those houses that had paint was just something to protect the wood from the weather. A generation of children had come to majority—or died short of it—never having seen a view through a window that hadn't been mitred into grids by tungsten bars. The place was done in a thousand shades and all of them were gray. It needed Ted Turner.

The officers who answered an anonymous tip that night had found Dale bleeding on the sidewalk with his head on the edge of a burned-out lawn belonging to a frame house with its shades down. He'd lost a gallon of blood by the time the EMS unit came and hadn't regained consciousness when they put him in the ambulance. He had three .32 slugs in his chest and stomach—not much penetration power, but one had pierced a major artery. The bullets had come from just the sort of lightweight piece a computer expert might carry when visiting a place like Mullett Street late at night. Of course a search warrant turned up no such weapon and no record surfaced of Earl North's ever having purchased a gun of any kind; but guns without pedigrees are as hard to buy in Detroit as stolen tape decks. Dale's car was found the next day parked around the corner with his .45 locked in the glove compartment.

Kid, the only thing wrong with knowing as much as I do about living is I got no excuse for dying.

It was still dark when the call had come through—the place marked NEXT OF KIN in Dale's old personnel file at the sheriff's department had more strikeovers than a Teamster with a short memory, and his daughter was hitching her way across Europe—and when I drove up, the strobes mounted on top of the parked cruisers were making their own dawn. The chalk line was fresh. I'd just missed the ambulance. I was talking to a young plain-clothesman named Battle when the report from Receiving Hospital came over the radio in his unmarked unit. He acknowledged it and returned the microphone to its hook.

"Sorry," he said.

"Thanks," I said. "I don't feel anything yet."

"It'll come. It's like stubbing your big toe. They'll want you down at County tomorrow for the positive."

"Did you know him?"

"Everybody downtown knew him. There aren't a lot left like him. Class of Forty-five, you know?"

"I know."

Twenty years of rain had washed away the chalk, but not the rusty stain. That had soaked deep into the porous concrete and would remain there until the earth finished reclaiming it, as it had begun to do, crumbling the corners of the sidewalk into perpendicular wedges like dry bread. Any day now someone would get a bright idea and fling the pieces off the nearby expressway overpass at the windshields passing below. It was one of the few pedestrian walkways not yet enclosed by a barrel-shaped grid like the razor wire on top of a penitentiary wall. In time the whole city would look like the approach to Sing Sing.

The house was still there, but the next Devil's Night would take care of that; it was ripe to burn. At the time of the shooting it had sheltered two families separated by a firewall with not a witness between them. It was empty now and had been for a long time, its windows cataracted with yellow plywood, gray clapboard splintering through stubborn traces of paint on the siding. Day-Glo graffiti—urban ivy, nocturnal cousin to the variety that grows on brick walls at Harvard—had spread across the front. There would be crack vials rolling around on the floor inside. Running sores just like it existed all over the city, drawing flies and hatching maggots. Evil abhors a vacuum.

I paced off the distance from the stain on the sidewalk to the fence surrounding the basketball court. That was the approximate location of the three cement steps that had led up to the front door of the American Eagle Motor Lodge. The forensics team had concluded from the angle of entry and depth of penetration that all three bullets had been fired from the top step; or from the bottom, provided that the shooter was at least eight feet tall.

I climbed those steps in my mind, turned, drew the Smith & Wesson, and sighted down my arm at the stain on the sidewalk. There had been a quarter moon that night and no clouds. Following North from the spot where he'd parked his car—a block and a half in front of Dale's, if I knew anything at all about his tailing method—Dale would keep to the shadow of the house, but there wouldn't have been much of it at three in the morning when the moon was at the top of its arc. Arthur Rooney, North's lawyer, had made a lot of noise before the grand jury about the marksmanship involved and his client's unfamiliarity with firearms; but the distance was less than twenty feet and North was shooting down. An ape could have done it.

But an ape hadn't, and Rooney was on the ground floor of a career that would eventually put him in charge of the legal affairs of several prominent local corporations. A courtroom is not a motel on Mullett Street. A courtroom is an orderly place where facts are sorted into primary colors and geometric shapes. It stands on an antiseptic platform at the opposite end of the universe. No indictment. All rise. All except Dale.

I had stood on that same spot before, when I didn't have to imagine steps or the high disinterested eye of a broken moon. It was twenty-four hours after the shooting and there was still a motel and occupants in the duplex and yellow police tape everywhere, circumscribing the last few yards between the cradle and the grave. And, forty-five degrees to my right, directly across the street from the duplex, there had been a brick house, well kept for the neighborhood, with windows looking right out on the spot.

And there still was.

Still well kept for the neighborhood: Windows scrubbed, shutters painted, roof and gutters in good shape. After twenty years it looked like a color photograph taken the day after the murder.

Couldn't be.

Everyone moved.

No one stayed in the same place for two decades.

Well, hell.

I holstered the .38, buttoned my coat over it, and took a walk.

The steps to the screened front porch were wooden and solid and had been repainted about the same time as the shutters. The screen was a heavy nylon one without rips or patches. The door fit snugly in its frame. I rang the bell. I had rung ten thousand doorbells, and no two sounded alike. There were lonely ones that echoed hollow as hope in houses where dusty smiles lay in state in frames on the mantels; happy ones that chirped like parakeets; sullen ones that snarled like dyspeptic dogs; sexy ones that purred; terrified ones that gasped and clutched at the door; broken empty ones that coughed deep from the lungs and said come ahead in, there's nothing left worth stealing anyway. This one sounded as if it had been through all that, with a cheerful little flirt at the end, like an old man at Hospice insisting he had no regrets. I couldn't remember if it had had that last bit the first time I'd rung it.

The inner door opened and someone came out onto the porch. Small bright eyes peered at me through the screen, and then that door opened too. It almost hit me in the face. I'd expected an interrogation. People in Detroit don't open their homes to just anyone, even in the better neighborhoods.

The small bright eyes belonged to a round black face, unapologetically female, set square on a lot of print dress with a blue plaid apron tied around the waist. The odors of lemon wax and hot butter curled out from behind her, enveloping me in a cloud of bittersweet nostalgia. The place had smelled exactly the same twenty years before.

"I know you," said the woman. "You're that detective. Did you ever find that man that shot your friend?"

16

I didn't have a comeback for that one. I had spoken to her for maybe five minutes when I was twenty-five. She had been about fifty then and had to be knocking on seventy now, not that you could place her age by looking at her. There wasn't a crease in the plump face, moist from the heat of a stove, and the shine in her eyes was not the soft luminescence of old age but the new-penny glitter of childhood.

The jolt jump-started my own memory. I could almost see the blue spark arcing from hers. "Mrs. Spurling," I said. "Mesta."

"Nesta," she corrected. "Mrs. Clark, now. Well, the

widow Clark. I married Mr. Clark in eighty-three. Buried him last year. Mr. Cooper, wasn't it?"

"Close. Amos Walker."

"That's it. I'd of had it in a minute. Things that happened, folks I met when I was ten, I see all that like I'm looking at a picture. I can't tell you what I had for supper last night."

"It's not last night I want to talk about. May I come in?"

She thought about it. She had a checkered dishtowel in her hands and the muscles in her forearms jumped as she kneaded it. She could have arm-wrestled the bartender at the Erin. "Devon wouldn't like it. That's my son. He told me not to let nobody in unless I knows them. But I guess I knows you." She held the screen door for me and when I had it she turned and went in through the inner door, leaving it open. Her feet were wide and flat in cheap low-heeled black pumps. The veins on the backs of her knees looked like Renaissance crackalure.

The living room was small and oppressively warm. The heat was blowing hard through an old-fashioned floor register the size of a subway grate. An inexpensive broadloom rug lay on the floorboards and the furniture was old enough to have had several owners, but the wood glistened and the upholstery was clean, doilies pinned conscientiously over the worn spots. One of those pictures of Jesus whose eyes open and shut hung above the sofa. When they were shut I felt abandoned. When they were open I wondered what He thought of my visit. I unbuttoned my coat and put my hat on the coffee table supporting a three-year run of *Reader's Digest* in neat stacks.

"I'd offer you a drink of water, but Devon's coming to

pick me up in a few minutes. It's only two blocks to church but he don't like me walking nowhere alone." She came out of the adjoining kitchen minus the apron and dishtowel and bent her knees to look in a mirror while she pinned a felt teardrop hat to her hair. The mirror, flaking in an oval Bakelite frame, should have been hung three inches higher for convenience. Probably it was hiding a crack in the plaster. "Devon's my oldest. He had a older sister but she got ran over on her way home from school. Lordy, she be fifty come next month."

"I'm sorry."

"Ain't no reason you should be, unless you was driving. I done forgave that man forty years ago. Can't love the dead more than the living, that's what Walter said. He was Aline's father. Aline, that was Devon's older sister that got ran over."

"Walter was Mr. Spurling."

"Lordy, no. Mr. Spurling was Devon's father. Walter done stepped on a mine in Korea. Colored troops went in first them days. I married Lucius in fifty-six. That was Mr. Spurling. He had a hardware store on Twelfth Street till the riots. They found him under a burnt rafter."

"I'm sorry."

"Can't love the dead more than the living." She took a green cloth coat out of a closet and put it on. The hat was gray but that was all right. She was a summer rummage sale in the middle of a bleak January. "Lucius made four good children, not counting miscarriages and the one that was born dead. They all coming home for Easter. Well, except Manvil, he's still in Jackson. They caught him with a gun on probation."

"I'm sorry."

"It wasn't even his gun. He was holding it for a friend.

But Manvil's a good boy underneath it all, just angry on account of not having no daddy. I was carrying him when Mr. Spurling got burnt up. Manvil he never got on with Mr. Clark. Cut him once over some little thing."

I wasn't going to say it again. "Can we talk about the night of the shooting?"

"Shooting?" The bright eyes flickered. "Oh, your friend. What you want to talk about?"

"I asked you some questions the day after it happened. You said you were asleep and didn't hear the shots. You told the police the same thing."

"I said that." She nodded, and went on nodding as if she'd forgotten to stop. She was thinking about something.

A dim bulb flared deep in my skull. I didn't move. A wire might be loose and I didn't want to jiggle it. "Who told you to say that?" I asked. "Devon?"

" 'Stay out of it,' he said. 'Ain't nothing to us what one white man does to another.' "

My nails were digging into my palms. I opened my fists and flexed my fingers. "What did you see?"

"Devon ain't no racist, reverse or no otherwise. I raised him according to the Good Book. He's just had him a hard life. Folks say things they don't mean when they're mad. Devon's mad a lot."

I took in a lungful of lemon wax and hot butter and let it out slowly. Waited. The furnace fan clicked, hummed, then cut in with a whoosh. I figured it was mocking me.

"I ain't missed a sunrise in forty years," she said. "I was chief cook at the House of Corrections eighteen years, had to be at work at four ayem. Took early retirement on account of my legs. That was twenty-two years ago, and

I still can't stay in bed much past two. I was in the kitchen washing cups."

The sink, an old-fashioned white porcelain one with separate taps for hot and cold, was visible through the kitchen arch. The window above it looked out on the basketball court. It hadn't been a basketball court then. I could feel the revolver in its holster on my belt. It throbbed as if it had nerve ends.

"It was dark," she said.

The fan cut out, wobbling a little against its bearings as it slowed to a stop. When it became obvious she wasn't going to go on I said, "There was a light over the front door of the motel. It was burning that night."

"It wasn't much of a light. The bulb was dirty. Anyway the light was behind the man. I couldn't see his face."

"Which man?"

"Oh, the man on the motel porch. I seen your friend clear enough when he turned. He looked like the picture they run in the *News* the next day. He was on the sidewalk and the light kind of slid acrosst his face when he turned."

"Turned which way?"

"Away from the other man. They been talking."

"Talking?"

"Uh-huh." She was fooling with her hatpin, adjusting the angle of the hat.

Dale and North talking wasn't the police take, or mine. Dale had followed him to the American Eagle, been spotted, and got shot. That was as close as anyone had been able to piece it together without an eyewitness.

"You were the one who called the police," I said.

"Uh-huh." She'd found a pair of gloves in her pocket and put them on, taking time with the fingers. "I called

Devon after. He was mad. He said I shouldn't of called the police at all, even if I didn't leave my name. Said—"

"What were they talking about?"

"The men? I couldn't hear. I don't even know they was talking, not to swear to. They just kind of looked like they been. I mean, two men standing that close on a empty street just naturally got to say something to each other, even if it's just the weather."

"Twenty feet isn't close."

"Oh, they wasn't twenty feet apart. Not at first. Your friend he was at the bottom of the steps that other man was standing on top of. He was just turning away when I looked out. I remember thinking, now what's them two doing out there at no two-thirty in the ayem? Your friend he walked away some and then the other man called out to him and he turned around and that's when the other man shot him."

"You saw it."

"I seen it. Wisht I hadn't."

"What did he call out?"

She shook her head. "It was cold out. I had the window shut. But the man that was walking away stopped quick and turned around like you do when somebody calls your name. So I figured that's what the other man done, called his name. I guess they was twenty feet apart then. Them shots, they sounded like a popgun. I wouldn't of knowed they was real except your friend jerked and fell down."

"What kind of gun?"

"I don't know nothing about guns. Anyway it was clear acrosst the street. It was shiny, I seen that. The light hit it just before he shot it."

I unbuttoned my peacoat, took out the revolver, and held it in front of her on my palm. "Did it look like this?"

"No. That looks like the gun Manvil had. I don't think this one had that cylinder thing."

"It was a semiautomatic?"

"If that's what it's called. I don't know nothing about guns."

That checked. The slugs the medical examiner dug out of Dale were copper-jacketed. I put away the Smith. "What did the shooter do afterwards?"

"Run, I guess. I didn't see on account of I ducked down under the window. I didn't want to see no more. I heard a car start up and drive away fast. The tires screeched."

The screen door banged. I jumped out of my shoes. The big man who came into the living room stopped when he saw the gun come out.

"What the hell," he said. "It's Sunday."

He had on a corduroy coat over cleaned and pressed work pants and a black tie on a white shirt; not a tall man but big in the chest and shoulders with a short thick neck and hastily blocked-in features, as in a charcoal sketch. He had a strong mouth, suspicious eyes, and the general air of a man who was carrying around ten or fifteen more years than he was, if he was who I thought he was. His skin was the color of dull slate.

"Devon, this here is Mr. Cooper. He's the man whose friend got shot out there that time. He come to ask some more questions."

"With that?" He tipped his head toward the gun.

I put it away again. "Sorry. You came in kind of loud and it's that sort of neighborhood. The name's Walker."

"What you tell him, Ma?" His eyes stayed on me.

"The truth, Devon. Just the Lord's own truth."

I saw how he was going to play it, a point in his favor. If you can manage to grow up in that part of town without hiding your emotions under a bucket, you're an authentic individual. He wouldn't be caught holding a gun for someone else. No one would find him under any burned rafters.

"You better not pay no attention to what she says," he said. "She don't think so good these days."

She shook a finger at him. "I was in labor with you for sixteen hours, boy. That was my worst day for thinking and I still thought better than you on your best. So don't you skin my shins."

I grinned. " 'Skin my shins'?"

The finger came my direction. "I lived on this street a long time. I walk past whores and gang-bangers to get to the bus. Ain't no buttons on these shoes."

"You a cop, let's see your badge." Devon hadn't looked away from me yet.

I got out the folder and showed him the ID and county buzzer.

"You ain't no sheriff."

"The metal's just for serving papers. This is a private investigation."

"Uh-huh. Who's the private?"

"I'd like to tell you," I said. "The only thing holding me back is it's none of your goddamn business."

I got a finger shook at me again. "No G.D. in this house. Not on the Lord's day and not ever."

I apologized. That made Devon madder. "I knowed you wasn't no cop. What you doing busting in on people?"

"He didn't bust in. I let him."

"Shut up, Ma."

She took two steps and backhanded him across the mouth. She had to go up on tiptoe and she was wearing gloves, but the noise was like a pistol shot. "You don't tell me shut up, boy. Your daddy told me shut up once and I bust a bread board over his head. I got another bread board."

It was a picture: Big, coarse-featured Devon, built like an earthmover, rubbing his mouth and getting a finger shook at him by an old woman who could have sat in his hand. I didn't laugh.

"She won't have to tell it again in court," I said. "She can't identify the shooter, and anyway a teenage defense lawyer would make coleslaw out of an eyewitness testimony twenty years after the crime. They don't let you smack people in court."

"I should of said something then." She adjusted her hat again. "Only mistake I ever made in my life was letting men do my thinking for me."

I said, "Maybe that's why your brain's just like new."

She smiled then. You hardly ever see gold teeth anymore. "Well, now, if you wasn't quite so pale and had some more moss on you, I'd ask you to come to church with us."

"He ain't no Baptist," Devon said. His lower lip had begun to swell and he was trying to stop the bleeding with his finger.

"You'd better get some cold water on that." I looked at his mother. "What are they collecting for this year, a new roof or a new building?"

"Both. Well, when you gets a new building the roof just naturally gots to go along."

I gave her the emergency fifty I kept in the ID folder. "For the collection plate."

It went down inside the front of the print dress like a pelican diving for breakfast. "Maybe not *all* of it," she said. "God's house ain't got no toilet needs fixing."

"I said I'd fix it, Ma."

"I never thought you wouldn't, son."

I put on my hat. "Thanks, Mrs. Spurling. I know a little more about how much I don't know."

"Clark. Nesta Clark. Don't you mention it." She put on a scarf that didn't go with the gloves or the coat or the hat. The outfit made perfect sense now. "What you figure them two was talking about that time of night?"

I used the doorknob. Cold came into the house like a bill collector. "That's one of the things I don't know," I said. "They're piling up."

17

Mondays are okay. They come at you scrubbed, bright of eye, and wearing a clean shirt. Unlike Saturdays they don't ram a crowbar between rich and poor, between a broken windowpane waiting to be replaced and an eighty-foot Criscraft burbling its twin Chryslers in a Grosse Pointe slip. Nor do they, like Sundays, demand a frantic effort to stuff as much recreation into a twenty-four-hour period as the human body can stand. Everybody's a working stiff come Monday.

As weekdays go, this one was starting better than some I'd had lately. My sinuses were open, nobody shot at me, and there weren't any second-generation Deadheads who put their babies in the snow waiting for me in the outer office. The asbestos crew was back at work, whistling the theme of the flying monkeys from *The Wizard of Oz* as they pulled the pink stuff out of the ceiling like entrails and packed it into yellow industrial-strength Hefty bags labeled WARNING—TOXIC MATERIAL. Even the mail had come early. I picked it up from under the slot and carried it into the heart of the great machine that keeps me in socks and cigarettes.

Dumping the mail on the desk I remembered that four days had passed since I'd asked John Alderdyce to pry Harold Boyette's address out of his leasing company. I was reaching for the telephone when it rang and it was John. This string couldn't last.

"So bright, so early," said the inspector. "I was under the impression you private types slept off the weekend till Wednesday."

"You public types ought to read a higher grade of fiction. What's the word on the street?"

"Same one that's always there, the only one the scum can spell. I've got good news and bad news."

"Like hell. Cops never have good news."

"Well, drive this one around the block and see how it corners. We found your client."

The *we* said it all. I put both feet on the floor, centering my gravity. "Just read me the method and time of death. I'll ask where later."

"You got a reason to think he's dead?" He kept it light. John's rattle is often mistaken for bells.

"Just playing the percentages. There are a lot more people dead than alive. So is he?"

"Someday before I retire, which I can't ever on account of my daughter tells me she's in love with a sculptor, I'd like to poke around inside that skull of yours with a flashlight. I bet I find Jimmy Hoffa in there. Sure Boyette's dead. Reason we think it's him, the Toyota he turned up in has the license number you gave us."

"Natural causes, of course."

"Of course. They mine lead, don't they? Diggers in the coroner's office mined ninety-eight grains of it out of his brain this morning. It went in behind the right ear, mob style. Fired from the back seat or else from the passenger's side in front when he turned his head, which would make the shooter a southpaw."

"My ballistics is rusty. What's that come to in calibers?"

"Thirty-two, jacketed."

I changed hands on the receiver. It was getting slippery. "The mob doesn't use thirty-twos."

"Oh, hell, nobody follows the rules anymore. They never used to cap them at home either, but we're pulling them out of their kids' nurseries these days." Air stirred on his end. "Maybe you've got an alternative."

"Where'd he bob up?"

"O'Hair Park. Kids went there to toss the football around yesterday and found him slumped over the wheel of his Toyota."

"That's not far from where I lost him. How long?"

"Since before the rain Thursday. The car looked like an iceberg. A car can stand a long time before anyone looks inside. When we know what time he ate last we'll know what time he died."

"What about the bundle he had with him at the Tomcat?"

"No bundle. No illuminated manuscripts either, unless you count the owner's manual. Care to meet me at County and positive him?"

I said I'd see him there in a few minutes. But a minute

later I was still sitting there, turning over the facts with a
fork.

Not that many premeditated murders are committed
with a .32. For reasons best left to the consumer research
team at *Guns and Ammo,* it lacks both the velocity and
the accuracy of the much lighter .22, currently the assas-
sin's weapon of choice for close range work because of
the low noise quotient. I'd asked questions in maybe
three killings in which a .32 was used. Two of them in
the past twenty-four hours.

The Coroners' Court Building, erected seventy years ago
at the corner of Brush and East Lafayette, is a gray Deco
box of the type that the city delights in tearing down in
favor of something sleek and glossy with the life ex-
pectancy of a campaign poster; only new charnel-houses
don't skew politically, so it stays. Somebody in those
Prohibition days had had an inkling of what was to
come, and although the morgue's capacity is often
strained, the attendants haven't had to resort to stacking
the clientele on the sidewalk just yet. They came close
during the race riots of 1943 and 1967.

Improvements have been made since fedoras. These
days there's no reason to visit cold storage unless you're
actually a customer. In a rare fit of sensitivity, the coroner's office has installed a closed-circuit TV system so
spouses and children and parents can view the remains
of their loved ones on monitors and avoid carrying away
the sting of ammonia in their nostrils. Everything's tele-
vised today: births, deaths, court trials, police beatings,
the act of love. The joke's on George Orwell. Big Brother
is us.

I found Alderdyce standing by the monitor, in conversation with a small man who looked like a circus barker. This was Noel Beman, the county's chief medical examiner. His shaved head, waxed mustache, and padded shoulders appeared on the TV news whenever a dismemberment or a satanic sacrifice made the evening deadline, lingering over the graphic details with all the loquacious poise of a man who truly enjoys his work. Which of course he did. Nobody winds up carving on cadavers by accident.

"Fascinating case," said Beman after the introductions, gripping my hand with his small strong one. "I just got my hands out of his insides."

I put mine in my pocket and wiped it on the lining. "I thought you preferred them with their heads cut off and stuffed with garlic."

"Wrong case," John told Beman. "Walker's here for the head shot we brought in yesterday."

The examiner's black Eastern European eyes lost their shine. "Oh, that. Boom-boom, no imagination. His fatty tissue would have killed him in ten years anyway. What is *your* cholesterol count, Mr. Walker?"

"I don't know right now. I'm hoping for the record."

John said, "Thanks for your time, Doctor. We'll call you first if any more parts turn up."

"A single metacarpus would tell me a great deal. You'd be surprised." Beman offered his hand again but I pretended not to see it and he left.

"That the jigsaw case?" I asked John.

He nodded. "Ford plant maintenance found the torso this morning clogging an intake pipe at Rouge. We're still missing the head and hands but it looks like we've found Hector Matador's missing bodyguard. Part of the payoff for the Acardo killing. You ought to remember that one."

"I testified against Matador. If those Colombians held a grudge as long as the Sicilians, you'd be spiking up pieces of me all over the metropolitan area."

"I hope not. It's a bureaucratic pisser. We're still hassling with the cops in Warren and Dearborn over who has jurisdiction based on the importance of the body parts and whose backyard they turn up in. Let's see what's on TV." He flipped the switch to an intercom. "Okay."

The screen snowed over and suddenly cleared. I was looking at Harold Boyette's face for the first time in days.

Encountered unexpectedly in tall weeds or on the floor of a city apartment, corpses in general look like mannequins. Powdered and painted under the pink lights of a funeral parlor they look asleep. In the morgue they just look dead. This one's eyes weren't quite closed, allowing thin semicircles of white to show with a gluey shine through the lashes. The hair was slicked back and darkened with water, but I recognized the putty cheeks, and his complexion wasn't that much paler than it had been when blood was feeding it. The full lips were gray as liver and pulled back from his teeth in a kind of surprised smile.

"That him?"

I nodded and lit a cigarette. Twelve inches of block wall separated us from the cooling room but I smelled formaldehyde anyway. I always did, even upstairs in the inquest rooms.

The inspector inspected me. "You look like you lost someone close."

I shook the match and my head. "Not as close as the ten thousand."

"Yeah, you're a mercenary son of a bitch. Rolexes up

to your elbows and diamond faucets in the kitchen. Save the act for those bent cops up in Iroquois Heights." He flipped the switch again. "Show's over." The screen went dark.

"What shape's the slug in?"

"Good enough to match, if we find something to match it with."

"Try the one in the wall at the Tomcat. I doubt they bothered to dig it out even if they mortared it over."

"I almost forgot about that. Who do you like for it?"

"Boyette's boss at the DIA told me he fired him six months ago for passing off phony manuscripts as genuine. Maybe his partners thought he was getting ready to crack."

"Why would they think that if the DIA chose not to prosecute?"

"Maybe he was shaking them down. He wasn't happy with his cut and threatened to turn them in if they didn't sweeten it. The ransom drop was just a gag to get me to back him up when he went to the theater to collect. I never saw inside that mailer. He might have been carrying his shirts."

"It fits the facts. So you think this Hours of the Virgin thing was a fake?"

"That's the part I don't like," I said. "The page he showed me could have been anything. I wouldn't know the real article from a letter to *Penthouse*. Why the elaborate forgery? He could have made up an easier story to support."

He grunted. He had a whole vocabulary without an intelligible word in it.

"How sure are you the Blessing woman killed Gilly for the reason she said?" I asked.

"You're barking down the wrong hole there. Any one of his tootsies could have been the one that got the bee up her pants over the wife in Corktown. It was Viola's bad luck it turned out to be her." He adjusted his cuffs; more or less than an inch and a quarter could spoil his day. "Did you ever track down that woman with the eyes?"

"I came to the conclusion I fell asleep and dreamed her up."

"That'd be a first."

"Which one, dreaming or concluding?"

"Take your pick. You own a thirty-two?"

"I ditched it right after I shot Boyette. How'd that work its way around to me?"

When he moved a shoulder it was as casual as pushing over a tree. "I have to ask. Sometimes I get lucky. Not today, though. Boyette's address was on his driver's license in his wallet. It checked out with what I got from his leasing company this morning. You want to come along? I'll let you work the siren."

"If it's all the same to you I'll follow. You drive like an axe murderer."

"Go to hell. When I was on the mayor's detail I took the Bondurant driving course. The diploma's in my office."

"You must've worn your gun to the graduation ceremony." I shook out my keys.

The address was in Madison Heights, a community of tract houses and sidewalk-planted trees fighting the noxious clouds drifting north from Detroit. On the way we stopped at a precinct station and Alderdyce picked up a local named Smithson, regulation sideburns and fresh academy creases in his uniform. The house was a small ranch on a quarter-acre near the end of a cul-de-sac: vinyl siding, clumps of broccoli planted between the flagstones and the foundation. John peered through the window of the attached garage, shrugged, rang the bell on the little front porch. When no one answered he tried the knob. The door opened. He looked at me. "Trusting little fart, wasn't he?"

"Either that or somebody beat us here," I said.

He scowled at me just for the pleasure of it and lifted his eyebrows at the Madison Heights officer, who tipped his palm in a gesture of invitation. I got the impression he wasn't as green as he looked. John pushed the door the rest of the way and we went in.

A fresh lead is like the bright wrapping on a gift package. Too often, when you finally get it open, the paper turns out to be the best part. The house was five rooms in search of a personality. Boyette had slept in one, cooked in another, watched television in a third, washed and performed his bodily functions in the fourth, and done his laundry in the last, leaving only his clothes, a pile of *Smithsonians* and some books, scholarly and otherwise, and a French fry moldering behind the electric stove to mark his passage. There were no papers of interest, no telephone messages on the machine; not even a smeared glass on the coffee table with a lipstick stain on the rim for pepper. That opened another possibility, but there was just as much nothing on the premises to indicate his tastes had turned in any other direction. No pornographic publications of either kind, no sheep smell on the unmade bedding. No signs that anyone else had tossed the place either. The furniture and wall art looked as if it had come straight from the showroom. He hadn't even bothered to remove the tags from the armchairs and sofa.

"Furnished rental," said John when we gathered in the living room. "I didn't know a house could stand mute."

"What about his redial?" I started going through the books on the built-in shelves."

"Tried it. The memory on some of them only lasts for a couple of days. I'd say this clown was some kind of deep cover if anyone was hiring."

"I can start knocking on doors," said the uniform.

I held a copy of *Huckleberry Finn* by the covers and shook it. "Witness Protection Program."

"Christ, I hope not," John said. "If it's a choice of commies or feds I'll take commies. But I'll put in a call to the Justice Department. Seeing as how he's dead maybe I'll have an answer by next leap year."

Nothing came out of *The Murder of Roger Ackroyd*. I put it down and hoisted *The Iliad*. The guy was eclectic. "Some people just don't make much of a dent. I thought that when we met."

"Terrific. His whole life was a waste of physical space and now he's wasting my time."

"What about those doors?" asked the uniform.

When I picked up *The Bridges of Madison County* something slid off the top and landed on the rug without bouncing. I put my foot on it. The uniform was looking at Alderdyce and Alderdyce was looking at his watch.

"No sense getting the neighbors riled up until we've had the grunts in here with toothbrushes," John said. "I've already put in too much time on this. Only reason I got interested at all is his name was still fresh in my mind from last week. I don't miss this hands-on shit at all. I like my desk just fine."

"Okay, Inspector."

As they turned toward the door I bent down quickly, scooped up the object, and put it in my pocket without looking at it. On the way to the car my fingers traced its triangular shape. That completed the set in my collection.

18

I stopped for lunch at a chain place on the Detroit side of Eight Mile Road, a maze of booths and latticework and movie lobby cards on the walls. I sat in the considerable shade of Audrey Hepburn's left eyebrow, ordered a glass of milk and a Reuben named after Erich von Stroheim, and examined the essential clue while I was waiting. I held it up by the post and let the triangle spin at the end of its tiny chain. The post ended in a hairpin bend jewelers call a French hook. The earring matched the one I'd found at the Tomcat Theater.

"What a pretty earring! Where'd you get it?"

The waitress had returned with my milk. She was blonde, eighteen, and boyishly slender in a green velour jerkin, nylon blouse with puffed sleeves, and a pointed hat with a feather. The theme for January was *The Adventures of Robin Hood.*

"I just picked it up somewhere," I said. "I'm thinking of having my ears pierced. Does it hurt?"

She touched the jade button in her right lobe and looked serious. "You don't want to do that."

"Yeah, I thought it hurt. I found it on a floor, but not here. If you lost an earring, how long would you go on wearing the other one?"

"Depends on how soon I missed the one I lost. I'd take the other one off right away then. I'm not into punk."

"How soon would you miss one like this?" I put it in her hand.

She held it up to her ear, moved her head up and down and from side to side, then gave it back. "It tickles my neck when I turn my head. I think I'd notice pretty soon if it was gone."

"So if you lost it on Telegraph Road in Detroit you wouldn't still be wearing its mate in Madison Heights."

"It'd be like walking around with one short leg. I guess some people wouldn't mind."

I thanked her. She left. When she came back with my sandwich she had a crease in her forehead. "Are you some kind of detective?"

"Some kind."

"What can I do to get somebody to leave me alone?"

"Old boyfriend or wannabe?"

"Old boyfriend. He's a computer hacker. He trashed my credit record and orders things sent to my apartment. Embarrassing things. My neighbors—"

"You could get a court order. If it happens again you could have him locked up."

"I tried that. They said I needed proof it was him."

"Any other hobbies?"

"Him?" The crease deepened. "Well, music. He collects old records. You know, the big ones. Opera and like that. He said they're worth a bundle."

I put a pickle slice on the Reuben and replaced the bun. "Know where he lives?"

"I still have a key. I gave it back but he sent it to me in the mail."

"That makes it easy. Go in there sometime when he's out. Bring a cordless electric drill with a three-eighths-inch bit and bore out the holes in all his records. It'll make Caruso sound like Dean Martin on a bat."

"Who's Dean Martin?"

"I'll eat now," I growled.

She took her crease away. When I finished my lunch I left ten bucks on a $6.80 check, wrote Dean Martin's name and the address of a nearby Sam Goody's on a page in my notebook, tore it out, and left it with the money, pocketing a copy of the check as a business expense.

I drove back to the office through a mix of rain and snow the consistency of curdled milk. The greasy pavement kept my hands on the wheel and my thoughts on the road. My subconscious poked at such details as women's jewelry and corpses.

The concept of Boyette double-crossing his partners in the forgery scheme was just a piece of raw meat to throw at John Alderdyce. If I'd added that Earl North may have been one of those partners, he'd have wrinkled his nose and tied a tin can to my tail. Cops allow only one coincidence to a case, and Merlin Gilly's death had used it up. The earring in Boyette's house stank even higher. I hardly needed a waitress too young to know Dean Martin from Morton Dean to tell me Laurel Strangeways hadn't worn the widow all the way across town and then lost it like the other, on top of a book no less. There wasn't a carpet pad this side of Flubber that could make one bounce that high.

It was a plant and a good one, meant to be found by someone who would take the time to look. Which presented me with Maid Marian in the clutches of the dragon or one fat dragon with a yen for detective for dessert. All I had to do was step into the trap and all would be known.

The office smelled of asbestos and dry rot and nobody getting rich on the double. I sat down and stared at the mail, still unopened from that morning; looked but didn't touch. Envelopes with windows, an insurance offer from a post office box in Pueblo, Colorado, and a package the size of a metropolitan directory that would be the stationery I'd broken down and ordered at cost from a printer I'd done a favor for, never mind which printer or the nature of the favor. Nothing elaborate, just A. WALKER INVESTIGATIONS and the address and telephone in blue on granite stock, no beady eyes or crossed machine guns. There was a chance the professional look would speed up payment on some of the statements I sent out. In the mood I was in I'd probably get a paper cut opening the package and bleed to death.

I dialed the service and asked for messages. I had two, both from a Mr. Strangeways, both saying the same thing. Call back.

*   *   *

"I thought you might wish to avoid me." The colonial accent was especially heavy on the line. "I'm afraid I came off pedantic the other night."

"Host's prerogative," I said. "Have you heard anything from your wife?"

"I was going to ask you the same question."

"I'm still backing and filling. Nothing concrete yet." I opened the belly drawer and dropped the second earring next to the first one in the pencil trough. I was getting tired of listing to one side.

"I'm more than a little concerned. She's never stayed away this long without word."

"Did you call the friends in Baton Rouge?"

"A woman answered, thank God. She acted surprised. She said she hasn't seen her in years and wasn't expecting her. She doesn't know Laurel that well. The woman works for a studio where she had some shots taken for her model's portfolio. They weren't social."

"Did you believe her?"

"The surprise was very low-key. Most people, when they dissemble, err on the other side. I think she was telling the truth. What do you think it means?"

"What do you?"

He breathed some recycled air. The machine whirred in the background. He was among old friends in the library. "It begins to sound as if you were right when you said she planned her disappearance. She knew I was too much the gentleman to call and check up on her until it was too late. We pornographers are sensitive about our court manners. I never saw them as a weakness until this moment."

I said nothing. I was getting too old to play Pat O'Brien to his Jimmy Cagney.

"I should like to pay you to find Mrs. Strangeways," he said then.

"I'm already looking. But if you'd care to pick up my expenses, a retainer of fifteen hundred will do it." I told him where to send the check.

"Who's been paying them until now?"

"Boyette. But his credit ran out this morning. He's in the county morgue with a hole in his head where a bullet used to be."

"Good Lord. Do you think Laurel's in danger?"

"I'll ask her when I find her."

"You will of course notify me when the fifteen hundred runs out. I love my wife, Mr. Walker. I'm certain there's a satisfactory explanation for her behavior. Even if there is not, I wish to hear it from her. If I had to visit the morgue to see her, I wouldn't have any reason to come back out."

"I'll call you."

"I nearly forgot the other reason I called," he said. "I've heard from Earl North."

I'd been in the process of hanging up. I screwed the receiver into my ear. "Heard how?"

"Over the telephone. This morning. The cheeky son of a bitch decided to take me up on my offer to provide him with a letter of recommendation."

"How did you handle it?"

"In a courtly fashion." He nearly spat out the adverb.

"Did you ask him about Mrs. Strangeways?"

"I asked him if he knew where she was. I did not ask him about their relationship."

I waited. His British understatement had begun to crawl under my skin.

"He said the last time he saw her was the day he finished cataloguing my library. I'm not as sure about him as I was about the woman in Louisiana. His astonishment may have been feigned."

"Anything else?"

"Certainly. I apologized for suspecting him and said I was overwrought. I shouldn't need to tell you that was one of the most difficult things I've had to do since my physical therapy. In any case I invited him here to collect his reference. He'll be at the house this afternoon at four o'clock. Will you be available?"

19

A group of women in arctic boots and quilted overcoats were patrolling the gravel apron in front of Gordon Strangeways' gate, carrying signs with inscriptions like PIGS EAT HIGH ON THE HOG and WOMEN ARE PEOPLE TOO. One of them was pushing a stroller containing a small human being in a pink snowsuit who looked like Broderick Crawford.

"Who'd he run on the centerfold this month, Mother Theresa?" I asked Ben, the welterweight security guard. The protesters stood in a cloud of spent breath watching him pat me down. The day was sunny, the air steel cold, and there wasn't a TV news crew in sight.

"Just the usual weekday crowd. You should see 'em

when it's warm." He led the way to the Jeep, where Vernon, his partner, was waiting to come out and strip the gears on the Cutlass.

The estate looked less woodsy by daylight. Some of the trees had protective wire around their trunks and a tent of professional-grade plastic had been stretched over a section of adolescent sod to protect it from frost. No wildlife put in an appearance.

This time, Ben and I entered the house together without stopping to knock. "He's waiting in the sun room," said the guard.

The sun room took up half the southwest wing. The contractors had laid terra-cotta on a football field, enclosed it with girders and glass, and inserted a roof twenty feet up to keep the room from colliding with the sky. On chunks of ancient masonry arranged along the base of the ceiling, orators in laurel wreaths and naked charioteers practiced their crafts in crumbling relief; plunder from some Mediterranean ruin, torn from its setting and transported a third of the way across the world to balance out the greenery growing in blue Pewabic pots. In that room it was always June. The glass magnified the sun into dusty yellow bars with dust-motes swimming around in them; a dream of summer against the snow clinging to the trees outside.

Gordon Strangeways lay in the center of all this on the brocaded cushions of a chaise longue bent in the shape of a gondola. It had broken loose of its moorings in Venice and drifted to shore here by way of the Thoroughfare. Its owner wore a thick white terrycloth robe that set off his tan and a pair of emerald-colored plastic cheaters behind his aviator's glasses. A blue blanket as thin as a napkin covered his legs. They would be covered most of the time; scarred, wasted things, whiter than the robe, too thin to make creases in the blanket. The motorized scooter stood close. It was too loyal to its master to wander off and graze.

Jillian Raider, the lawyer and general factotum, sat nearby in a white wicker armchair with a laptop computer open on her knees. She had on a gray linen blouse to match her eyes, tied at the throat with a figured scarf, and a mulberry skirt with a slit that buttoned and just enough of the buttons unfastened to expose a round knee and a well-toned calf in sheer hose. Her shoes were plain black, again without heels. She glanced up briefly as we entered, then returned to the keyboard.

The man on the chaise didn't stir, even when the guard cleared his throat. It was shirtsleeve weather in the room, but the welterweight left his coat zipped and his fur cap stayed put on his head. He was the kind that didn't break a sweat before the third round.

"I know you're there, Ben. I can feel the cold coming off you even with my eyes closed. Thank you. Please return to your post."

Ben's feet made no more noise going away than dust settling. The sliding door whooshed twice and shut with a click.

"Thank you, too, Jillian. I'm sure you're needed at the office."

She looked up. "Not as much as I'm needed here."

"This isn't legal business. I'd prefer it to be private."

"I hope you know by now you can count on my discretion."

"As my attorney you're entitled to all my secrets. As a woman you present complications. Please respect my feelings in this."

She closed the laptop with a snap, rose, said her good-byes in a crisp cool voice, and left.

Strangeways sighed. "What makes lawyers so damned territorial?"

"DNA." I unbuttoned my coat. "Nice room. Who waters the philodendrons?"

"Someone comes in twice a week with a can and a spraygun. Damned nuisance, but Laurel thinks the oxygen the plants put out is good for me. Actually I think it has something to do with her name. The heat feels good on my legs."

"No Laurel yet?"

"No."

"How are the plants on nicotine?" I fished out the pack.

"They breathe carbon dioxide. One more poison shouldn't harm them."

I committed arson and spiked the match in a pot. "No North yet either, I guess."

"I thought detectives never guessed."

"That's Sherlock Holmes. Are you going to give North that letter of recommendation?"

"Certainly. A man who is not as good as his word isn't good for much. He did do an excellent job with the library."

"That's awfully New Wave of you, considering you suspect him of stamping the Dewey decimal system all over your wife's body."

He colored under the tan. "I don't see a reason to be crude about it."

"Sorry. A day that starts with a visit to the morgue never does much for my social skills."

"I said before I've made my peace regarding the urges

of a healthy young woman chained to a crippled husband nearly thrice her age. Not to extend the same un-
derstanding to the other man would be hypocritical in
the extreme."

"No argument." I dropped ash on the floor. "Funny
thing about blankets. Unless they're pretty thick they just
make a gun look more obvious than it already is."

"Bloody uncomfortable as well." He pulled it out from
under and laid it in my palm.

It was a sleek semiautomatic that could have been
mistaken for a water gun, but not when you were holding it. The checked rubber grip was new and the metal
had been reblued recently, unless it had spent the last
sixty years in a vacuum. It was a Walther P38, the nine-
millimeter parabellum. I figured out the catch on the fat
magazine slung beneath the frame, inspected it and the
chamber, sniffed the muzzle, and tipped sunlight down
inside. It was clean except for a frost of dust in the stri-
ations. Nobody had fired it in a while. I handed it back.

"Pretty. First one I've seen outside of photographs.
Your grandfather's?"

"My father's. Prize of war. He acquired it from a Home
Guard who took it off a dead German flyer and carried
it from Dunkirk through El Alamein, where he was in-
valided out and chose not to return to England. Shot
himself with it in 'fifty-two, never found out why. Always
hoped it was an affair of the heart. Resented him for
years, of course. Still do, I suppose." He reached over
and laid it on the seat of the scooter.

"Were you planning to shoot North right away or talk
first?"

"I hadn't decided. Thought I'd play it by ear."

"No good. You've got to have a plan. Do it quick before

you change your mind, and bury him back there in the woods. Ben and Vernon can take care of that. You'd have to cut them in anyway. They'd know he was here. You can rig it to look like breaking and entering, but that's tough to stage when you haven't had experience, and you'd probably go down for it in any case. The trespassing defense isn't what it used to be. What am I, corroboration?"

"Possibly. My accuser, perhaps. In case I developed cold feet when the time came to turn myself in. No doubt you're convinced I'm a prize ass."

"A romantic. Same thing." I flicked my cigarette again. The white ash did a jerky little dance on the terra-cotta. "I never bought the civilized act. A man who would fight for his life would fight for his wife."

He smiled his water smile. "Not bad. A tad long for a bumper sticker."

"Too short for a country song," I said. "You weren't going to shoot him right away. First you'd find out if he stashed Mrs. Strangeways and if so where."

"True. That much of an ass I'm not. How would you suggest I go about finding out?"

"Ask him."

"I tried that. Do you suppose a gun would get me a different answer?"

"I've seen him under cross-examination. If a grand jury couldn't shake some truth out of him, I doubt artillery would. That might work on a computer expert. Not a killer."

"She's dead, isn't she?" he said. "He killed her to cover up the affair."

"The motive's thin. Twenty years ago he had a marriage to protect, but not now. If he was afraid of you he wouldn't have called. If he killed her he was throwing a muzzle on something worse than plain old adultery. Grand fraud, for instance."

"So you do think he was in league with Boyette."

"It's just a hypothesis. I still don't know why Boyette wanted me in, or who suckered me into calling on him if not him. As the DIA's resident authority on fifteenth-century manuscripts, he okayed the forgeries for purchase. Probably he gave advice during the process so the fakes would look good enough to pass at first glance. North might have done the actual faking."

"He didn't strike me as any kind of artist."

"Artists are obsolete. An eleven-year-old with a Mac can run up a copy of the Mona Lisa that would fool a layman. You said yourself North's a wizard with a keyboard."

"A computer can't inlay letters with gold and semi-precious stone," he said. "It can't duplicate ancient parchment and vellum."

"Glitter-dust and Elmer's glue-all and poster paint. New parchment baked in an oven. Most people don't even know what vellum is. All they had to do was fool the eye. Boyette was the expert. The scam's as old as the original art. Technology's taken out most of the grunt-work."

Strangeways lifted his glasses and removed the cheaters. His eyes looked bruised. "Then you believe he killed Boyette to wipe out his trail."

"It'll work for a loaner until I get something better."

"But what has any of this to do with my wife?"

"I'll answer that one when I find out what she was doing in the Tomcat the night Boyette dropped out of sight. And why she can't seem to keep these in her ears." I held up the earring I'd brought.

He took it, slid his glasses down his nose, and examined the triangle on both sides. "I had them made for her on the occasion of our first anniversary," he said. "The shape symbolizes solidity and love ever-renewing. Where did you find it?"

"In Harold Boyette's house this morning."

He poked his glasses back up. "Ah. The link."

"You don't seem surprised."

"Nothing has surprised me since Little Rock. Do the police know about it?"

"No. They don't know about the other one either."

"*Now* I'm surprised," he said after a moment.

"She lost the other one when I elbowed her in the Tomcat. I didn't show it to you the other night because I wasn't sure what side you weighed in on. The Walther sold me." I dropped what was left of my cigarette in a pot full of Spanish bayonet. "I'd like the earbob back. I'm hoping to return both of them with their owner."

He put it in my hand. "Laurel isn't usually so careless."

"The first time was carelessness. The second time she meant for it to be found. She's leaving a trail of breadcrumbs. For who I don't know, but it makes her look like less of an accomplice than she looked last week."

"Is there a reason you haven't told the police?"

"I don't know what kind of jam she's in. I've got nothing against cops except they're too public. There are some holes a plastic badge can fit through that a brass one can't. Then it's plugged for everybody. I need to get a look at the hole. Would you rather I called them?"

He shook his head. "They keep coming back to ask the same questions and they never listen to the answers."

"They listen."

He shook his head again.

I breathed some plant oxygen. "Did your wife and Boyette ever meet to your knowledge?"

"She accompanied me once to his office when I consulted him on a putative Richard the Third letter someone wanted to sell me. I saw no spark between them, if that's where you're heading. You know by now how sensitive I am to that sort of thing."

"When's your birthday?"

"December. Why?"

"That's a long lead time if she was planning to buy a manuscript from him and give it to you as a present. Anyway it wouldn't explain the fact that the earring in his house was a plant. Also he didn't have any—" I stopped.

"Yes?"

"Forget it. Something I should have noticed." I looked at the earring. "I thought sixty was platinum. What made you choose it for the first?"

"The first is paper. I have too much of that in my library to make it anything special. I'll be one hundred and twelve when we celebrate our sixtieth. I thought it unwise to wait."

I pocketed the piece. "I'll find her in plenty of time for the party. She's the thread that ties Boyette to North. Who by my watch is ten minutes late for this meeting."

"Eight, actually. I'd have thought you'd discovered quartz technology by now. But then you and your partner always were the wind-up kind."

This was a new voice. The room was just long enough and empty enough for it to echo, but neither of us had heard the sliding door open. I turned to face Earl North. The leaves on the potted plants rose and turned in the stirred air that Dale Leopold wasn't breathing anymore.

Part Three

The Hours of Iscariot

20

A cloud, prescient as hell, sucked the sun from the room as he came our way down the long passage, the plants on both sides shrinking away from his slipstream. He'd lost some hair and gained some waistline since his day in court, but there was still a haze of carroty orange at his temples, and his eyes looked exactly the same, a faded gray-blue like two flat pieces of tin left out in the weather, no shine in them. He wore a tan topcoat open over what might have been the same Robert Hall suit, a brown worsted that pouched behind his neck, and a bow tie that could have been red if it had the energy. He looked as if he'd spent the past twenty years in a drawer somewhere, growing blurred and brittle like Dale's favorite cartoons. He would smell—if you wanted to get that close—like old ledgers.

I didn't let him get that close. When he got within arm's reach I hit him with everything I had.

I didn't have a lot. I was still recovering from the flu. But it was enough to take him off his feet and demolish two pots; one with his head on the way down and another when he struck the tiles. A third, top-heavy with some kind of miniature palm, went over on its side and rolled around in a half circle, coming to rest against one of his sprawled legs. The hanging pot he'd hit swung crazily from its chain, spilling black earth down on him where he landed, half-sitting with his back against the heavy glass wall.

I was shaking the sting out of my hand when Ben came barreling in behind his gleaming hogleg of a magnum. He had on his outdoor gear. He stopped and swung the gun from me down to North, then flushed from his cap to his collar and threaded the long barrel into its holster. He was chugging like a pressure cooker.

"Lost him in the hall," he said. "You all right, Mr. Strangeways?"

"I'm fine. You forgot Mr. North knows all the shortcuts."

North was shaking himself out of his stun. He ran a hand over the lower half of his face, looked at the hand, then spat blood into it. He'd bitten his tongue. He looked up at me with the beginnings of an animal glimmer in his dull eyes and smiled. One side of his face was still numb and it made the grin crooked, like a hyena's. The smears of black earth didn't help.

"You're Walker," he said. "I wasn't sure at first. I only saw you that one time, and we didn't speak. I guess I'm sure now."

"Get up and I'll convince you some more."

"That will be enough," Strangeways snapped. "Ben, help him up."

The welterweight hesitated, then bent down and stuck out a paw. North grasped it and hauled himself to his feet. He brushed at the dirt on his suit.

"He's a tricky one," Ben said.

Strangeways said, "Next time don't take your eyes off them. Leave us now."

He left. He was always leaving.

"What did you hope to prove by that?" asked the billionaire.

"I think he's talking to you," I said.

North smoothed back his thinning hair with both hands, then stuck them in the pockets of his coat. I wondered about those pockets, about that little side trip through the house after Ben had patted him down outside.

"Just grandstanding," he said. "A long time ago I got into some trouble. It left me with a bad impression of people in uniform."

"He might have shot you."

"I didn't say it was smart." He was still looking at me. "I've been following your career."

"Hard to do, with a naked eye." I wasn't looking at his face. *You read a lot of bullshit about killer's eyes, kid. Forget the eyes, eyes don't kill. Watch their hands.*

"You're too modest. You went to jail that time that TV news reader's son was killed; something about protecting a client. And you were right in the middle of it when Timothy Marianne got shot in his own auto plant. You made the papers a few other times."

"You didn't. I kept checking the obituaries."

"Where is my wife?"

The washed-out eyes left me for the first time, went to

Gordon Strangeways. On the way they took in the P38 resting on the seat of the scooter. "I don't know," he said. "I thought you might."

"What does that mean?"

"We were supposed to meet in Louisiana last week. I rented a bungalow, but she never showed up. After three days I came back here. I thought she'd lost interest."

"You damned liar." The London polish had begun to flake off the Mossel Bay.

"On the flight back I started to wonder if something had happened to her. That's the real reason I called you this morning. You asked about her before I could work around to it." He nodded toward the Walther. "Is that what you used?"

A second's silence plunked into the void. Then Strangeways reached for the gun. North's right hand moved in his coat pocket. I stepped between the chaise and the scooter, blocking Strangeways' reach.

"No shooting in here," I said. "Too much glass. You might hit a picketer and then we'll all have the feminists on our necks."

A little of the tension drained out after that. North's topcoat smoothed out. Strangeways fell back against the cushions. I picked up the P38. The topcoat moved again. I was sure now he was right-handed.

"Is this the only gun you own?" I asked Strangeways.

"The guards have an arsenal in the hall closet."

"Locked up?"

"No. They'll need quick access in the event of a siege."

"Uh-huh." I put the semiautomatic in my coat pocket. Kept my hand there.

North looked amused. "Pompous old eunuch.

America's czar of sex, dead from the waist down. How long did you think you could keep Laurel a prisoner?"

"She's always been free to come and go. Perhaps you killed her to prevent her from coming back."

"Let's find out if she's dead first." I strolled out of the line of fire, circling to North's left. Now he'd have to turn to start something. "Louisiana's an odd choice for a tryst. Why not Florida? That's where most of Michigan goes when the snow flies."

"It's home to her," North said. "I guess she thought she'd feel more comfortable there. Also Strangeways would buy the excuse. If he got suspicious and checked the roaming charges on her cell phone they would check out."

"Apparently the last twenty years didn't make a dent in your hormones. Your tastes are more expensive, though. That why you threw in with Boyette?"

"You don't give a damn about Boyette. Ten years after Leopold was killed I was still getting a greeting card on the anniversary of his death, without a return address or a signature. Why'd you stop?"

"Postage went up. Why'd you kill him? The worst he could have done was put you on the wrong side of a sloppy divorce. It wasn't like you had far to fall. That computer records job didn't pay anything."

"If you have to ask *why*, you should ask yourself *if*. I didn't kill him."

I wanted another smoke, but I'd never gotten the knack of lighting up one-handed. The European gun felt odd in my palm. I missed my comfortable Smith & Wesson. It was in my glove compartment again, a hundred yards and a thousand miles away. "I've thought about it," I said. "A lot. Up until Dale your case history reads like an insurance pamphlet. It starts to get gaudy around age thirty-one. No more home at five-twenty. Mysterious withdrawals from your savings account: fifty here, ninety there, then fifty again. Always one or the other. The dates slide around but they jibe with your late nights. It's all in the record of your divorce proceedings."

"You read it." He nodded. "You would."

"I couldn't put it down. You went from an insurance pamphlet to a bestseller. A pavement princess like Star LaJoie would have been forty bucks a turn tops, maybe eighty for all night. The extra ten would have paid for the room. Nothing new there, the song was around a long time before they invented lyrics. Not for you, though. A gray statistic of a man sees his first streak of scarlet. He's nervous, but that's part of the thrill. Then he finds out he's being tailed."

"I'm going to spoil the ending for you," he said. "He lays off and goes home like a good statistic. He winds up getting divorced anyway; it's not that kind of an ending. But he doesn't kill anyone. Sorry, Walker. It's not exactly blockbuster material."

"Not this statistic. This one bought a gun. It went off three times. One would have been enough for a professional at that range, or two if his aim was off. Three is a nervous finger on an unfamiliar trigger. Just the kind of messy job a computer programmer might make."

He smiled dustily. "There's a saying in the computer field: A theory is just a wet dream with numbers."

"Gentlemen. What has this to do with my wife?"

We looked at Strangeways. I think we'd both forgotten he was there. He'd used the time to touch up the bare spots in his breeding. He was sitting up with his hands folded in his lap and no expression at all behind his glasses.

I said, "It's an indirect link. Every other crime gets easier once you've committed the granddaddy and gotten away with it. Forgery and fraud, for two. Ruddy at the DIA caught North going through the files of wealthy patrons. That clicks with what Boyette was up to. Once he was nailed, he lost his best customer in the DIA, but there were plenty of gullible private collectors in those files who would buy the manuscripts North faked if Boyette confirmed them. Boyette probably figured the board of directors did him a favor when they chose not to go public with the scandal."

"But I knew about it," Strangeways said. "It was common gossip in the trade."

"Boyette probably found that out the hard way. That's where the Hours of the Virgin came in. Back a little." I looked at North. "The fakes had to be good enough to survive a first glance. Boyette could give you pointers and show you examples, but you'd need time to become intimate with the real thing. That's why he got you the hands-on job here. Only he got caught before either of you could get rich, and his credibility as an expert was blown. That ended his usefulness. But there you were, still gainfully employed at the museum, with a stack of forgeries under your arm and a drawer full of suckers to unload them on."

"A lot of good they'd do me without someone to authenticate them."

"It eliminated some buyers, no doubt, and probably lowered your asking price," I said. "There would still be collectors who would actually be intrigued by the missing pedigrees."

"Provenances," Strangeways corrected.

I waved my free hand, even as I found the Walther's

safety catch with the other and thumbed it off. "They would suspect they were being offered stolen goods, and you wouldn't say anything to discourage that suspicion. A lot of upright people come down with rickets of the ethics when they smell a bargain. As long as you had the manuscripts and the greed of your customers, you didn't need Boyette. It didn't even matter when you were discovered and dismissed. You'd put together enough of a list to get started.

"That didn't sit well with Boyette," I went on. "He'd lost his reputation, and he didn't have the manuscripts, except one page of the Hours, which he might have been carrying around as a sample. Probably there never were any other pages. He couldn't sell it; everyone in the collecting world knew he was a crook. When he found out you were peddling the stock without him, using his know-how and his scheme, he decided to shake you down. Jump right in anywhere if I get the order wrong."

"Go ahead. This story is even more entertaining than the one about Leopold." As he spoke, North turned my way a couple of inches. I tightened my grip on the P38.

"He set up a meet," I said. "Maybe he sweetened the offer with the first page of the Hours, so you'd have a complete set when you cut him in on the action. I like it that you were the one who suggested the exchange take place at the Tomcat Theater. It appealed to your hormones as well as your sense of irony. You'd know it was owned by your former temporary employer. You'd give him his cut, he'd give you the page and the promise not to tip off the cops."

I gave Strangeways the corner of my eye. "This is where I get to your wife. Somebody had to let Boyette know what sort of man he was dealing with. Somebody had to scare him enough to bring me in as his bodyguard with a trumped-up story about a museum theft and a ransom drop. I don't know why it had to be me or how Boyette connects to the man who set me up for it, but I know who was the one person who knew North and Boyette both, and was intimate enough with North to have heard him boast about what a big bad killer he was."

"Laurel." Strangeways' tone was barely a whisper. "My God."

"She played you both," I told North. "She warned Boyette about you, but she helped you out too. You had to have been watching when I entered the theater behind Boyette. You recognized me, put two and two together, and sent her in to distract me while you made your play. That was a smart choice. I never even saw you come in. Tell me, if Boyette had hired anyone else, would you have tried to kill him?"

He said nothing. He was facing me full on now. The right side of his coat hung six inches higher than the left. Mine did too, by now.

"You missed," I said, "but I went to the floor like any ambushee with brains, and the place emptied. Boyette was one of the last out, having had to run all the way from the front row, and you were waiting for him. You marched him to his car at gunpoint and got in the back and told him to drive. He didn't drive far. You directed him to O'Hair Park and capped him when he stopped."

"He's dead?"

I couldn't read him. All that time with just an electronic gizmo for company had dulled the impulses between his face and his brain.

"What rot! Laurel may be capable of infidelity, but not accessory to murder."

I didn't look at Strangeways. "Anyone's capable given the right circumstances. Let's say these weren't them; she didn't know murder was what North had in mind. Even when you know his history, it's hard to accept him as a desperate character when you're face-to-face."

"You didn't seem to have any trouble." North limped his injured tongue around the inside of his mouth, tasting blood.

"I've had plenty of practice. Anyway, that's why she ran when you shot at me. Or why you killed her. Beautiful women make great witnesses. Especially if you're unlucky enough to draw an all-male jury."

For a long time after I finished, the room was silent. Even the leaves on the plants hung motionless, totally enervated. Then from somewhere in the room came a low bubbling, like thick liquid coming to a sluggish boil. Earl North was chuckling.

"It's a great yarn," he said. "There are only three things wrong with it. I didn't kill Boyette and I didn't kill Laurel, to start. And I didn't fake the Hours of the Virgin. If Boyette's dead, it isn't because he tried to hold me up. It's because he had the Hours, the real thing. Or knew where he could get it."

The liquid chuckle turned into a cough, deep and racking. He took his hands out of his pockets. I raised the Walther. He unscrewed the cap from a portable inhaler, brought it to his mouth, and pumped it twice. He took a deep breath and let it out with a rattling sigh.

I flipped the P38's safety catch back on and laid the pistol on the seat of the scooter. I felt as played-out as the flora. I couldn't tell whether it was relief or disappointment.

21

I took off my coat then and draped it over the scooter's handlebars. My skin felt dank under my clothes. I thought about having that cigarette but my lips were too dry. I looked at our host. "Can a man get a drink around here, or is that just for the shrubbery?"

He groped a hand under the cushions and came up with a cordless telephone. "Ben? Bring the cart." He punched out.

"Ben's the butler?" I said. "I thought he was security."

"He does most of the things I can't do for myself, including serve drinks and turn away bullets. He's been with me since Little Rock. Before that he was the subject of a feature in the first issue of *After Six* I edited. He fought

Sugar Ray Robinson just before Robinson retired and coached the U.S. boxing team in the 1976 Olympics. I hired him away from the finest security firm in the country. If I were to stop trusting him I would give up entirely."

Ben entered in shirtsleeves, pushing a jingling cart on rubber wheels. I asked for Scotch and soda, Strangeways a glass of water, which he used to chase a pill he took from a prescription bottle standing among a forest of them on the shelf below the bottles and siphon. North wanted nothing. Ben served us and left. The Scotch tasted like smoked heather. I didn't know what kind of fighter the guard had been, but he was wasted in anything but a bartender's coat.

"The Hours of the Virgin is too risky to fake," North said. "Boyette and I specialized in lesser rarities; manuscripts valuable enough to justify the time and expense, but not so interesting they might attract attention from outside. I'd just as soon copy *The Last Supper* as the Hours."

"You admit to the scheme?" Strangeways was becoming interested despite himself. He had the collector's bug.

"I admit to forgery. It's not illegal unless you try to sell a copy as the real thing, and you'll have to prove that. I missed my calling when I became an accountant. Programming fifteenth-century-style monastic lettering into my hard drive, even the thousand little irregularities needed to make it look like hand work, was comparatively easy. Getting the printer to feed through the right kind of paper was the hard part. I had to redesign the machine from the ground up, and of course I didn't use the real thing or the rollers would have eaten it. Then there was staining and aging, which required certain dyes and acids and a conventional oven."

I drained my glass in a lump and filled it again from

the cut-glass decanter, not bothering with the soda this time. The Scotch wasn't working as fast as Strangeways' pain pill. I was spending a social afternoon with Lucifer. "You were telling us about the Hours."

"Boyette didn't tell me much about it," North said. "Only its complete history back to Richard the Third. He said the other scholars were wrong when they said it disappeared at the time of the Reformation. He had it on good authority a band of rebel monks spirited it away before Henry the Eighth ordered the monasteries destroyed. They smuggled the entire Plymouth Book out under their cassocks, a page at a time, and hid them in the walls of the houses owned by sympathetic noblemen, dividing up the sections among several houses for safety. When the danger had passed, all the sections were retrieved except the Hours of the Virgin; the monk in charge of that section had died without telling anyone where he took it, and whatever nobleman had possession conveniently forgot to come forward. It remained, largely forgotten, in the attic of the ancestral home of a prominent family until an American serviceman helped himself to it in 1944. He brought it home to Detroit as a souvenir."

"That's where the story crosses with the one Boyette told me," I said. "Why would he lie about that?"

North went into his liquid chuckle. "He was an egghead. He did his homework after the manuscript worked its way around to him. He was good, probably as good as he said he was. He was going to publish the real story when he announced the find. Then they fired him. Knowing him, I'd guess getting back his reputation became even more important in the end than making a bundle. He wouldn't jeopardize that by spilling it all to a cheap private eye."

I went to my shirt pocket for my pack of Winstons. I smiled when he shrank away from the sudden movement. My knuckles still ached and I didn't think his jaw felt any better. "If he had the real Hours, why didn't he try to peddle it? He said it was worth a million at auction."

"He couldn't, legitimately," Strangeways put in. "It belongs to Great Britain. The World Court doesn't recognize the spoils of war. He would have had to return it."

North said, "He couldn't sell it under the table, either, if he wanted to make hay out of the discovery. So your idea about me killing him to keep him from going to the police doesn't hold air. Academic fame meant more to him than blood money."

"Ideas are like cigarettes in a machine. There's always a fresh pack right behind the last." I lit one and blew smoke at the junior Acropolis along the base of the ceiling. "Like, you waxed him because he refused to fence the Hours and split the take."

"What would that get me, aside from a moment's satisfaction? Certainly not the Hours."

"He had a bundle under his arm when he went into the Tomcat. He didn't leave it in the theater and it wasn't found in his car when he was. It wasn't in his house. He had no manuscripts there of any kind. I didn't even think about that until a little while ago. That's when I figured out you had them all."

"Not all. I don't have the Hours. And I was never in the Tomcat Theater."

A movement from the chaise hooked my attention. Strangeways had picked up the gun from the scooter. It wasn't pointing at anything, just resting in his hand in his blanket-covered lap. "I remind you both that the purpose of this meeting is to determine what happened to my wife. I shall pay the sum of one million dollars to the man who produces her alive and in good condition. It no longer matters whether that man is the one who took her away in the first place. I wish to have her back. If she's dead, I shall spend that million to bring the person who killed her to justice."

Something shifted in North's dull gray eyes, a shadow of a suggestion of a glimmer. His hands, which had gone back into his pockets, came partway out. I wasn't paying any attention to them now, they were just hands. It was the glimmer I didn't like. It was equal parts avarice and worry. It should have been one or the other, but not both. It wouldn't have been split if he knew where Laurel Strangeways was, or *if* she was. Then I decided I was trying to get too much out of something that could have been just a reflection of the pale sun going down outside the glass room.

I swirled the liquor in my glass and drank it. "A million to you is a hundred to me. I'll throw it in. She shapes up to be the last person who saw Boyette alive, not counting the passenger in the back seat."

Strangeways wasn't listening. He'd traded the P38 for his cordless telephone. He punched out a number, waited, and said, "Jillian Raider, please. This is Gordon Strangeways. Good afternoon, Jillian. I want you to draw up a letter of intent for my signature." He waited again, then repeated his offer word for word. He asked her to read it back, listened, said, "Splendid," and rang off. He looked at us. "It will be notarized and placed on file in the safe with my will." Without waiting for a reply from either of us, he pressed another button. "Come in, please, Ben. Your hat and coat."

That made it last call for the guests. I put on my coat

and we went out, North first with the welterweight bringing up the rear. We waited on the front porch while Ben went to fetch our cars.

"You didn't get your letter of reference," I said.

"Didn't expect one. I came here to find out what happened to Laurel. I still think that son of a bitch killed her. It doesn't cost a cent to offer a million-dollar reward no one will ever collect."

"So it's love."

A beige Pontiac was coming up the driveway with Ben at the wheel. North faced me.

"At least I care. You don't give a damn if she's alive or dead or what happened to the Hours of the Virgin. Unless you can use them somehow to nail me for your partner's murder."

"Any old murder will do. It doesn't have to be Dale."

"He isn't worth it, you know."

The Scotch had reached my nervous system at last. My face felt warm in the bracing cold. "You only knew him long enough to take aim."

"I knew him longer than that."

I waited. His smile looked as if it had lain on a windowsill for a week.

"I don't like being followed," he said. "Even when I'm not doing anything, and—hell, it was a long time ago and my ex-wife has remarried—I was doing something. Immoral, yes; illegal, no. Nobody's business but Mr. and Mrs. North's. But every time I glanced up in my rearview mirror, there was that beat-up Fury, as easy to shake as an ulcer. So one day at a stoplight I got out and went back and offered Leopold a thousand dollars to paint me up as Ward Cleaver for my wife. He accepted before the light changed."

I grinned. "That the best you can do? If Dale had a price it was a lot higher than a grand."

"I said it was a long time ago. Carter was president. I was living on a clerk's salary."

The Pontiac slid into the curb and Ben got out, leaving the door open. North stepped down. I said, "Thanks for clearing that up. It explains why he wasn't following you that night on Mullett and why he's home right now clipping coupons."

"Try this. If he was holding me up for a grand, chances are he was holding somebody else up for ten. See, that's the problem with raising the ante. The kind of person who can afford to cover it didn't get where he is by making a habit of paying off chiselers."

I took a step toward him. He scrambled to get into the front seat and slammed the door. I gave him a moment to find his spine, then tapped on the window. He cranked it down two inches.

"You're going down," I said. "If not for Dale, then for Boyette. For Laurel Strangeways too, if she's dead. If I could get you for Star LaJoie, she'd do as well. Death's been too good to you. The bill's on its way."

There was no life in his eyes. They might have been penciled in. "He was your friend. If I had a friend I'd like to think he'd do the same for me. I don't think he started out crooked, if it means anything. Just burned out. Maybe you feel that way sometimes. God knows I do. That's why I've made the mistakes I've made."

"Quit kidding. You don't know what it's like to have a friend."

"If you hit me again I'll kill you."

He cranked up the window and pulled away.

22

Just another Dagwood

Just another Dagwood Bumstead with a snake

Just another Dagwood Bumstead with a snake in his pants, kid. Don't worry your pretty little head about it.

The drive back to Detroit from Downriver is always longer than the drive out, especially when it's getting dark. The attenuating shadows always seem to be moving faster than the car. Tonight it was Lindbergh's crossing, Columbus' first voyage, the trek up Everest. I was going ten miles over the limit, but the Cutlass was standing still on the back of an elderly tortoise with bunions. I snapped on the radio and ran the indicator all the way right and left, but everywhere it stopped, Dale Leopold's voice came out of the speaker. *Just another Dagwood Bumstead with a snake in his pants, kid.* As much as I knew about the Earl North divorce case until I got the call to come down to Mullett Street.

A generation reared on the smug politics of *Doonesbury* and the lunkheaded jock humor of *Tank MacNamara* probably skipped right over it on the way to the Ninja Turtles, but my crowd and my father's grew up following the adventures of Dagwood, the quintessential harried husband, through the daily obstacle course of marriage, work, fatherhood, and life in the suburbs. It was his comic strip, even if it was named for his wife. Six times weekly and in four colors on Sunday, *Blondie* pushed this lanky cowlicked Everyman off stepladders, got him in Dutch with his boss, and propelled him into a collision with the equally hapless mailman on his way to catch the morning bus, all in the cause of old-fashioned family values and the Puritan work ethic.

What was less known, and that only to readers ancient enough to remember the strip's debut in the twenties and the odd trivia fanatic like Dale, was that Dagwood had started out rich. Heir to the fabulous Bumstead fortune, he had given up his birthright to marry Blondie, the airheaded flapper beloved of the newspaper junkies of Prohibition, and sentenced himself to life among the proles for the sake of love. Dale had won a couple of hundred dollars from unbelievers by producing a copy of the premiere panels, clipped from a Permabound history of the comics and stashed in his wallet. When it began to grow tattered at the fold, I had told him he was in danger of losing his investment if he didn't have it laminated. I never knew if he took me up on the suggestion or if it had worn out finally and he had thrown it away. It wasn't in his wallet when his body was found.

I thought about it for fourteen or fifteen blocks; then I pressed down the accelerator.

The prosecutor who'd failed to indict North hadn't given it his best shot. He didn't like the motive. A computer clerk with a colorless background made a poor candidate for a murderer. Divorce on grounds of infidelity didn't pack the punch it had during the Victorian era, especially at the height of the sexual revolution of the 1970s. North, mired deep in the low end of the middle class, had stood to lose his small tract house in the suburbs and five-year-old Plymouth two-door, but he was young enough to start over. Double the loss, triple it, and it still didn't add up to three bullets fired from a gun in his hand.

Don't worry your pretty little head about it.

Reverse psychology.

Dying clue.

To hell with that. Dale never reversed anything. A county survey crew could have plotted a road along the progression of his thoughts, and he'd been just as direct about expressing them. Not the world's most enviable virtue; it had cost him two marriages and more friendships than most people made in a lifetime. But to quote the late CEO of the Midwest's largest vending machine distributor, just before he went to prison for tax evasion, "You knew where you stood with the son of a bitch." Dale had no use for cryptic codes.

But if North was right. If Dale could be bought. If somebody with a lot more to lose didn't agree to his price. That would be a motive.

Nuts. A handful of snowflakes shaped like tiny cartwheels flattened out against the windshield and turned to water on contact. I flirted the wipers, sweeping away the drops and the doubts along with them.

But assuming what Nesta Spurling Clark had told me held air, what were Dale and North talking about just before Dale died?

He wouldn't leave a clue, not on purpose. But there had to be a reason he had Dagwood on his mind. Why the strip that had won so many bets hadn't shown up among his personal effects.

No wife, Blondie-type or otherwise, greeted me at the door with a drink when I entered my kitchen from the garage. I had thought once or twice about getting a dog, but you never know when a tail job might end in California and I didn't have anyone I'd trust to feed and walk the pooch without helping himself to the TV and VCR; so no big clunky paws muddied my shirt and no sweaty tongue licked my face either. The only greeting I got came from a bulb in the ceiling fixture that jinked and went out when I flipped the switch.

Time enough to replace it later. I went into the living room without taking off my coat and switched on the floor lamp. The little bookcase stood on the edge of the pool of light.

Dale wasn't a book collector except by accident. He could never understand why anyone would pay hundreds of dollars for a first edition when he could buy the same book in paperback for a buck and a half or borrow it from the library and read it for free. But he was a John O'Hara fan most of his adult life. It began with a beat-up edition of *Appointment in Samarra* without a jacket he bought in a used book store to look busy while he was tailing someone and started reading on stakeout. He'd gotten so hooked he almost missed his subject, and had never again read on the job, although he usually had an atlas or a road map spread out in front of him in case anyone wondered what he was doing sitting in his car. But he finished the book at home, then went to the library and checked out *Pal Joey* and read that in one sitting. When he'd exhausted the early titles he started buying each new one as it appeared, in the end amassing an impressive collection of first editions in pristine jackets because he couldn't wait for them to show up at the library or come out in cheaper editions. Something about the writer's plain style and honest presentation of the flawed human creatures with whom Dale shared a planet touched a nerve. When O'Hara died in 1970, he moped around for days, then went back and reread *Appointment in Samarra,* whose fatalistic epigraph, borrowed from Somerset Maugham, was later read aloud at his funeral. At the time he was killed he'd read them all two or three times.

Other books he read and discarded, marking his place by turning down the page-corners. He treated the O'Haras like fragile children, removing the jackets when he read and using bookmarks. The bookmarks themselves didn't matter. He never bought the decorative ones on display at the cash registers in bookstores, just grabbed whatever was handy or tore a piece off a newspaper and stuck it between the pages.

I might not have thought of any of this if I hadn't had recent practice going through the books in Harold Boyette's house. I started with the top shelf left to right. The battered, jacketless copy of *Appointment in Samarra* yielded nothing, even when I held it open upside down by the covers and shook it. I replaced it and pulled out

The Farmers Hotel. A triangular tear of colored newsprint fluttered out. When I picked it up and examined both sides I learned that someone was offering something for $1.98 a pound. *Hellbox* and *Hope of Heaven* were even less communicative. One of Dale's old business cards fell out of *A Rage to Live.* Nothing was written on the unprinted side. At that point I thought about the jackets. I stripped them from the books I'd checked already, spread them out, and looked at them under the lamp. All I got was a paper cut off *Hellbox.*

By *Pipe Night* I was pretty sure there was a special place in hell for prolific writers. It would contain one typewriter, without keys. Then I slid out *Butterfield 8*—and there it was, sticking out of the top a hundred pages in.

It was too fragile to pull out without tearing. I opened the book to that spot and looked at it and didn't touch. In the second panel, thumb-blurred and faded, a very dapper Dagwood, in dark sport coat and white flannels with his hair slicked back and parted in the center like Valentino's, was dragging a ditzy, curvy bombshell of a Blondie into the room to meet his father, a ferocious old baldy who resembled J. P. Pennybags on the *Monopoly* box. The narrow strip of paper, yellow-brown and beer-stained, was worn soft and ragged where it had been folded too many times into Dale's wallet and was coming apart at the edges. I lifted it free, cupping it in my palm, closed the book gently, and slid it back into its place on the shelf. The strip was rubbed so thin I could tell without turning it over that something was written on the back.

I carried it to the lamp and turned it over. Dale's writing—it had been done with one of the cheap skippy ballpoint pens he bought by the package in drugstores—

was just rooster-scratches to most people, but I had had
plenty of practice typing up formal reports from his hasty
notes. Some printing and a piece of another comic took
up part of the back, but he had written a series of letters
and numerals on the blank part in a vertical column:

DMB—9
CNB—8.5
NBD—9
DSB—9.5
AAF—8
AAB—8.5
TSB—9.5

I put on the table lamp beside the good armchair, laid
the comic strip on the table, and went into the kitchen
and fixed myself a drink from the bottle in the cupboard
and two crisp ice cubes from the refrigerator compartment. I brought the drink out and sat down and picked
up the strip and looked at it and drank. When the glass
was empty except for two half-melted cubes I got out the
directory and looked up Tom Burnchurch.

He wasn't listed in Detroit. I called Information and
gave the operator the name and said I wasn't sure what
city but that it should be in the metropolitan area. She
gave me an argument, but I waited her out.

"I have a Thomas Burnchurch in Royal Oak." Without
waiting for a response she hit a button and a female
voice with all the personality wrung out of it read me the
number off a recording. I let Ma Bell do the dialing.

"Burnchurch residence."

A youngish male voice. It would always sound young

until it soured overnight, somewhere around sixty. He had twenty-five years to go.

"Mr. Burnchurch, I wonder if you remember me. My name is Amos Walker. We met once or twice at your father's house when I went there with Dale Leopold. You were fourteen or fifteen."

"Dale's partner? Oh, hell, yes." He sounded younger still. "He always talked to me like I was an adult, even when I was twelve. Dad thought the world of him. What are you doing these days?"

"The same thing I was doing then. This is business, I'm afraid. Your father and Dale passed away about the same time, didn't they?"

"About six weeks apart. Dad had a massive stroke and dropped into a coma. He hung on for thirty-six days before they pulled the plug on him at Receiving. He had no more brainwaves than a cauliflower. He was just forty-eight. The job killed him."

The job was director of the regional office of the Federal Bureau of Investigation. Dale had once done Frank Burnchurch a good turn—neither man would ever say what it was—and the G-man repaid the debt by allowing him access to information denied the president of the United States: bank records, IRS files, sealed Justice Department cases, personal medical histories. If any of the services he provided got back to Washington, Burnchurch had stood a better-than-even chance of being prosecuted under the Espionage Act. Whatever the favor had been, it was big.

"You aren't by any chance with the Bureau yourself," I asked.

"Oh, hell, no. The old man would haunt me right out of the office. I'm an investment counselor."

"This is a longshot. Do you know if your father kept any records of cases he was investigating at the time he had the stroke?"

"Oh, sure. The Bureau was just starting to put everything on computer then. He never trusted those big mainframes. Made hard copies of everything. I've still got boxes and boxes in the cellar. About once a year my wife tries to talk me into getting rid of them."

I excused myself, laid the receiver in my lap, and mopped off my palms on my trousers. When I picked it up again my voice was normal. Breaks like that are too good to last. "I wonder if I could come over and take a look."

"Tonight?"

"I'll try not to disrupt your evening too much. I'll go through the stuff myself if you'll trust me."

"Is this about Dale's murder?"

I said it was.

He gave me directions to his house. "I'll look for you in twenty minutes. How good's your lead?"

"It looks promising. I may have found the Bumstead millions."

23

It was one of the older homes in Royal Oak, a narrow brick two-story with a steep roof and a trellis up one side where ivy would grow in summer, dense as a blanket. The front was calm and honest in the glow of the corner streetlamp. From attic to basement it was one-tenth the size of Gordon Strangeways' shack in Grosse Ile.

A small pretty woman of about thirty, with curly dark hair, let me in. She was Tom Burnchurch's wife and she didn't like me any better than a splash of purple among the muted grays and earth tones in her living room. But her husband had invited me, so she excused herself and went into the kitchen while we shook hands. Burnchurch was tall and fair and going prematurely bald in a steel-gray cardigan, brushed blue jeans, and expensive Italian loafers that had been demoted to comfortable house shoes when his toes began to wear through. He had his father's blue eyes and cleft chin.

"Jean doesn't like anyone from the old days coming around," he said. "Her father was a fire chief in a small town. She's afraid somebody's going to take me away in the middle of the night."

"Does anyone come around from the old days?" I asked.

"Once every couple of years. Dad used to slip his snitches cash when they needed it, whether they had any fresh information for him or not. The survivors never forget. Jean keeps after me to get an unlisted number."

"Do you give them money?"

"Yeah, but don't tell Jean." He raised his voice. "The basement's through here. I pulled the stuff out from behind the furnace. Hope you don't mind dust."

I followed him through a kind of den. I recognized the huge yellow-oak desk from his father's house. The wall above it was plastered with photographs and documents in frames: Frank Burnchurch shaking hands with J. Edgar Hoover, a much younger Frank in a fedora and shoulder holster, posing with another agent on either side of a bed with pistols and hand grenades and a Thompson submachine gun laid out on the mattress, a letter typed on White House stationery congratulating Special Agent Francis X. Burnchurch on the breakup and arrest of a band of kidnappers called the Tri-State Gang. It was signed by Harry S. Truman. There were certificates of merit, a front-page spread from the old *Detroit Times* with a picture of Burnchurch escorting mobster Sam Lucy into the Federal Building in manacles, the top half of a silhouette target from the FBI range with six holes bunched together where the heart had been.

"It's a shrine," admitted his son when I paused at the desk. "Dad would have hated it, especially the shot with Hoover. He stuck it in a drawer and forgot it. He said the old sham stood on a box so he wouldn't look like a circus midget."

"He'd be happy you're proud of him."

"He'd never say it. Jean complains about it all the time. They'd have gotten along a lot better than she thinks."

We descended a flight of unpainted pine stairs into a basement recreation room with walnut paneling and a Ping-Pong table. I followed him through a door in a partition into a bare concrete area lit by hanging bulbs, with a furnace and water heater in the corner and next to it a washing machine and electric dryer. The room smelled of detergent and slightly of mildew. A mountain of dusty cardboard cartons stood on the floor with jagged towers of file folders and stacked sheets sticking out of the tops.

"Sorry it's such a mess. Dad was a bloodhound as a field agent, but an absolute pack rat as an administrator. It's a little more orderly than it looks. Do you know what you're after?"

I took a sheet of notepaper out of an inside pocket and handed it to him. "I copied this from Dale's scribble. What do you think?"

He looked at it under a bulb. "They're bank initials," he said after a moment. "Detroit Manufacturers, City National, National Bank of Detroit, Detroit State. Two *A*'s, that'd be Ann Arbor; Ann Arbor Federal and Ann Arbor Bank. TSB, that's Toledo State Bank. What do you think the numbers represent, deposits? Thousands?"

"You tell me."

"Thousands. Nine, eight-point-five, nine again, nine-point-five. Never ten. You know why?"

"Ten thousand's the cutoff point," I said. "Whenever an account reaches ten thousand, banks are required to report it to the IRS. You can hide millions from the government as long as you break them into increments of less than ten thousand and don't run out of banks."

"Not hide. If the spooks from Internal Revenue smell something, you're better off burying the money in your back yard or in a Swiss bank. But you can stash it this way for a while. You need to monitor the accounts, make withdrawals or close them out before the interest pushes them over the red line. It's a lot of work. Almost as bad as earning it honestly." He handed back the sheet. "Is this what Dale was working on when he was killed?"

"That's what I'm hoping to find out. He couldn't have gotten this information without a court order unless your father helped."

He nodded. "Clear violation of the Privacy Act, and what's worse, Bureau policy. But Dad and Dale operated by their own set of rules." He stopped nodding. "Of course, there's a different interpretation."

"I'm trying not to think about that. What's your take?"

He gave it a blink of thought. Then he shook his head. "I'd sooner imagine Dad hiding money than Dale. And Dad made me walk halfway across town to return a package of baseball cards I stole from a drugstore when I was ten. I had to apologize to every clerk in the store."

"Ever steal anything after that?"

"Not even first base. I lost my taste for the game." He pointed. "You'll find most of the financial stuff in the second box from the top. If you don't find what you need there, I'm afraid you'll have to go through the rest. Like me to give you a hand?"

I took off my coat and draped it over the dryer. "I've already taken up part of your evening. I don't want to be named co-respondent in your divorce."

He looked relieved and regretful. "It's tax season. This is the first night I've been home this early in a week. Jean's got a crazy idea husbands and wives should see each other now and then."

"She'll grow out of it."

"Now you sound like Dale. Raise a whoop if you need anything." He left me.

I got the top carton onto the floor without stirring up a cloud, although the contact smeared my shirt with dust. I upended a wicker laundry basket, sat on it, and dived into the second carton with both hands. The TV set was directly overhead. They were watching a medical drama; lots of people yelling "Stat!" and bickering with one another. I'd spent enough time in emergency rooms to use them as voting addresses, and I'd never heard anyone raise his voice in one. But you can't get a thirty-nine share of the ratings asking patients about their insurance.

The contents of the box provided plenty of entertainment if you were interested in the credit history of some white-collar felons and a politician or two who had long since cleaned out the war chest and gone home to spend more time with their families. The really juicy stuff, about organized crime figures and money launderers, would fit onto a three-by-five card. Racketeers deal strictly in cash and don't leave paper trails. There were a lot of names I didn't recognize, a few I did but couldn't remember why, and an occasional surprise, including a police commander with a running tab at a male escort service and a cardinal who seemed to have been paying the bills for a woman named Heather.

It was at times like those that Frank Burnchurch's honesty hit me like a clean gust of wind. He could have climbed that pile of paper into a four-acre house in Grosse Pointe, but he had lived all his adult life in a shotgun-style ranch house in a Sterling Heights development and went to his rest in a three-hundred-dollar coffin in a plot earned by his military service.

I didn't find what I wanted in that carton or the next. At the end of two hours I stood, stretched out the kinks, and walked around the basement until my right leg woke up. The studio laughter of a late-night talk show broke overhead like surf. I sat back down and tackled the third box.

It was in a bulging cardboard file folder right on top. I pulled out a sheaf of green-bar computer printouts, removed the king-size paperclip, and shuffled through them. Each sheet bore the name of one of the banking institutions whose initials Dale had written on the back of Dagwood. The deposits listed had all been made within four weeks in April 1978, in the form of computer transfers drawn on the corporate account of Paul Bunyan Mutual Life and Property, the insurance firm Earl North had worked for at the time Dale was following him for North's wife. The total on each page matched the numbers Dale had written next to the initials. It came to $62,000 all told. The names under which the accounts had been opened were nigglingly familiar. Burroughs. Pitney. Bowes. Adler. Victor. He'd lacked even the imagination to choose his aliases from beyond the names stenciled on the office equipment he used.

Upstairs the TV noise cut off abruptly. The basement

door opened and the stairs squeaked under a pair of worn Italian loafers. Tom Burnchurch came in and asked if I was having any luck. I handed him the sheaf without comment.

He paged through it. He figured it out in half the time it had taken me. He was an investment counselor; he worked with numbers every day. "Dale must have suspected something to put Dad onto this," he said. "Do you think North's wife tipped him?"

"Maybe. She'd want her cut. Or maybe Dale suspected there was more involved than the divorce settlement an ordinary clerk could afford and started digging. He must have told her about the sixty-two thousand. It never would have occurred to him he was naming the price of the alibi she gave North in front of the grand jury."

"I bet I know how North did it. He was a computer whiz at a time they were few and far between. He transferred the money electronically from company files into these accounts, then went back and erased the transactions from the company computer. Paul Bunyan was a big company. The loss would have been investigated, but when it dead-ended they might have charged it to sloppy record keeping. We're talking Stone Age here, before the microchip; there was a lot of ignorance about the whole technology. In any case the company went bankrupt paying off fire claims in California in the early eighties. Sixty-two grand was a drop in the bucket."

"North's bucket was smaller. It would have made a bigger splash." I picked up my coat. "Somebody told me he was caught pulling off a scam similar to this at the DIA. It turned out to be a lie, but this may have been where he got the idea. North might have bragged about it."

Tom Burnchurch curled the sheets into a roll and slapped it against his palm a couple of times. "This would have made a difference if the grand jury had known about it, wouldn't it?"

"It would have given the prosecution some backbone. The cross-examination of North's wife would have been sharper. She might have caved. Money's a motive everyone can understand."

"If Dad hadn't had that stroke he would've come forward with it. Hell." He unrolled the sheaf and looked at it as if he were viewing a corpse in state. "It feels like he just died all over again."

"It wasn't his fault. If I'd been thinking straight I would have run down this angle at the time. Dale said something about Dagwood the night he died. He didn't mean it as a clue; the strip was just on his mind because of what he'd written on it. Your father must have given him the information over the telephone. I wasn't the detective Dale was. I'm still not."

"That's a dead-end street," he said. "I went down it myself. I'm not my dad, you're not Dale. That doesn't mean we're not as good. Just different. Are you going to take these to the police?" He held out the sheets.

I took them, folded them into quarters, and slipped them into one of the saddle pockets in my coat. "It won't do any good without a murder weapon. I need to put that thirty-two in North's hand."

"Do you think it still exists?"

"It's a thin hope. But it's better than none at all." I stuck out a hand. "Thanks."

"Thank my father. He was the one who couldn't throw anything away." But he shook my hand. He didn't seem to mind the dust.

24

It was as good a job as I'd seen in a long time. Getting around a deadbolt requires two picks, one to hold back the granny shield and another to work the tumblers. If you've got the control to do that without leaving telltale scratches on the outside plate, you could probably clean out the Federal Reserve in a fortnight.

Of course, there was a bare chance I'd gone out without locking the office, but that was less than likely. I'd lived in Detroit a long time.

It was the first sour note of the morning. I'd gone home and straight to bed from Tom Burnchurch's house and slept until the sun hit me in the face. What clouds there were were high, feathery, and easy to ignore.

Shelves of icicles as long as javelins leaned in from the eaves on both sides of the street, refracting sunlight into colors unseen since last summer. I felt a hundred percent for the first time in a week.

I hadn't paid much attention when I found the door unlocked to the outer office, even when there was no one waiting inside. Rosecranz might have let someone in who'd decided to fade when I didn't show up by one minute after eight. The business I lost for lack of a secretary meant less than the luxury of not having to say hello to the same person all day long. The lock on that door had come with the building. The building had come with gargoyles, and it wasn't a revival.

I extracted the Smith & Wesson and swiveled into the Holy of Holies. I checked all the standard places: behind the desk, in the space between the window and the file cabinets, inside the little water closet. The face above the sink was scrubbed and clear-eyed, with a fresh dusting of talcum on the perpetual five o'clock shadow. The eyebrows were too high. I put them back where they belonged, holstered the revolver, and got to the inventory.

You couldn't call it a ransacking. Nothing had been torn or broken, and whoever had frisked the place had done it in order. Drawers had been pulled out and dumped, furniture turned over, the heat register unscrewed from the hole that had no duct connected to it because the 1967 renovation had been interrupted by the riots before the old-fashioned heating pipes could be ripped out. The joke of a safe had been sprung with a toenail and my change of shirts rumpled.

Something crackled underfoot. I glanced down at a

sheet of my new stationery. There had been a major snow-
fall on the floor. That saved my opening the package.

I went out into the hall, where one of the asbestos
workers sat perched on his stepladder drinking coffee
from a Thermos cap. His protective hood lay crumpled
at the foot of the ladder. I asked him if he'd seen anyone
go in since he came on.

He swallowed coffee and thought. He had a broad, intelligent forehead and a full red beard. His name might
be Randall Adams Stonybrooke III, but everyone would
call him Red except his mother. He thought a long time
and then shook his head. "Been on since seven. My
partner didn't show up. Quietest building I ever worked
in on a Tuesday."

"It's that kind of building. I stuff pillows for Hudson's.
The guy down the hall crochets engine blocks for bull-
dozers that operate in hospital zones. Aren't you afraid
of breathing asbestos while you're on a break?"

"It ain't asbestos. It's rock wool, you could pad a crib
with it. Don't tell no one, okay? Me and Julio need the
hazard pay."

"Your secret's safe with me, Red."

"Clarence," he corrected.

I went back in and set the swivel on its wheels and
dropped into it. The belly drawer of the desk hung open
like a tongue, but the earring I'd left there was still inside.
So was the pint of whiskey. I tossed the cap over my
shoulder and tilted the neck. The container tasted like
water, bad sign. I got down on my hands and knees to
find the cap and screwed it back on. Standing, I shook the
last Winston out of yesterday's pack, lit it, looked around
for the wastebasket, and righted it so I could dispose of

the match and the crumpled pack. The tidy eye, I. That made me grin for as long as my face could hold it.

I leaned back against the desk, folded my arms, and smoked. Out there on the cusp of the millennium a siren gulped, a set of brakes locked with an animal yell. The air went thud and the building shook a little, exhaling a vapor of plaster dust from the ceiling; either a sonic boom from Selfridge or the Detroit Bomb Squad detonating a suspicious package on Belle Isle. The old pipes in the walls groaned soul-deep, passing rust like a kidney stone. And some called it a dead city.

They hadn't found what they were after, whoever they were, and who didn't matter yet. You don't pull up a couple of buckled linoleum tiles hunting for a secret compartment unless you've looked in all the easy places, and I hadn't had anything in the office valuable enough to get cute with in a long time except a pair of platinum earrings, and I had the mate in my pocket. Anyway they weren't looking for anything that small because they hadn't dismantled the telephone or taken Custer's Last Stand off the wall to pull the frame apart. The mail I hadn't bothered to open yesterday morning was scattered on the floor, the envelopes intact. Only the package of stationery had interested them and they'd given that a toss when they found out what it was.

Something about that size.

No larger than ordinary drugstore bond.

The telephone rang. I got my hackles down and answered it. It was John Alderdyce.

"It's alive," he said. "I tried to reach you a couple of times yesterday and last night at your dump. I thought you'd died or hit the lottery."

"I've been lucky so far and not lucky enough. Why didn't you leave a message with the service?"

"I did, twice. Why pay them if you don't call them once in a while?"

"I'm a little unorganized this morning. What's the rumpus?"

"I thought you'd like to know we took your advice and dug that slug out of the wall at the Tomcat. The manager wanted to call Strangeways but we convinced him we'd be in and out between the travelogue and the color cartoon. That was before I found out the head of the forensics team is a Marilyn Chambers fan. But we got both of them out finally."

"Was it a thirty-two?"

"Way too big. It weighed out at 240 grains. Thirty-eight at least, and maybe bigger. Hard to tell for a certainty. It lost all shape when it hit the mortar. No copper jacket. Even if we had another slug from the same gun we'd never make a match."

"So whoever killed Boyette had two guns. Or a partner."

"I'd go with a partner. It's an odd set, like wearing one wing tip and one espadrille. As a general rule those large-caliber boys are hung up on size."

I remembered my cigarette smoldering in the ashtray, a souvenir from Traverse City that had stood on the end table next to my father's favorite chair for ten years. I broke off a long column of ash and hauled in some smoke. "How's my balance sheet look on favors?"

"Friend to friend?"

"Whatever." I'd had it with semantics and it wasn't even nine o'clock.

"Ask."

"Send somebody down to the sub-sub-basement and

shovel out the file on the Leopold murder, April seventy-eight. Find out if the slug the M.E. dug out of Harold Boyette lines up with the three you got from Dale."

I couldn't hear his brain turning over. He kept the shaft well oiled. "I'm pretty sure I'd remember if you told me there was a link between this case and your partner's shooting." He sounded as cold and flat as a flagstone.

"Just a wild hair. Not that many killings take place with a thirty-two."

"I'll lend you the files. Where should I send the fork-lift? Are you withholding evidence again? Go ahead and lie. It shortens the balance sheet on your side."

"Ideas aren't evidence. There's no law against hanging on to a hunch."

"What was his name, North? If he is the one who pulled the trigger, he got rid of the gun ten minutes later. It's growing zebra mussels at the bottom of the river."

"Probably. He's smart enough."

He jumped on it. " 'Is'? When was the last time you saw him?"

"It's a small town," I said. "They say if you hang out at Carl's Chop House long enough you'll see everyone you know."

"The way I heard it, it was a café in Paris."

"I don't like French restaurants. They put ice in the butter and give you a hard roll. Thanks, John. Leave a message when you know anything."

I hung up quickly. The telephone rang again ten seconds later. I let the service get it. I got up, kicked shut one of the file drawers, wrenched up the window, and stuck my head out into the crisp sunny cold. A pigeon sat on the ledge of the building across the street, drying its feathers. It was puffed up as big as a squab. I pulled my head back in and closed the window and turned the latch. Pushing the reset button on my brain.

I turned around and poked at the mail on the floor with my foot. I would have done the same thing with a spray of clover. Bills, a marriage-mailer circular on Missing Teenager No. 1,000,008, bills, an offer to join a video club and receive the Horst Buchholz Collection, bills. No wonder they hadn't bothered to open them. I didn't want to myself. Not a four-leafer in the bunch.

I separated them with my toe, the way they said William Randolph Hearst used to read his *New York Journal*. Two of the bills were stuck together with something sandwiched between. I stooped and peeled them apart. Standard white envelope, letter size, addressed to me in block capitals with a Detroit postmark, no return. The machine stamp was at the end of its ink run; it might have been Wednesday's date. That was the day Boyette disappeared. The longer I looked at it the less sure I was about the number. Comparative graphology wasn't in my resumé, but when I felt like it I could go down to the bank and look at Boyette's signature on the document in my safe-deposit box. That would be as useless as the document, because he'd signed it in cursive.

I sniffed the envelope. It smelled like paper and ink. That was as much as I could get from it without going inside. I ran my thumb under the flap and pried it loose.

There wasn't anything inside but a business card. It was cheap white stock, not much thicker than notepaper, printed in smelly black ink with a Dearborn Heights address on the bottom and a pair of thickly lashed eyes, curving lips, and a comma of a nose decorating one corner. It looked like a tattoo on the arm of a sailor who still had his baby teeth.

THAT TOUCH OF VENUS
117652 Woodbine
Massage • Sauna • Body Shampoo
Discreet Service

That's the thing about looking for a Virgin. She always turns up in the last place you'd think.

25

The security man in the veined marble lobby of the *Detroit News,* lean and black and hardy in a medium-gray uniform with dramatic hollows under his cheek-bones like an Indian in an old western movie, took my license out of its folder and read the fine print front and back. I didn't think anything was printed on the back, but then I never looked at the thing. He returned it. "Who'd you say you came here to see?"

"I didn't. I came to buy a newspaper."

"There's a box out front."

"It's got today's paper. I want yesterday's."

He didn't like the sound of that at all. "How come?"

"I want to see if the weather forecast was right."

"Down the hall on the end. Don't leave this floor."

I started that way. I had to turn back and lean on his desk. "You know, no one's laid siege to a newspaper since Dodge City."

He thought about that. Then he brightened. "Dodge City papers didn't have security."

I quit even and waited in line behind a woman looking for Classifieds and an old man leaning on a quad cane who wanted the issue containing the obituary of a man named Bud, but didn't know which issue it was and couldn't remember Bud's legal name. When I finally drew face-to-face with a small, dish-faced blonde behind the counter I forgot what I wanted and had to think. She ducked, smacked a copy of Monday's paper onto the counter, and took my money without saying thanks. On my way out I smiled at the friendly guard.

In the car I turned to the city section, found the mug shot they'd run with the piece about Harold Boyette's body turning up in O'Hair Park, and cut it out with my pocket knife. The *Free Press* hadn't used any art and the *News* had bumped the story to a paragraph on a back page in the latest edition; the First Lady was coming to town and her fan club was all over City. The picture was a standard ID shot, obtained from the DIA, but for once it was a good likeness. You can describe someone the same way to forty people and leave forty different impressions of what he looks like. How detectives got along before Mathew Brady is anybody's guess.

There are a lot of Jeep Rangers around town, so I didn't draw the connection right away. Sport utility vehicles are a Detroiter's answer to all those suppository-shaped go-buggies buzzing out of Kyoto and Tennessee; the four-by-fours are made of steel, not beer cans, and you can roll them all the way over and maybe have to straighten your tie afterward. An eight-foot-tall tank will rumble up to the curb and a woman the size of your thumb will step down from the driver's seat and feed three meters.

This one pulled away from the curb on West Lafayette just as I shut myself into the Cutlass, which was parked behind it. The light at First was just turning yellow when the Jeep got to it, but the driver braked anyway; a careful motorist, credit to a busy downtown. When the light changed again he started out slow and I passed him on the outside. He let a panel truck get between us before switching to my lane. I had two blocks on him when we switched lanes again and turned onto Washington and again when we hooked up with Michigan. There he stayed all the way past the Edsel Ford Freeway, where the traffic picked up and he narrowed the gap. He was pretty good.

I still wasn't sure, so I wobbled the front end as if I were losing a wheel and pulled over and stopped. The driver of the Jeep didn't look right or left as he passed me. He'd changed clothes and that threw me for a minute because I thought he slept in that uniform; but I recognized the profile, the gray sidewalls, the skin starting to sag under the granite chin that had had more fists bounced off it than a wall at Betty Ford.

He was parked on the gravel on the other side of the C&O tracks when I started up again and passed that intersection. A couple of minutes later I saw him in the mirror in the inside lane. I couldn't tell if he were trying to call attention to himself or if he didn't care. They call it an open tail, and it's the toughest to shake.

I fought a little war with myself. For four blocks it was

anyone's battle, but then detective's curiosity lost; I didn't want company where I was going.

I slowed up for the yellow at Schaefer, then banged the accelerator to the firewall and swung right from the inside lane. A Mayflower van rushing to make the light from the other direction laid down horn and a red Ford Escort crossing on Schaefer panic-braked and stalled, but I threaded the needle and powered north as far as Colson, jogged over to Neckel, crossed Ford Road, and hung out in the parking lot at Fordson High for a while, smoking a cigarette and watching for Jeeps. Three came by in five minutes, but they were all the wrong color. I ditched the butt out the window and took Alber back to Schaefer and turned north. From there Warren Road led west to Dearborn Heights.

Dearborn is where it all started, where an apprentice machinist tinkering nights and Sundays in the little shop behind his house transformed some scrap metal and a set of rickety buggy wheels into the largest industry in the history of the planet. Overnight, Detroit stopped manufacturing stoves and started making potholes. Dearborn Heights was founded exclusively to shelter the overflow when hunkies and hillbillies came to work at the mammoth River Rouge plant and started raising families on Mr. Ford's generous paychecks. Now Rouge Park and its succession of golf clubs wind green through the city's belly, but it's still a factory town, all two-story storefronts and attached garages, where a Hyundai parked in a driveway means someone's entertaining a visitor from out of town.

That Touch of Venus was hard to miss. The name was scrolled in yellow Day-Glo across a blue plastic canopy running the length of the building, flanked by a Jiffy

Lube and a used paperback emporium. There was a light behind the canopy and another in the window, where a placard read OPEN MONDAY THRU FRIDAY, 10 A.M. TILL 12 P.M. in black press-on letters. They never get that right.

I parked next to an exhausted-looking station wagon in the little gravel lot behind the building and walked around to the front. The glass door was plastered over with decals: Elks, Lions, Shriners, Kiwanis, Rotarians, some others I couldn't identify. I pressed the button. It took me a second to place the melody that chimed out. "Venus, If You Will." I grinned at my reflection in the glass. It looked properly predatory. Silence, then a pair of slippers slapping on linoleum. The net curtain behind the glass stirred. A latch clicked, the door opened.

"Hello, honey. You want massage?"

She might have made five feet with heels. There weren't any on her red Chinese slippers with gold drag-ons on the toes, so it was more like four-nine and ninety pounds. Black hair worn long and straight and glossy, cut in bangs across her eyebrows like Anna May Wong. Yellow kimono covered with pink cherry blossoms, tied at the waist and ending at mid-thigh. She was a light-skinned Korean, stretching for sixteen under the makeup. They beat the law with the highest turnover this side of fast food. The girls were paid off and gone long before the warrant came down.

"How much?" I asked.

She opened the door wider and stepped aside. I en-tered. She closed the door, flicking the latch, and pulled back a thick maroon velour curtain hanging in a door-way to the left. The opening was cut out of a partition as thin as a cracker. I went through it and waited for my pupils to adjust themselves to the fifteen-watt light. It

was a sailor's berth of a room, just wide enough for a
padded table with a tiny lamp and bottles of lotion on
top and a kitchen chair. Those places always smell of
scented oils and boiled cabbage, the main staple of
Seoul.

"One hour, sixty. Half hour, forty."

I took out my wallet, but I couldn't see the bills. I
groped at the wall until I found a toggle switch and
tipped it on. Fluorescents mounted above the frosted
ceiling panels flooded the room to the corners. In the
angry light the girl's paint looked like a Greek mask. I
gave her two fifties.

"Ah." Into her pocket they went. Off came the robe.
She was all sharp ribs and tiny breasts like brass bells,
and shaved her pubic hair. That made her look more like
eleven.

"You massage me, yes?"

"No." I showed her the newspaper shot of Boyette.

The robe went back on. "You are police?"

"I'll ask the questions, China doll," I growled. "You
seen this man?"

She glanced at the picture barely long enough for the
face to register, if it did. She turned and fled through the
curtain. I didn't follow her.

Time went by, quite a lot of it. I got some tobacco
burning and dropped the match in an incense burner
shaped like Buddha on the stand among the bottles. A
white chip marred the imitation gold leaf over Buddha's
right eye, making him look a little like a battered pug. I
resisted the urge to give his head a brotherly pat and
looked up. I couldn't tell if anyone was watching me
through the frosted panels. That would be part of the

menu. If you couldn't afford the forty you could pay twenty and watch.

The odor in the room had color and texture. The cabbage smell was brown and greasy, the perfume creamy pink and as thick as motor oil. Faintly, Del Shannon was singing "Hats off to Larry." It might have been a radio wave that had been bouncing around the cosmos since 1961. It might have been just in my head. I figured I was getting a contact high from the hashish that was burning somewhere on the premises. Either that, or someone was incinerating a rope.

The curtain stirred finally and a silver cloud drifted into the room. This one was eight inches taller than the Korean and thirty pounds heavier, which made her just right. She was Occidental, but her Hollywood Chinese costume jumped the culture gap: silver high-heeled slippers, silver satin pajamas with white embroidered doves on the shoulders, glasses with silver inlays in the tilted frames. Her glittering page boy wig was made entirely of tinsel and looked like one of Cleopatra's headdresses. It would have a label stitched to the lining reading *E. Taylor—Property 20th Century Fox*. Her long silvered nails, razor sharp, caught the light like a dragon's tears. It was quite a special effect; but it might have been the second-hand smoke.

For a long time after she entered—it might have been fifteen seconds—neither of us said anything. Eyes like blue planets smiled behind the clear flat placebo lenses of the spectacles. She could have been twenty or forty; the eyewear and wig were just distraction enough to smear the difference.

I held up the newspaper picture in lieu of greeting. "Him deadee. You knowee?"

That surprised a laugh out of her. She had small white even teeth with sharp incisors. Abruptly she stopped laughing. "Are you a policeman?" She had a breathy voice like Marilyn Monroe's, but without the aggressive innocence. It sounded artificial, as if she were hiding a speech impediment.

"Just a man." I put away the picture. "The name is Walker. Amos to my friends."

"I know."

I watched her. After a little silence she showed her teeth again in one of those switched-on smiles they hand out with the naughty underwear. She held out one of her slim razor-nailed hands. When she turned her head the light found a slight swelling along the left side of her jaw, shadowed under makeup expertly applied.

"I'll be your friend, Amos. Around here I'm Madelaine." She pronounced it with a long second *a,* like Lily Marlene.

I left the hand where it was. "Who are you other places?"

"Depends on the place."

"The Tomcat Theater, for instance."

She lowered her hand then. The smile stayed. I plummeted on.

"I never get over modern science. How in the middle of chasing down a cure for AIDS and stopping up the hole in the ozone it's always got time to invent the little things, like cloned sheep and colored contact lenses. These days no one with money has to go around looking at the world through eyes that don't match. Do they, Mrs. Strangeways?"

"Please," she said. "Call me Laurel."

26

"What gave me away?" she asked. "Don't just say you're a detective and let it go at that. I need to know, to avoid slipping up next time."

She'd ditched the husky whisper, also the wig, running her fake nails through her short black hair to give it lift. The accent was back, like windchimes on the verandah of a plantation house. She took off the glasses, which hadn't done that much to change the shape of her face anyway. She was twenty again—nineteen, to be accurate. She had the complexion of a little girl and the whites of her eyes were as pure as clarified milk.

"When you changed your look, you should have changed your perfume too. I've never smelled magno-

lias, but if they don't smell like that, I'll be disappointed."
I breathed some of it. "What next time?"

"Let's go someplace. These walls wouldn't stop a noisy thought."

I followed her out of the room and down the linoleum hall to a brightly lit kitchen at the end. The cabbage smell was coming from a covered stainless steel pot simmering on a two-burner electric range. There was a sink and cupboards and a laminated table with three vinyl-upholstered chairs split and repaired with fiberglass tape. It might have been a kitchen in any low-rent apartment in the city. Another Korean woman, twice as old as the first and stout, got up from the table when we entered and left without a word. Her fuzzy pink robe had all the animal allure of a bathmat.

I took her chair. "Slow night."

"It picks up on payday." Madelaine/Laurel sat down and folded her arms on the table.

"Who are you hiding from?"

"Gordon. Well, everyone. I never should have left Louisiana."

"Did you ever go?"

"I mean before. I moved up here with my mother. She didn't tell me, but I think she knew she was dying then. Some people are like wild creatures. They want to die where they were born."

"She came from Detroit?"

She nodded. "She wasn't really my mother. She raised me after my real mother died when I was eight. She came from Detroit too. They were friends here before. My real mother came down to stay with her when she was pregnant with me."

"In Baton Rouge?"

"New Orleans. We moved to Baton Rouge, Mom and I—my second mom—when I got my first modeling job. I supported both of us after that."

I felt a tingle. It might have been the hashish.

"Are you a drinking man, Amos?" She got up and opened a cupboard.

"Just water. I didn't have lunch." I was beginning to enjoy the sensation of blood singing in my brain. Einstein must have skipped breakfast the day he cracked the secret of the atom.

She took out a square bottle of gin and two glasses. She filled one glass from the tap, splashed an inch into the other, and topped it off from the bottle. She carried the glasses to the table and sat down. She lopped off half an inch, rolled it around her mouth, and swallowed. That first sip of nine parts gin to one part water is like jumping into an icy mountain lake; it makes your breath catch. Not hers. She'd swum plenty of laps for someone still two years away from legal age.

"I'd offer you some cabbage," she said, "but I think I'll keep you on a liquid diet a while longer. Tit for tat. You hit me pretty hard in the theater. I still can't chew anything on that side."

"It threw off your friend North's aim. If it hadn't, the worms would be chewing on me."

"Earl didn't—" She stopped and took another swallow from the glass. It brought a flush to her pale skin. "I didn't go there to distract you. I went to warn you. I was pretty sure Harold didn't tell you the whole story."

"It's Harold, is it? Earl and Harold."

"Protective camouflage," she said. "It's easier to get information out of people when you know them well enough to use first names. That shouldn't be news to a detective."

"You seem to know a lot about me. Am I famous?"

"You're not Madonna, but you've had your fifteen minutes. I saw your picture in the paper when you testified against that man Matador. Of course, I heard your name before that. If I told you how *long* before that, you'd call me a liar."

I changed my mind about the gin. I got up and dumped out my glass into the sink. Then I filled it from the square bottle on the drainboard and returned to my seat. It wasn't my favorite drink—I don't like the smell of junipers, let alone the taste—but it was more honest than a Bubonic Plague and it kicked. "You haven't asked me how I found you."

"Haven't I?"

"Up until a little while ago I thought it was Boyette who sent that card. I figured he'd stashed the Hours of the Virgin here before he went to meet North and sent the card as insurance. If everything went as planned, he'd have made away with it long before I got the card, but if it didn't and I recovered the manuscript, it would be safe for posterity. Whatever else he was, he cared about such things. Only he didn't send the card. You did. Why?"

"I didn't want you to find the manuscript. I wanted you to find me."

"I passed a telephone in the hall."

"Yours might be tapped. Gordon doesn't trust anyone."

"You're hiding from your husband?"

"I'm hiding from everyone, except you. Not that that

made much difference. The card was a last resort. I was running out of jewelry."

I reached into my pocket and tossed the earring onto the table. "I left the other one in the office. Did you lose that one on purpose too?"

"No, but it gave me the idea. I couldn't go to see you; you might be watched. But I know enough about you to know you could come to me without anyone following."

I thought about the Jeep Ranger. "If you wanted to be found, why'd you send your luggage to Louisiana and have it sent back to Detroit?"

"Because it had to be you who found me. As long as Gordon thought something had happened to me down there before I could get on the plane, he wouldn't turn Detroit inside out looking for me here. His love for me—dependence, call it what you like—it's frightening. He'd never stop to think that bringing all that attention might put me in more danger."

"He's offering a million dollars for your safe return."

"Only a million? Well, he has stockholders. But you see what I mean."

The doorbell rang. "Venus, If You Will." I got up and went to the swinging door and pushed it open a crack. The little Korean girl slapped out into the hall from another curtained opening and unlocked the front door. She led a heavy-shouldered brute in dirty overalls through the curtain by one huge hand. I went back and sat down.

"Some hiding place," I said. "Strangeways owns That Touch of Venus."

"He owns the whole chain. If you were him, where would be the last place you'd expect to find your wandering wife?"

"That only works in fiction. What makes you think no-body's tipped him?"

"No one here knows who I am." She smiled with a kind of shamefaced pride, and I remembered with a start how young she was. "I got the job on my own merits. The woman who raised me was an experienced masseuse."

"Who was she?"

"You wouldn't recognize the name. When she was younger than I am now she worked in a house of pros-titution in Detroit. That's where she met my mother."

"Your mother was Star LaJoie."

She wrinkled her nose. "That awful name. Her real name was Ariadne—that's Greek. She knew a little mythology. That's how she came to name me Laurel. Laurel North."

27

I emptied my glass, taking care to drink slowly. I didn't want to get the bends. I set it down just as carefully. A thump seemed disrespectful. "Earl North's your father." It wasn't a question. It wasn't a response of any kind. It was just four words to drop into the long dark shaft with my brain at the bottom.

"He didn't know my mother was pregnant when she left. She cleared out in a hurry. She was on the morning train to Florida four hours after my father killed your partner."

"So you know about that."

"Of course. Did you think you were picked at random?"

That invited a question, but I parked it for now. I almost knew the answer anyway. "The cops in North Carolina found her body."

"It wasn't her, obviously. A lot of working girls in Detroit made that Miami run in winter. Mother was no fool. When she'd had time to think, she knew North would look for her in Florida, so she changed trains and went to Louisiana instead. She had a friend in New Orleans: Mama Carrie. That's what I called the woman who raised me. Mother had a bad heart, though you wouldn't know it judging by what she'd seen and done."

"She saw North shoot Dale Leopold?"

Laurel drank without taking her eyes off me. "I'm repeating family history here. What my mother didn't tell me, or what I forgot, Mama Carrie filled in. Hookers have a reputation for keeping quiet, but not inside their own circle. Mother was standing at the window of the motel room looking down on the porch. She saw everything."

"Did North and Dale speak?"

"Briefly. She couldn't hear what they said and North didn't tell her afterwards. He ran into the motel and up to the room and gave her the gun and told her to hide it. He said he'd be back for it and left. She was packed and gone ten minutes later."

"Did she pack the gun?"

"Uh-huh." She drank.

"North didn't kill Dale because Dale knew he was stepping out on his wife. He killed him because he knew North was robbing the insurance company he worked for. That's helpful, but the courts would need the murder weapon to convict. That gun can send him to Jackson for life."

"Uh-huh."

The gin was working. My arteries were opening,

flooding my gray cells with oxygen. "So that's why you're hiding out. You're using the gun to blackmail him."

"That's the short form. Would you like to hear the long?"

"What the hell. I'm not due on the slopes for an hour." I sat back.

"The gun's a family heirloom. I've never had it out of the protective case Mother bought for it, to keep it from rusting and to preserve the fingerprints. When I moved up here with Mama Carrie, I packed it along with my lingerie and makeup without giving it much thought. Gordon doesn't know about it. The Napoleonic Code isn't in force here, a woman doesn't have to inventory her possessions when she marries. I'd just about forgotten I had the damn thing when I saw Earl for the first time."

"When he came to work for Strangeways."

"No. Before that, when I went with Gordon to talk to Harold Boyette about a manuscript Gordon was thinking of buying. He was in Boyette's office and introductions were made. I didn't hide my emotions very well when I heard the name; I'd been hearing it all my life and never expected to meet the man it belonged to. I'd assumed he was dead. Everyone else was. Mother was, and by then so was Carrie."

"Carrie Triste."

"Yes. I took her name. Mother gave me North's because she was old-fashioned about that kind of thing— respectability counts high with reformed prostitutes—but she kept her own. Anyway, my reaction made him suspicious. Otherwise he might have chalked up these damn freak eyes of mine to coincidence. I inherited them from my mother."

"The clerk at the motel didn't share that with the cops."

"According to my mother, he wouldn't have been able to describe an orange elephant. He was higher than the Milky Way three-quarters of the time and strung out the rest. Anyway, I could see Earl's brain working. He went as white as a sheet, but he recovered quickly and left the room. I can't say I was surprised when a week or so later he came to work at the house."

"Strangeways said he sensed something between you," I said. "That's the only thing he got right."

"Gordon's rather a Victorian, in spite of the way he made his fortune. Maybe because of it. I think he believes I'm the only truly respectable thing in his life. I couldn't tell him who my mother was, or what she was involved in. He'll always be recovering from what happened to him in Little Rock. I'm afraid this would kill him. Can I count on your confidence?"

"It'll come out," I said. "From some other source if not from me. This has been too big for a family secret since the beginning."

She drained her glass. "You're right. I should have told Earl my mother got rid of the gun before I ever saw it."

"He wouldn't have believed you. Killers always believe the worst. And there was money to be made."

"Go to hell. Is that what you think this is about? I'm married to two and a half billion. I wouldn't bargain with a snake like my dear father for anything less than my freedom."

I looked around the kitchen. "So this is freedom. It smells like cabbage."

"I mean freedom from Gordon."

The stout Korean in the fuzzy pink robe came in, went to the stove, lifted the lid off the pot, stirred the bubbling contents with a wooden spoon, then replaced the lid and went out, shuffling the soles of her dirty white sneakers on the worn linoleum. She would be a hard woman to shut up once you got her started talking. Getting her started would require twelve volts from a Delco.

"I've been to his place on Grosse Ile," I said when the sound of shuffling faded down the hall. "I didn't see any bars on the windows, but I didn't see the whole house. I forgot to bring a compass."

"He wouldn't try to keep me if he knew I wanted to leave. He cares too much for me to do that. But it would kill him. All my life I've had to take care of someone: first my mother, then Carrie. I've been a working model since I was thirteen. Gordon has nurses, but he needs someone he isn't paying to coo over him and fluff his pillows and ask him if he needs to take a pill. I thought that was me. It isn't. I need a life for myself. I don't want his money. I've turned down more than a million in job offers since I married him.

"There's no way I can make leaving him easier for him," she said. "But I can give him a parting gift, one a collector like him can appreciate. I can give him the Hours of the Virgin."

I'd started to light a Winston from the new pack. The cooking smell was getting to me. I shook out the match and let the butt hang off my lip. "You have it?"

"No. But I know where I can get it, and at a bargain. What's the current market price on a Beretta thirty-two-caliber semiautomatic pistol, twenty years old?"

"So that's the deal."

"It was. It can be again. I don't know how much Harold told you about the setup at the Tomcat."

"He said he thought North stole the Hours and he was going there to ransom it back for a hundred thousand in cash. He carried a thick mailer into the theater, but I never saw what was inside. I think I can guess now."

"Earl was still working at the house when he bragged about the Hours. He said knowing what I knew about illuminated manuscripts thanks to Gordon, I'd be proud to know my old man had something my husband would trade his legs for if they worked. He liked saying that: *your old man*. He's a gray little person except when he thinks he's cock of the hill. Then he's slimy. They say some chromosomes skip a generation. I may not have children."

"This one might not have skipped."

She thought about getting angry. In the end she just got tired.

"You've been living with that night twenty years. That's a long time to you, but it's my whole life. I just want out from under. Whatever happens to that pistol once he has it is no concern of mine, as long as I get the manuscript and my ticket out. But it's where yours begins. That's why I brought you in."

"I've been wondering about that. A man named Merlin Gilly tipped me to the job. What was he to you?"

"My uncle."

I struck another match then and lit the cigarette. I didn't want it anymore. The action gave me time to think. I took a drag, poked the match into my glass, and parked the burning weed in an old scorch-groove on the edge of the table. "I heard Merlin had a sister who died."

"He was just a boy when she left town, but they kept

in touch through letters. She used her real name, of course. The only one the cops cared about was Star LaJoie, and they didn't care about her once they thought she was dead. Which she was. She never used the name again, and she never turned another trick after that night. She was a legitimate masseuse in Carrie's parlor."

A Gilly on her mother's side, a North on her father's. She ought to be sterilized. But I had a headache and the atmosphere in the kitchen was thick. "What made me your Lancelot?"

"You were always the hero in the family story. Mother bought all the out-of-town papers and followed the story until it dropped off the back page. They did a little human-interest on you to keep it alive. She was afraid to come forward, afraid even if she sent you the gun anonymously that North would suspect she was still alive and come looking for her. She was always after Merlin to throw work your way."

"He charged me every time."

"You can't expect Merlin not to be Merlin. I had to pay him to tell you about Boyette. I was pretty sure he'd put the arm on you too, but I was too busy making way for my new life to try and change his."

"Why Boyette?"

"I needed someone who could authenticate the manuscript. I made him a deal: He could publish his research about the Hours, but Gordon would maintain possession in secret until his death. Then he could go public with the 'discovery.' Gordon isn't a well man. We're talking ten years here." She rolled her glass between her palms, making wet rings on the table. "I liked Harold, despite his flaws. He realized his mistake and wanted to get back what he'd sold for money."

"It must have broken your heart when North used the gun he got from him to put a bullet in Harold's brain."

"I'm not through telling my story."

I couldn't take it anymore. I got up, went over to the little window above the sink, and heaved up the sash. It only opened two inches, but it let in a knife of pure cold air. I turned off the burner and moved the pot to the cold one on the other side. I circled the room and finished where I'd started, a familiar route. "Who frisked my office?"

"Frisked?"

"Searched. Tossed. Turned it on its ear. Conducted a thorough and professional investigation involving both mitts. From the French *friskadoo,* meaning to cause the building cleaning service to give notice. You know, frisked."

"It wasn't me. I'm not looking for anything."

"What were you looking for in Boyette's house?"

"What I found." She stood, brushed past me, and opened the second drawer below the drainboard. It contained a divided tray full of flatware, which she removed and set on top. She peeled back a section of newspaper lining the bottom of the drawer, and lifted something out. Something that required both hands, even though it was no heavier than the newspaper. I looked at the wrinkled, buff-colored sheet, the enormous inlaid *L,* the uneven Gothic pointed letters in ancient brown ink. It had a pungent odor all its own, a cloying brownish stench of decay, distinct from the cabbage permeating the room. I hadn't noticed it when Boyette showed it to me in the DIA, and I remembered what he'd said about the destructive properties of uncycled air and pollution. The Secular Age was killing the sacred text.

Just to put the realistic point on things I bent close and located my old friend the crab louse.

I straightened. "I've seen it before. Boyette said North sent it to him to prove he had the manuscript."

"That part was true. He wanted money then. Earl told me about it, and that's when I went to Harold and made our deal. Earl was quick to accept the counteroffer. The existence of that gun has been haunting him all these years. That's why he wanted to get close to me, to find out if I knew anything about it."

"Is that what he was looking for in my office?"

"Wrong twice. You're looking at what I was looking for. And I ain't North."

This was a new card in the deck, one who walked lightly and knew his way around locks. Laurel and I turned and looked at Ben, the aging welterweight who guarded Strangeways' gate and mixed his drinks. He was hatless and wore a civilian mackinaw over mufti that didn't fit him nearly as well as his uniform. He had his big magnum trained on us, but I was more interested in the much smaller pistol stuck in his belt, a semiautomatic whose square brown butt cut a notch out of the hard fat of his stomach.

"That's the part of the story I didn't get to," Laurel said. "I don't have the thirty-two. Ben took it after he shot at you in the Tomcat."

28

The square battered face, scorched deep umber by outdoor duty and seamed all over like a duffel, was profes-
sionally dead; anesthetized into that nerveless mask
common to poker players and prizefighters, as if to say
that striking it would be like kicking a granite gargoyle.
Only the eyes, splinters of light folded in scar tissue, appeared to be wired to anything as complicated as a central nervous system. The shining revolver looked as big
as a T-square in his small hard fist, broken many times
and healed over shiny across the knobby knuckles.

Laurel Strangeways, still holding the first page of the
Hours, let out her breath in a shuddering sigh. In every
dreaded confrontation there is an element of relief.

I said, "I must be getting old faster than usual. I thought I lost you at Ford and Schaefer."

"You did. I done a load of driving up and down before I remembered what's here. Get them hands away from your sides."

I'd managed to unfasten my overcoat with my left hand. I was turned halfway toward him, putting that side out of his line of sight. But fighters are used to watching hands. I spread my arms. "You went with Laurel to the Tomcat?"

"I followed her. I'm good. People forget I was a store cop a lot longer than I boxed. Nobody pays much attention to the help, not even Mr. Strangeways. I hear things. That house of his has got no doors."

"Why'd you shoot at me?"

"That was your fault. When she sat down next to you and started talking, I figured you was there for backup. I was just going to lay the barrel alongside your head. Then you started moving fast and I pulled the trigger instead."

"That's why I ran," Laurel said. "I was blind with pain and I thought you were shot, you went down so fast. Then I saw Ben. I thought Gordon had sent him. Everybody was running for the exit. I panicked."

"Ben didn't." I was watching him. "The only way out of the theater was the way everyone came in. Boyette had to run all the way from the front row. Naturally he scooped up the package he'd carried into the place. Ben intercepted him in the aisle, took it away from him, and made Boyette drive him to O'Hair Park, where he took the thirty-two out of the mailer and shot him with it. That was a break," I told Ben. "You couldn't be sure the thirty-two was loaded. Even if you brought cartridges, there was no way to predict if it would even fire after all those years."

The corners of the pug's slit of a mouth tugged out in a smile as tight as a turnbuckle. "I didn't even know about the gun till I pulled it out. I had it all wrong; I heard her when she called Boyette from the house. They was talking about this twerp Earl North. I thought she was going to run away with him and Boyette was help-ing. I seen the way she and North looked at each other that time I went with her and Mr. Strangeways to Boyette's office. I knew it was trouble when North come to work for Mr. Strangeways."

Keep him talking. "North is Mrs. Strangeways' father."

"I said I had it all wrong. Boyette set me straight when he was begging for his life. I got the whole story. He said if I let him go he'd give me a page of a manuscript Mr. Strangeways would pay big money for. That it?" He jerked the magnum's barrel that direction.

"Ben," she said.

"Shut up. I never killed nobody before but I'd do it again if they talked about soaking Mr. Strangeways. The gun was loaded, all right. Trigger pull was stiff. It needed oil. But it done the job."

"You wanted to hang it on North," I said.

"No need to thank me. I know about your part in it too. Boyette talked right up until he stopped."

Laurel said, "I don't want to soak Gordon. I wanted to give him the Hours."

"I said you shut up. You run out on him. I knew you would the day he brought you home. I followed your cab when you said you was going to Louisiana. For a visit, you said. The driver put three bags on a cart at the airport curb. You went in behind the skycap and come out ten minutes later with one bag and got into another cab. I followed you to your motel. I slipped the desk clerk a hundred bucks to call me when you checked out and to give you the stall till I got there."

"He said my bill was misfiled."

"Clerks are smart. I was a house dick two years." He backed off on the turnbuckle. The tight smile went away. "I got there just in time to tail you to the theater."

"You didn't park in the lot," I said. "It was empty after you left with Boyette in his car."

"I parked around the corner and walked back from the park. North knew the Ranger. I didn't want to scare him off."

"You did anyway. How much does Strangeways know?" I measured the distance between me and the big revolver. It was easier to get to than the Smith & Wesson on my hip. Two long strides against a half-centimeter pull on the trigger.

"I ain't told him a thing and I ain't going to. Mr. Strangeways is a great man. He don't treat me like I'm a punchy, the way they done where I worked before; good enough to take a bullet for a paying customer but not nothing important, like carry money or use my head. He talks to me like a man. It was his magazine got me my first and only shot at a title. He stays clean of this."

"What do you want?" Laurel asked.

"I want you to *shut up!*" He yelled it. Then he looked at me. "Where's the rest of that manuscript? I seen you and North talking on Mr. Strangeways' porch like old buddies. I figure you made some kind of deal. I'll give you the same terms she and Boyette gave him: the thirty-two for the pages."

The gun was just something in his hand now. He

wanted an answer. I came up very slightly on the balls of my feet. "What happens once you have them?"

"I give 'em to Mr. Strangeways. That one too. From what I hear he can buy a thousand hillbilly whores worth more than her for what it's worth."

"I mean, what happens to us?"

"That's your lookout. If I never lay eyes on either of you again it'll be too goddamn soon."

"Too thin. You've been talking too much to just let us walk. What if we walk straight to the cops?" I tensed the muscles in my calves, shifting my weight forward from the waist. Glaciers never moved more slowly.

"And tell 'em what? Even if they believe I said what I said, they won't buy a word of it when they question me. I'm just a busted-down old canvasback that took one too many shots to the coconut. I'll pour it on thick." He shook his square head. "You won't go to the cops. They'll just laugh you out of there like the last time."

"What if I don't know where the manuscript is?"

"Then everything changes." He tightened his fist on the magnum. "Back on your heels, bub. You ain't nobody's Fred Astaire."

I relaxed my muscles. He was as punchy as a cat in an aquarium.

"One kill doesn't make a character," I said. "You can be out in three on Boyette. That was passion. The Frank Murphy Hall of Justice has a drawer full of happy precedents there. Loyalty, that's a novelty even a tired judge might buy. Strangeways will probably pop for your defense. Lawyer Raider took on the United States Supreme Court and won. She'll grease you through the system on her lunch hour. Two more murders is a complication you don't need."

"I don't butter that easy. You saying you ain't got the thing?" The slits he saw through went stormy.

"Not with me. I can't tell you where it is. But I can show you."

"Well, that was the idea," he said. "You think I was going to let you tell me where to look and then say thanks and go off and leave you here?" He motioned with the gun. "Let's see some footwork."

I said, "There are other people in the building. If you march us down the hall waving that cannon, we won't need to go to the cops. That part's okay. It's the shooting that comes after I'd like to avoid. My mother told me to stay out of crossfire."

"Mine told me to go for the eyes." But he considered. Then he holstered the big revolver under his mackinaw and took the .32 out of his belt and stuck it in his coat pocket. That's when I scooped the pot off the stove by its handle and threw it at him.

The lid came off and the cabbage flew out like chain-shot, plastering him from head to knee. It scalded him and he roared in pain, but managed to deflect the pot with his free hand. By then I was coming in low and hard.

My shoulder went into his belly. He said woof and I smelled what he'd had for lunch, but he didn't bend. He retreated two steps, then pushed back. I was sliding on cabbage. The padding around his middle was just for show; two inches in he was coiled steel, like the forearm I grasped in both hands to keep him from twisting the gun around inside his pocket. It was like trying to hang on to a tree limb in a tornado. He lashed around, breathing hard, but not as hard as I was. A bench vise clamped my forehead on both sides and squeezed. It was his free left hand, trying to get juice out of my skull. My eyes were swelling out of their lids when I let go of his arm with one hand to grope for his face.

That was a mistake. His arm turned right out of my grip, as if he'd gotten tired of carrying me and it was time for the referee to start counting. The hard flat smack of the pistol going off was like a heavy book hitting the floor. A hot wind slapped my ribcage. I jerked away, an involuntary reaction, like jumping when a snake strikes at the transparent glass separating you. But I wasn't through. I tore my coat away from its buttons, reached back and felt the rubber grip of the .38 in my kidney holster, snapped it out and jammed it deep into the hard roll around his middle and squeezed the trigger. The report was as muffled as if I'd stuck it into a pile of earth. The heat blew back over my hand. I smelled sulphur and saltpeter and scorched cloth and cooked meat. I got another whiff of his lunch, a curse of surprise and pain behind it. He struggled to level the pistol in his pocket; I think the barrel had gotten snarled in the hole he'd made when he fired through the lining. I didn't wait to confirm it. He was as strong as a bull and as desperate as a trapped grizzly. I fired twice more, feeling the cylinder turn both times. He stopped struggling then. A string broke inside him and he fell away from the gun. I followed him down with it, just in case it was a trick. Three bullets seemed hardly enough.

Three bullets had been plenty. He knelt almost reverently on the scuffed linoleum, clutching at his stomach with threads of smoke uncoiling between his fingers, his other hand still in his pocket but not doing anything. After a while he fell forward. His forehead hit the floor like a rock. Then he was very still, kneeling there with his buttocks pointed at the ceiling; and I remembered a ring commentator somewhere sometime saying: *When they go down on their face, they don't get back up.*

Ben Whatever. Loyal as a police dog, shot like a rabid stray. All he wanted was to make his master happy.

Phooey on him. I inspected my side. The .32's muzzle flare had burned a hole the size of my hand through my coat, scorching a black triangle onto the shirt beneath as if it had been done by an iron. There was no blood. I might have a second-degree burn. A little Neosporin would do it. A little Neosporin and a couple of months with a police therapist. I leaned over Ben, got his fingers unclamped from the pistol in his pocket, gave it a quick glance, and put it away in my coat. Beretta 81. I didn't worry about preserving the original fingerprints. Ben's hand had been all over it, and anyway latent prints evaporate in a few days or a few weeks. But North wouldn't know that.

And then I remembered that I wasn't alone with Ben, and how quiet a room containing three people shouldn't be when only one of them was supposed to be dead.

29

Only the deaf know silence.

When the soundtrack drops out of an old film you still hear the frames ratcheting through the gate of the projector. In forests deep inside the Arctic circle the wooden trunks groan as they crystallize. A hundred feet below the earth's crust in a bomb shelter with walls six feet thick, your breath roars and your heart is a dead-blow hammer; your blood whistles through your veins. True silence is as rare as roc's eggs, as piercing as a steam blast. Compared to the complete and utter cessation of sound, a boiler factory may as well be a pillow fight.

For a time as I stood over Ben's body, silence rang like a brass bell. The first real sound I was aware of was my brain cells clicking to life, tickity-tick, followed by the buzzing of electrical impulses in my nerve-ends. Then the whole system—heart, capillaries, digestive mechanism—kicked in with a thump and a shudder like a refrigerator coming back on. That was when I remembered Laurel Strangeways.

She was sitting on the floor in front of the sink, breathing in quavering gasps and gripping her right leg above the knee. Her hands and the slick material of her silver pajamas glittered with blood.

I knelt by her side quickly, fished out my pocket knife, slit the hem of the pajama leg, then grabbed it in both hands and tore it up to the thigh. I spread her hands gently for a look, but there was too much blood. I found my handkerchief and used it as a sponge. I turned the leg carefully, pulling a gasp and a little whimper out of her. I'd have yelled. The bullet had passed clean through. The blood wasn't pumping, so it hadn't nicked an artery. I tore the satin another six inches, wrapped the handkerchief around her thigh above the wounds, unclipped the Smith & Wesson from my belt, and used the four-inch barrel to twist the cloth tight, tying it off so the tourniquet would hold. I looked around. Pink Robe was standing in the kitchen doorway. There was blood on the floor amidst the cabbage and she was looking at it all and the corpse as if here was one more thing she had to clean up before business got lively.

"Call nine-one-one," I said. "Ambulance. You know ambulance?" I spaced out the syllables.

"EMS." She withdrew into the hallway. The door flapped shut.

Laurel was sitting with her back against the sink cabinet. She shivered. I stripped off my coat and draped it over her shoulders. "Chinee girl feely rousy?" I asked.

She made a ghost smile. "I've been shot. How do you think I feel? How bad is it?"

"It's all flesh. That's more serious than the westerns make out, but it's how I'd take a bullet if I had the choice. They won't have to do any more damage digging it out. If it had been the magnum, the leg would be gone. You'll be running for those hills in a month."

"Do you have a cigarette?"

I got one going and held it for her while she puffed. She was hugging herself under the coat. "Strangeways said you don't smoke."

"I think we can tell him now, don't you?"

She took a few more puffs and then she closed her eyes. I made sure she was breathing—shock can kill—then I went to work.

The first page of the Hours of the Virgin had come to rest on the floor by the stove, where some cabbage had soaked through from beneath, adding a fresh stain to the inventory. I picked it up carefully, brushed off some clinging morsels, sandwiched it between the newspaper pages lining the drawer, and laid the tray on top. I closed the drawer, then knelt again, excavated the .32 from the pocket of my overcoat, and rearranged the coat across Laurel's shoulders. She was breathing evenly. The tourniquet was holding.

Finding where the slug had gone after it passed through her leg was more difficult. It had gone into the linoleum in a corner near the baseboard. I carved it out with my pocket knife and threw it out the window.

I heard the first siren then; time to go into high gear. I rummaged among the items in the overhead cupboards until I came across an ancient box of Special K at the back. The contents were alive with weevils. I slid the pistol in among the flakes, then pushed down the flap and returned the box to its place on the top shelf.

When I turned around, Laurel was watching me. "Think you can get away with it?" Her voice was strained. The shock was wearing off; the pain was starting.

"If the cops don't get too hungry. Another drag?" I took the cigarette out of my mouth. She shook her head. I went over to Ben, leaned across him again, and slid the magnum out of its holster. Two more sirens had joined the first. "Can you stand a little noise?"

She nodded faintly. I crossed to the open window, aimed the big revolver at the sky, and hit it. I used the corner of Ben's mackinaw to wipe the butt and then to hold the barrel while I curled the fingers of his right hand around the butt. I managed to get gun and hand into his coat pocket with the muzzle poking out through the hole the .32 had made just as the first siren swooped into the little gravel lot outside.

Neither the cops nor the EMS crew would have heard the report over the sirens. One or two neighbors might bring up the subject of a late shot, but witnesses were notoriously shaky when it came to timing. The Koreans wouldn't volunteer anything. Two shot people, two fired guns. That was too neat to tamper with.

I hoped.

"The Hours!" Laurel whispered harshly, looking around.

"Stay still," I said. "I couldn't find a better hiding place than yours in a week."

"They won't hear it from me." She closed her eyes again, smiling her ghostly smile.

Fists clobbered the front door.

Part Four

The Hours of the Virgin

30

I sat on a gray composition chair in front of a gray composition desk in a small bright room with a ceiling made entirely of fluorescent lights. A jumble of textbooks on the nature of citizenship and government stood on the desk between gray steel bookends. There wasn't a single personal item in the office and I suspected it was just taking up space intended for supplies.

Technically I was under arrest, but I hadn't been cuffed or printed and no one was guarding the door, which stood open six inches. I could walk out any time if I didn't mind leaving my personal possessions behind. The room belonged to a sleek brick building, not very old, in Dearborn Heights' civic center, which included

the library and city offices as well as the police department. It was as quiet as only an official building can be
at 3:30 in the morning. Somewhere in a corridor someone was operating a floor buffer; its pleasant soft whir
wanted to put me to sleep. I was only half resisting. I'd
been asked all the questions anyone could think to ask
several times. I'd answered them all pretty much the
same way, varying just a little here and there to give the
detectives something to chew on and to avoid sounding
as if I'd rehearsed the answers. The only question that remained was whether I was going to be let go or put
through the rest of the system on principle.

Of course, there was a bare possibility that the cops
would take it into their heads to search the massage parlor and find Earl North's .32 and the first page of the
Hours of the Virgin. I tried not to think about that. The
questions would come harder then, and I was running
low on tricky answers. I saved my thinking for Laurel
Strangeways. The EMS team had arrived ahead of the police, stuck a tube in her arm, and whisked her off to
Henry Ford Hospital, the nearest facility with a wound
trauma staff worthy of the name. Updates, filtered
through officers keeping tabs on when or if she would
be able to provide further illumination on what had happened at That Touch of Venus, had her in critical condition with a fever. The tourniquet I'd applied had saved
her from bleeding to death at the risk of creating infec-
tion. The rules kept changing about whether you should
release the pressure from time to time to let the impuri-
ties bleed out; I'd opted for the lesser risk.

I had no idea how long I sat alone after the last cop
took the air. They'd let me keep my watch, but I didn't
look at it much. I wasn't expected anywhere, and any-

way watch time is not cop time. At length a sole scraped the freshly waxed tiles outside the door and a short compact Russian came in carrying a cheap vinyl zipper portfolio and sat down behind the desk. I thought Russian because he had foxlike features and Tatar eyes of the palest blue, the irises nearly indistinguishable from the whites, sloping toward his nose under hooded lids. He had short pale hair combed forward into a point on his forehead and aristocratic nostrils. He wore a black knitted tie on a white button-down oxford shirt and a stiff black suit with a petroleum sheen. I hadn't seen him before. I didn't know his name or rank and I wasn't even sure if he was a cop.

"You're from Detroit." He placed the portfolio on the desk and rested his hands on it.

"Just barely. I live across the street from Hamtramck. My closest neighbor's Ukrainian."

It didn't do anything for him. The late generation of citizens of Eastern European descent was the first to show no interest in ancient alliances. Then again, I could have been all wrong about his nationality.

"The police in Detroit should have explained to you that a permit to carry a concealed weapon is not a permit to shoot people."

"I've had it for twenty years. This is only the second time I've had to kill a man. It was self-defense both times."

"You seem pretty casual about it."

"I've been awake for twenty hours. I could seem casual on the *Titanic.*"

"According to your own statement, this man Ben was acting out of loyalty to his employer. If you're as honorable as you want us to think you are, you might feel sorry you had to kill him."

"I never said I was honorable. The hell with him. He'd have killed us both as soon as he found out we didn't have what he wanted. He still managed to put a bullet through Mrs. Strangeways' leg. Have you heard anything lately from the hospital?"

"She was in serious condition as of thirty minutes ago. I'm worried about that bullet. A magnum round should have smashed her leg to pieces."

"Do a carbon test if you don't believe me."

"Thank you. I'd never have thought of it if you didn't suggest it." He drummed his fingers on the portfolio. It was big and bulky enough to contain a number of items, including a medium-caliber pistol and a page from an illuminated manuscript. "What gave him the impression you knew where to find this Hours of the Virgin?"

"My guess is he thought he'd looked everywhere else. I let him go on thinking what he thought. It was the best insurance I could get under the circumstances."

He drummed some more. "Let me tell you a little something about Dearborn Heights. We're ten minutes from downtown Detroit, less when they aren't tearing up the streets. There are people who have lived here fifty years who have never been there. Twenty years under that old crook in the mayor's mansion pushed that city clear off the map. We have our problems, sure, but we don't have any police chiefs in prison and nobody's been stomped to jelly in broad daylight for being the wrong color in the wrong neighborhood. We don't need fortune-hunters bulling in from the big bad city and dumping their trash here. We don't need it, and we certainly don't appreciate it."

"That's why you arrested me? Illegal dumping?"

"Shut up. I'm talking." His fingers did the opening lick from "Fever." He was a Russian-American Buddy Rich. Then he unzipped the portfolio all the way around, spread it open, and dumped out its contents on the desk.

My wallet and badge folder and the Smith & Wesson .38 bounced all over. I had to slap a hand down on the gun to keep it from falling over the edge. It was reflex, and as I did it a shard of ice went straight up my spine; it could have been a trick to shoot me down and claim I went for the weapon. But he didn't budge. He was as calm as twilight on water.

"Get out," he said. "We'll call you when we want you. And we will want you."

I put the wallet and folder in their pockets, checked the load in the revolver—it hadn't any—and stuck it into my holster. I got up then and went out without saying anything. Slavic people have a way of changing their minds without warning.

"Walker."

I had my hand on the glass door leading outside. I turned around and there was John Alderdyce standing in the sterile reception area, big as Gibraltar in Harris tweed and a woven club tie. He had a way of easing up on you unexpectedly, like a police cruiser in heavy traffic.

I found a cigarette and slid it into its permanent notch in the corner of my mouth. "Who's your daughter meeting with tonight, the Women's Wrestling Federation?"

"She's out with her sculptor. I don't need as much sleep as I used to. When I get a call at home I usually do something about it. How were you planning to get back to your car?"

"I thought I'd walk. The cold air will wake me up."

"Temperature's zero, with a wind chill you don't want to know. After two blocks you'll be a Popsicle. I'll give you a lift."

"I'll take it—if you promise not to ask any questions."

He spun his keys around his index finger. The ring was attached to a silver-plated whistle, an old memento.

The frigid air constricted my lungs like a blow to the chest. It frosted the hairs in my nose. In the sky the constellations were as clear-edged as holes punched in carbon paper. There wasn't even a thin sheeting of cloud to insulate the earth from frozen outer space. John unlocked his gray Chrysler and we climbed into the unthawed leather seats. After a few blocks he turned on the heater. The blower pushed warm air at our ankles.

"So the butler did it," he said.

Well, it wasn't a question. "He was a lot more than a butler." I found the cigar lighter and blew smoke. The cloud flattened out against the windshield. "He was Gordon Strangeways' legs. Three years of that can make you kind of possessive."

"I wonder what happened to North's gun."

"If it doesn't turn up among Ben's things, it's probably gone for good. Maybe North got it back. He's tricky enough to have conned a simple organism like Ben into trading it for a lick and a promise."

"If that had happened, Ben would have confronted him instead of you."

"North might have convinced him I had the Hours. He'd know how to play it so Ben thought the information was worth giving him the gun. Don't forget, he was able to fool a grand jury."

"He's not the only tricky one."

I said nothing. I found the button that operated the

window and snapped my cigarette out into the slip-stream. It made an orange phosphorescence and vanished. The window slid back up with a sucking sound.

"The slug we got out of Boyette matched the one in the Leopold file," John said. "I've been trying to reach you ever since. The way I see it, Ben would still be walking around and the Strangeways woman wouldn't be hooked up to half the equipment at Henry Ford if you'd told me what North had to do with anything."

"Maybe. Did you ever read a book called *Appointment in Samarra*?"

"What is it, a spy novel?"

"It's just a story about a handful of people in a small American city. John O'Hara wrote it. He got the title from Somerset Maugham. The point is you can't cheat destiny."

He drove for a while in silence. Turning onto Woodbine he said, "I thought you gave up on this white whale a long time ago. It won't bring Leopold back. For my money it wouldn't matter if it did. I talked to him a couple of times when I was in uniform. He had that squashed-hat, cigar-chomping bit down cold, called everybody kid. The rookies laughed at him."

"Not to his face."

"You can't love the dead more than the living."

I snapped my head around. "What?"

He said it again.

"Where'd you hear that?"

"My mother used to say it everytime someone died in the family. It makes sense."

"An old lady on Mullett told me the same thing. It made sense then too." We were nearing That Touch of Venus. There was a Dearborn Heights cruiser parked in the lot and a light was on in the building. I was too tired to worry if the cops were searching the place. John pulled up next to my Cutlass and stopped. I opened the door. "Thanks for the ride," I said. "And for not asking questions."

His face was a brutish mask under the domelight. "You're not finished."

"No."

"I know it's a question, but the ride's over, and anyway I don't have to play by your rules. If what the old lady said makes sense, why don't you just walk away?"

I thought about that. My brain was on low trickle and I had to push it to turn it over. "If everybody did the sensible thing, you and I would be out of a job."

"I wouldn't mind it," he said. "I'd learn taxidermy at home and stuff ducks for a living."

"It wouldn't work. By the third duck you'd be asking questions about how it died."

He drove off and left me there. I slid onto the cold seat and ground the starter and drove home. Before I went to bed I called the hospital, but I got a suspicious nurse who wouldn't give out patient information over the telephone. I woke up still sitting in the easy chair with the receiver squawking in my lap and hung up and went to bed. I didn't dream about guns or ducks or Occidental women got up like Myrna Loy in *The Mask of Fu Manchu*. I slept the dreamless sleep of the Undead, and when I woke up nine hours later I knew how I was going to play it right to the end.

31

I waited.

Over coffee and the *Free Press* I called my answering service and asked them to forward all my office calls to the house until I left for downtown. That's when the waiting started.

The story on the shooting at That Touch of Venus was a bundle of facts and misunderstood information, as usual. Gordon Strangeways' name was in the headline and lead, and a file photo ran from around the time of the Little Rock beating. Mrs. Strangeways was reported injured and a bodyguard slain, but Ben's name didn't appear and there was no mention of a third party. That explained why my telephone wasn't ringing off the hook.

Before calling the service I'd tried Henry Ford Hospital again and got a different nurse this time, who told me Mrs. Strangeways' condition was still serious but stable. I didn't bother calling Strangeways. If he wasn't at the hospital, the ringing telephone alone would throw his heart into the red zone. It would be like calling the father of a teenager at midnight Saturday. I didn't have anything to talk to him about in any case.

When I left the house I called the service again and told the operator to take messages. There must have been something in my tone, because she asked if she should keep whoever called on the line until I got to the office. I told her not to risk it lest the party think she was stalling for another reason. I also told her to come see me when she had her investigator's license.

The work in the hallway outside my office was finished. They'd removed the last of the ersatz asbestos from the ceiling, blown in fiberglass to replace it, and re-laid the panels in the grid. The sharp stench of fresh acetate stung my nostrils like airplane glue.

I had no customers waiting; either they'd given up when I hadn't arrived by two o'clock or they'd found another reason to go another day without a detective, along with the other ninety-nine percent of the local population. Back behind the desk I dialed the service. There were no messages. I told the operator to put all calls through until further notice.

I didn't go out to eat. I didn't go out for cigarettes, even though there were just three left in the pack and the carton I kept in the deep drawer of the desk was empty. I could smoke the horsehair stuffing from my chair until the telephone decided to ring. I doubled the carton over twice and stuffed it into the wastebasket. The basket was full but I didn't go out to dump it. When I used the water closet I left the door open in case the running water drowned out the bell. I hadn't felt this way since my last job interview.

The telephone rang at four o'clock, but it wasn't the call I was expecting. It was Jillian Raider, Gordon Strangeways' lawyer and general factotum. I asked her right off if there was any news on Mrs. Strangeways.

"Her condition has been upgraded," she said. "Her temperature is normal and she needs no further transfusions. Mr. Strangeways is with her now." The climate-control apparatus in her throat was working. I couldn't tell from her voice if she wanted to brain me with the Michigan Penal Code or offer me a partnership in the firm.

"Who's with Mr. Strangeways?" I asked.

"Vernon. The other guard. I suppose you could say he's been promoted." She paused, not long enough to invite interruption. "I need to meet with you in my office in an hour. Can you make it?"

"I'm waiting for a call. Can I get back to you?"

"I'm afraid not. It's extremely important I meet with you as soon as possible. You can forward your calls here, if you like."

"Where is your office?"

"In the American Center Building in Southfield. Suite 2670. Do you know the location?"

I said I did and that I'd see her there in an hour. Then I went through my desk drawers until I found my pager, called the service to test it, and clipped it to my belt on the side opposite my revolver.

Raider & Associates, Attorneys at Law, peddled its briefs from a suite occupying half the twenty-sixth floor of the

American Center Building, a black glass slab towering some forty stories above suburban Southfield. The employees would share the elevators with a couple of international credit brokers and a man known on Gratiot as Tony the Wop. The recession of the eighties had brought a relaxed attitude toward the references of certain prospective occupants.

The legal firm wasn't one of them. A pair of smoked-glass doors operated by an electronic system drifted open to admit me to a reception area done in steel gray with bands of mauve and shut themselves against rubber stops with all the noise of a feather floating down a well. The receptionist was a young man with close-cut blonde hair in a midnight-blue jacket over a slate-blue shirt and a pale orange tie. He took my name, gave it to someone over a gray telephone mounted flush with the top of his desk, and asked me to wait. I spent a couple of minutes admiring a framed panoramic shot of the Detroit skyline at night hanging opposite a panoramic view through a window of flat Southfield by day, and then the telephone purred and the young man answered it and said I could go in.

Jillian Raider's office was done all in white, with walls of brushed velvet and a pile carpet that retained footprints like a white sand beach. Books with white spines were arranged according to height in built-in bookshelves enameled white and a white leather sofa and pair of matching armchairs stood in a conversation area in one corner. More yet of Southfield spread beyond a window that took up the entire east wall, in front of which a sheet of plate glass laid atop two wicket-shaped pieces of white steel performed as a desk. Mrs. Raider was standing behind this with her weight resting on her fingertips on the desktop. Her red-gold hair was still combed back from the severe line across her forehead and her gray eyes had a sheen that looked almost—but not quite—like fresh tears. She wore an unstructured gray silk blazer over a white blouse with the top two buttons unfastened and a black suede miniskirt that caught her at mid-thigh. It was a young look for a woman close to my age, but in the indirect light she managed to get away with it just fine.

After a moment she said, "Do you undress every woman you meet, or should I feel special?"

"No undressing," I said. "Just checking out the armor. Something tells me I'm not walking out of here with a million of Gordon Strangeways' dollars in my pocket."

"I asked you here to discuss that. Do you mind if I have someone in to take notes?"

"Did Radio Shack repossess your recording equipment?"

"It's operating. But if I were a man I would be the kind of man who wears suspenders and a belt." Without waiting for my answer she pushed a button on an intercom no thicker than a Big Chief tablet. "William?"

A moment later a door I hadn't noticed opened in one of the white velvet walls and another young man, black-haired with a fashionable blue shadow on his chin, entered. He nodded to me without pausing and took a seat in one of the armchairs with his legs crossed and a steno pad open on his knee. He was wearing a white turtleneck, Australian bush jacket, and khaki slacks. Tan moccasins gleamed softly on his feet. I counted through the days of the week and wondered if it was Casual Friday.

"Have a seat, Mr. Walker," Jillian Raider said.

"Thanks, I'll stand. I sat all last night."

She frowned at that. The armchairs were lower than the padded white swivel behind the desk and she'd lost her edge. She remained standing.

"First of all, it may relieve you to know that as of ten minutes ago Mrs. Strangeways' condition is officially listed as fair. Her doctors hope to release her in a week."

"It's good to be young and strong," I said.

"Hospitals are rigid when it comes to language. They never use critical when they mean serious, nor fair when they mean good. Can you see where this is going?"

"I've worked for more lawyers than the plea bargain, Mrs. Raider. You're going to have to come out and say it."

She lifted a sheet of typewritten bond from the desk, but she didn't look at it. " 'I shall pay the sum of one million dollars to the man who produces her'—*her* meaning Laurel Strangeways—'alive and in good condition.' Etcetera, etcetera, signed Gordon Strangeways. You're aware of this document." It wasn't a question.

"I was with him when he dictated it."

"*Good condition.* The terms are specific. As you know, Mrs. Strangeways was critical when she arrived in the emergency room; a public venue which I think we can assume qualifies as a place of delivery. Translation: No million dollars." She laid down the sheet.

"Mr. Strangeways might have something to say about that."

"He won't have much to say about anything for a while. He's preoccupied at present. If at some future date he should decide to reward you regardless of the language in his letter of intent, the check will not be honored. I have access to all his accounts."

"That ought to keep you out of Wal-Mart."

"It might have been different had you not placed Mrs. Strangeways in the path of danger. Extortion and homicide are police matters."

"Strangeways said no police. But go on. You're paying the rent."

She smiled then. It wasn't by any stretch of the imagination a dent in her armor. "Let's not be enemies. I have another job for you. It won't pay a million, but I suspect you haven't the temperament for riches. It will pay your bills for a few months."

I said, "I don't know where the Hours of the Virgin is."

That rattled her right down to the carpet. She reached up and curled a coppery tendril behind her right ear. "The police in Dearborn Heights said you told Ben Broderick you knew where to get it."

"So his last name was Broderick. I didn't know that." I scooped one of my last two cigarettes out of the foil and held it up. She hesitated, then nodded at William, who put down his steno pad and went out through the trick door. He returned an instant later carrying a retro ashtray made of burnished steel with a lighter built into the center. He spun the wheel under my nose. I blew smoke at the ceiling and accepted the tray. "I was stalling for our lives, Mrs. Strangeways' and mine," I said. "I can look for it, if you like. I charge five hundred a day and expenses."

"I was thinking of offering a finder's fee of ten percent of the original estimate of a hundred thousand dollars. If you do know where it is and are hoping to sell it for more, you'll be in prison before you can spend a dime. The manuscript belongs to the British government."

"That's why I can't turn it over to you even if I find it. It would have to go to the ambassador from the U.K., or the State Department, or the DIA, which has a better shot at an appointment with either one. If as a citizen concerned that national treasures are returned to the nations that treasure them you're hiring me to recover the Hours, I can save you the couple of hundred dollars it would cost you to fill in another investigator on the background. Anything else would bend my license to the breaking point."

"I doubt that. Based on what I've seen, it's made of latex." She walked to the window and looked out. Then she turned back. The blazer was unlined and the light silhouetted her bust. She would be the kind that worked out at Bally's three times a week between the office and the cigar bar. "I might double the finder's fee. There's no telling what those pages would bring at an underground auction."

I looked at William, rapidly scratching Gregg on his pad. I set the ashtray on the glass desk and walked over to his corner. "May I see that? I want to make sure you're getting my answers right."

He looked at Raider, but before she could signal or say anything I snatched the pad out of his hand and tore off the top sheet. I gave him back the rest of it.

"That doesn't mean anything," the lawyer said. "Any judge would throw it out."

"Any judge except Strangeways. Does he know what you're up to?" I looked at the hen tracks on the ruled sheet. They didn't mean anything to me, but I'd flunked secretarial school. I folded it and put it in an inside breast pocket.

"I said he was preoccupied. When he's had a chance to think he'll agree with the decision."

"Were you planning to sell him the Hours or present it to him as a gift? That's what Laurel wanted to do, Ben

too. Everybody wants Mr. Strangeways to have that manuscript. I wonder if anybody has bothered to ask him if
he wants it."

"He was willing to part with a million to get back his
trampy wife, as if she'd stay afterward. He ought to be
willing to offer the same price for the Hours. Oh, for
God's sake, William, stop writing! You can go."

He was up and gone in ten seconds, like a bird star-
tled off a telephone wire. The velvet door closed behind
him.

Jillian Raider's gray eyes were bleak in her taut white
face. "I've held Gordon's cold-fish hand for fifteen years.
I fought the same fight five times from scratch: district
court, appellate, State Supreme, federal appeals, U.S.
Supreme Court, each time against a different prosecutor,
like a punch-drunk boxer facing fresh new opponents. I
won. I established a precedent that shouldn't have had to
have been established at all—that the First Amendment is
for everyone, regardless of what he does with it. In the
process I made Gordon a billionaire. He could have
brushed a million my way as easily as flicking lint off his
sleeve. Instead he offered it to get back that teenage
Bayou bride, and she doesn't even *want* to come back.
He can do whatever he likes with the damn manuscript
once he has it, lock it up in his basement or return it to
the Brits and get himself knighted. But he can pay me a
million dollars for the privilege."

My pager beeped. I turned it off and asked if there was
a telephone I could use.

"There are pay phones on the ground floor. You can
use one on your way out." She turned on the intercom.
"William, escort Mr. Walker back to reception."

I said, "I'll find it. I'm a detective."

Waiting for the elevator I took out the fold of steno paper and looked at it. I'd send it to Strangeways in the same envelope with Laurel's other earring and an explanation. Someone might be able to read it.

I watched the numbers change as I glided down in the car, but I was seeing Laurel Strangeways' hospital room, her husband sitting on his electric scooter beside the bed. You can get a lot of talking done under those circumstances, if you didn't mind health-care personnel getting an earful. I figured I'd read their decision in the tabloids.

In the ground-floor lobby I slotted some change and called my service.

"Mr. Walker, I have a Mr. Earl North on the line. Will you take the call?"

32

There were no official cars parked under the single security light in the lot of That Touch of Venus. I drew up next to a 1978 Dodge Club Cab pickup rubbed down to primer paint everywhere except for a four-square-inch patch of white on the hood, got out, and pushed the button. Hearing the chimes ring inside the building I was pretty sure it would be a long time before I could listen to Frankie Avalon without smelling blood and burnt gunpowder.

When the net curtain stirred I made sure I was standing too close to the door for my face to be seen. When the door opened and the little Korean girl with the painted features saw me, I wedged my foot into the

space and leaned with my shoulder until she gave up trying to push it shut. I went in past her and walked down
the linoleum hall toward the brightly lit kitchen. The
older Asian woman poked her head out of one of the
curtained doorways to watch me with no expression at
all on her face. She'd traded the old pink bathrobe for a
cobalt-blue kimono with peacocks printed on it.

The kitchen was unoccupied except for a fresh pot of
cabbage cooking on the stove. I opened the flatware
drawer and lifted out the divided tray. My heart missed
a beat when I peeled aside the top page of the newspaper lining the drawer and saw only more newspaper. But
the first page of the Hours of the Virgin was under the
second sheet, gleaming gold and blue on a cracked yellow surface that was already old when the *Santa Maria*
left its slip. I slid it into the cheap red cardboard folder
I'd bought at Office Max, stuck it under my arm, and
turned to the overhead cupboard. The cereal box was
where I'd left it. So was the .32. I blew the crumbs out
of the action and dropped it into my overcoat pocket.
The girl and the woman were standing in the open door-
way when I turned around, and I saw the family resemblance between them for the first time. Mother-daughter
operations are common in the trade. I didn't speak to
them on the way out. Korea would rise again before they
ran to the police with what they'd seen.

A torn fingernail of moon showed through a gauzy
break in the overcast when I got to the demolition site.
A twelve-foot board fence had been erected around the
remains of the Hotel LaSalle, but I worked two of the
boards loose without working up a sweat and slid sideways through the opening. A brimstone smell still lingered from the charges the mayor had set off.

I'd brought a battery-operated Coleman lantern, but I didn't want to use it yet in case someone saw the light and called the cops. I picked my way through the remaining rubble with my penlight and down fourteen feet of steps into the well of the basement. Power shovels and armies of workers had scooped the debris into dump trucks and carted it away, leaving a square hole lined with concrete where bottles of vintage wine had been stored in racks throughout Prohibition. Jerry Buckley might have taken a tour of the labels before he was shot down in the lobby, presumably for changing his broadcast position on the recall of Mayor Bowles on the night of the election in 1930.

I set down the lantern and walked around to work the cramps out of my muscles and listen to my footsteps bouncing back at me from the crumbling foundation. The cellar smelled of concrete dust, dry rot, and sulphur. Only a week had passed since I'd seen Merlin Gilly standing inside the fresh notch in the skyline where the building had stood for most of the century. It seemed longer. It seemed as if they could have put up a new structure in its place and used it for sixty years and knocked it down and started work on another, long enough for two or three generations of private detectives and small-change grifters to pass by. I thought if I got through this night I'd go back to the Erin Go Bar and order a Bubonic Plague and raise it in a toast to Merlin's memory.

I wouldn't, though. I'd choose an anonymous bar with no history and all the ambience of a Styrofoam cup and drink Scotch.

A nail came loose with a gasp. I switched on the lantern, adjusting the metal louvers so that the light shone down onto the floor, and stepped away from it into the shadows. I listened to my own breathing for a long time before the first scraping footstep struck the edge of the basement. A circle of yellowish light—the beam of a larger flash than the one I'd put away in a pocket—bounced over the top of the wall and found the stairs. Beyond it I saw the vague outline of a figure, black against the charcoal sky.

"Walker?"

Although he spoke quietly, the name echoed as if he'd shouted it down a canyon.

I moistened my lips. "I'm here. Turn off the flash. It's too big. Someone will see it."

"I'll break my neck."

"There's a light down here. Wait a minute for your eyes to adjust."

The circle of light vanished. After a moment he started down, reaching out with his foot to feel each step before trusting his weight to it. It seemed five minutes before he stood at the bottom. He didn't move from there. Very slowly I made out the features in the blur of his ordinary face, the banal mask the world saw when it bothered to look at Earl North. He wore a long dark coat and dark slacks and shoes, his body a blank cutout against the block wall behind him, barely illuminated in the glow of the lamplight ricocheting off the floor. Traffic swished by a dozen yards away. The downtown People Mover clattered along its circular run two stories above the pavement, its lighted windows a yellow crayon streak. The hour was early, for all the dark; some workers were still on their way home, shoppers were making their last purchases before dinner.

"You picked a lonely place to meet," North said. "I told

friends where I'd be, if you're planning to kill me." It was clear from his tone his upper lip was lifted.

"You don't have any friends."

Another silence. Then: "Did you bring it?"

"I brought it. Did you bring yours?"

Clothing rustled. He held up something wrapped in a bundle.

"How do I know that isn't last Sunday's paper?" I asked.

He fumbled with the package. His flashlight snapped on briefly. Part of an enormous capital *E* glittered, bejeweled and gilded. It matched the *L* on the page I had locked in my car. There were other pages behind it with puckered and uneven edges. When the light went back out I said, "It looks genuine enough in the dark. How's it look in the light?"

"It's the real thing. I wasn't kidding when I said the Hours is too risky to fake. Your turn."

I took the .32 out of my pocket and held it up. The flashlight snapped on and off. I felt the heat of it on my hand. Our breath steamed in the fading phosphorescence.

"How do I know that's the right gun?"

"Who else but you knew it was a Beretta?"

"My dear daughter Laurel." The lip was lifted.

"Well, you don't get to look it over until you let go of the Hours."

"You surprise me. I would've bet you wouldn't part with that gun no matter how much the manuscript was worth."

"Twenty years is a long time. You can't love the dead more than the living." I breathed sulphur. "Two questions."

"First question."

"You and Dale talked about something just before you shot him. What was it?"

"Who told you that?"

"No one who can do you any harm. Is that when you tried to buy him off?"

"I made him an offer. He took it. I said that. I had no reason to kill him."

"Then it shouldn't matter to you what I do with this gun. My guess is you offered him a good chunk. You had more than sixty thousand to spend. He knew how much you stole from your bosses at Paul Bunyan, so you couldn't poor-mouth him. All I want to know is what he said when you made the offer."

"I'll think about it. Second question."

"How'd you manage to get your hands on the Hours of the Virgin in the first place? You didn't steal it from Harold Boyette's office at Christmas like he said. He'd been fired five months by then."

"Poor Harold. He was a victim of poor timing. The priest who went to the DIA to deliver the manuscript didn't know Boyette from the Apostle Paul or that he'd been let go. He asked me for directions to Boyette's office. He had a bundle under his arm and a look on his face like he'd just robbed a bank by accident. It looked promising. I told him I was Boyette. After he left the manuscript with me I met with Harold to authenticate it. I couldn't go to anyone legitimate, or I'd have wound up with nothing except maybe a cheesy certificate of thanks with the Queen's signature. I offered him a split, but he didn't want that. He wanted to be the one who presented it to the British government and reclaim his reputation." He blew a jet of vapor and stamped his feet; the dank cold of the basement was worse than the open air at ground level. "Maybe it's the manuscript. Maybe it makes people see the light."

"Not you."

He shook his head. "Don't feel sorry for me. It's not so bad, this not having a conscience. If you're born with only one arm you don't miss the one you never had. I only got interested when he came back and offered me the gun in trade. I'm kind of nostalgic about it. I wondered what had happened to it all these years."

"I figure you got your cue from Strangeways to make up that gag about having a date with Laurel in Louisiana. You knew she was the daughter you fathered with Star LaJoie and that the gun offer came from her. After the exchange blew up at the Tomcat Theater you thought she still had the gun."

"Mistakes, I've made a few," he said. "Let's swap."

"You didn't answer my first question."

"Fuck you."

"What?"

"'Fuck you.' I'm quoting. That's what your dear old dumb dead dick buddy Dale said when I offered him twenty thousand to let me alone."

I filled my lungs with the clear stinging January cold and let it out in a thick cloud. Then I spun the pistol in an old-time border roll and held it out butt first. He extended the bundle. We reached out simultaneously with our free hands. As his fingers closed on the .32's butt he dropped the bundle.

I almost stooped to pick it up. I caught myself, but for a chair-warmer he was fast. I heard metal slide against metal, punctuated by a full stop of a snap. They were the noises made by a fresh clip sliding into the handle of a pistol and a shell snapping into the chamber.

"Let it sit. I'll pick it up after you leave."

I looked into the muzzle of the .32 and did nothing.

"I knew you were too smart to hand me a loaded gun," he said. "I bought an extra clip from the same back room of the same store where I bought the gun. I think it was even the same salesman. Funny how all the good restaurants have left the city while the illegal weapons merchants keep prospering. Maybe it's cause and effect. We accountants spend a lot of time studying that kind of thing. Now take your gun out and drop it at my feet."

The pistol was a rock in his hand. I reached slowly under my coat, slid the Smith & Wesson out of its holster between my thumb and forefinger, and bent to lay it atop the bundle containing the Hours of the Virgin. Then I straightened again and backed away.

"I'm greedy," North said, "but you knew that. I wanted the gun *and* the manuscript. If you thought I was going to settle for just one or the other you're just as dumb as your partner."

"I'm dumb." I nodded. "I soaked up a little culture there for a while, but it'll drip out. Don't you want the first page? It's in my car."

"That old wreck of a Cutlass? You'd put a Rembrandt in a J. C. Penney safe. Give me the keys." He snapped the fingers of his free hand.

I reached into my other coat pocket and brought out the hard heavy object that had been slapping my leg ever since I got out of the car. The light from the Coleman lantern painted a stripe along the oily blue-black barrel of Dale Leopold's .45.

North was one fast office drudge. The big gun had barely cleared my pocket when he pulled the .32's trigger.

Nothing happened.

Not even a click.

His mouth formed a round black hole in the pale blur of his face. The trigger lay flush to the back of the guard now and would have to be pried forward in order to be squeezed again, and it wouldn't work then either.

"If you thought I was going to put a pistol in your hand without removing the trigger sear first, you're as dumb as Boyette." I reached into the pocket from which I'd taken the .32, took out a plastic Ziploc bag, and shook it open. "Drop it in there."

When he obeyed, I doubled the bag around the pistol one-handed and slid it into the pocket. "I needed your prints on the gun that killed Dale," I said. "The ones you put on it before evaporated twenty years ago. There was nothing to connect you to the murder weapon until tonight."

And I hit him with the .45.

It was just a light tap along his jaw, but it dropped him like a piano. The Colt Army has a frame as heavy as an engine block; it pulled me off balance and I had to spread my feet to keep from falling on top of him. I thumbed back the hammer and waited. I had all night. That's why I'd picked a place as remote as the old LaSalle.

He was out only a few seconds. He awoke with a twitch, then pushed himself up onto his knees and looked around, as slowly as a dopey old hound coming out of a doze. When he lifted his gaze and it went up the big bore, his eyes grew as large as manholes. He pressed his lips together and tried to form a *P.* He was shaking from his head to his knees.

Just then a sour earthy stench mixed with the damp

odors of the urban underground, overpowering them. It was thick, primeval, unspeakably corrupt.

It was my signal. I placed the muzzle against Earl North's slick forehead and pressed the trigger. The pin snapped on the empty chamber.

My mouth was stretched into a rictus so tight I couldn't get the words out. So I thought them.

Bang.

You're dead.

33

"If I were you, I wouldn't be too proud about the way my job got done," John said.

I ate a mini-pretzel from the bowl and washed it down with Scotch. "Dale always said if you can't do it right, do it wrong."

"He was a rotten role model."

"He told twenty grand where to get off."

He looked around at the faux mahogany and tin advertising signs distressed to look as if they'd hung out in the weather for years. We were in the same cigar bar where I'd spoken with Merlin Gilly. "I don't know why we couldn't have this talk in my office. I keep expecting the Rough Riders to come charging through the door."

"I've had it with offices. I'm going to hang an out-of-order sign on mine and work out of my basement." I watched him shake snow off his camel-hair coat. "I guess it's still snowing."

"If you can call it snow. It looks more like gorilla turds." He sat down.

"I like January," I said. "It's the only time you can't tell Clairmount from Lake Shore Drive. Democracy in action."

"Don't you believe it. In Grosse Pointe it comes down white and stays that way. The servants come out every hour and spray it with appliance enamel. How's the cigar?"

I'd bought a package of Grenadiers in honor of Merlin, pulled twice on the first one, and parked it in the General Grant ashtray to smoke itself out. "Okay, if you can get used to the not-inhaling part. It confuses my lungs."

"You should quit."

"You never know where a thing like that will end. You might wind up with nothing left to quit."

"That statement you gave needs backup. If you get it we might not throw the Frank Murphy Hall of Justice at you for withholding evidence and tampering with a crime scene."

"It'd be worth it."

"See if you still feel that way when North walks in two years. Old crime, first offense, solid citizen. Assuming it gets that far. The jury has to buy his prints suddenly showing up on a weapon no one's seen in twenty years. Laurel Strangeways' testimony is hearsay. He might get a clean bill of health."

"I don't care. I killed him."

"You and Freud." He sat back and caught the eye of the woman bartender, the same heavily made-up blonde who had served Merlin and me. When she came over, he ordered Jack Daniel's. I tapped my glass of Scotch. She went away, disappointed again. When I'd sat down, she'd recognized me from before and came up eager to experiment with another trick drink. To hell with her, I thought. Molasses is for spreading on toast.

"Going over to visit Strangeways' wife before she leaves Henry Ford?" John asked.

I shook my head. "They've got talking to do. I'd be just somebody they met somewhere once and can't quite remember why they bothered."

"What'd they say at the DIA when you delivered the Hours?"

"I think Mr. Ruddy's beginning to warm up to me. He didn't have security throw me through a plate-glass display case. I'm getting a certificate to toss in the drawer with my army discharge papers."

"You should have turned it over to us along with North's thirty-two."

"Buy a ticket. You might check out the Goya exhibit while you're there. After that you can subpoena the manuscript and paper the police gym with it for all I care. If the Duke of Plymouth or whatever he was had bought his wife a chafing dish like any other bridegroom, there'd be two more vacant drawers in the coldroom downtown."

He drank Jack. "Like you wouldn't trade any number of Boyettes and Brodericks to nail Earl North."

"That's not how a friend talks."

"So we're friends again. What's my address?"

"Thirteen hundred Beaubien. Fifth floor."

"Go to hell, Walker."

We clinked glasses.

*   *   *

Outside the air had grown granite cold since the raw morning, slicing the descending clots of mixed rain and snow into rice-paper wafers that skidded on the air currents and folded themselves onto the Cutlass' roof and hood with a rustling whisper. They cloaked street and sidewalk blue-white, erasing sharp angles, filling potholes, and covering refuse. I left the motor to warm up while I scraped the windows, then drove away from the curb, plowing fresh twin furrows that filled in behind me; the captain of the only ship abroad on a virgin sea. The noon rush hour had come and gone.

It seemed a shame to mess up the office all over again, but I didn't cry over it. I locked the door, took out the desk drawers I seldom used, and upended them onto the square of rug. Then I sat on the floor and sorted squares and rectangles of old yellowed newsprint into a pile and dumped the rest of the stuff back into the drawers. I reached inside the cavities in the desk and rescued the crushed and accordioned flotsam that had spilled over the sides and slipped through cracks. When I was finished I had gathered enough of Dale Leopold's favorite cartoons and comic strips to fill a small anthology, the Dagwood strip on top.

I replaced the drawers, sat in the swivel, and studied each clipping. I stopped once to pour myself a drink from a bottle I'd left standing on the desk the other day, then resumed, giving each clipping its full measure of attention before moving on to the next. Probably I'd seen most of them before, but I'd forgotten many of them and I hadn't always paid attention when Dale showed me one; he was always doing it. I'd spent twice ten years pushing them around to get to something else in the drawers.

Some of them made me laugh out loud even now. Others didn't rate more than a smile, if they rated that, and were probably personal to Dale. One or two missed me completely. Humor's like that: a tailored prescription that works on different people different ways and sometimes not at all. As a profession it was almost as uncertain as sleuthing.

When I was through I drummed all the cuttings together, snapped a rubber band around them, and stuck them in the side pocket of my jacket, where they made a substantial bulge. I put away the bottle and went out, locking both doors behind me. Closed due to a death in the family.

The snow was picking up. I crawled home behind a salt truck. Rather than try to break through the berm piled up at the foot of my driveway by a plow, I left the car at the curb and waded up to the front door, soaking myself to the ankles. The living room smelled of stale tobacco smoke. I opened a window. Immediately the furnace gulped and fired and I closed the gap to two inches.

My bed was a tangle, the way I'd left it after two hours of tossing and twenty minutes of sleep. The tobacco stink was in that room too, along with the flat desperate odors of a wakeful night. I opened the almost-empty drawer in the bureau and looked inside; as if I had to, as if I didn't carry around a mental inventory of the contents. The snapshots could stay. I was casting off, not erasing. On my way out of the office waiting room I'd taken Dale's dented old hat off the peg, and now I put the cartoons in the White Owl cigar box that held his obituary and stuck the box inside the crown.

I tested the heft. It seemed insubstantial. I had a brainstorm and went through the kitchen into the garage, where one of Dale's old raincoats—he'd had a dozen in the time I knew him, kept leaving them places and snagging them on things—made itself useful protecting the lawn mower from dust. He wouldn't have minded the gasoline smell; he'd started Apollo Investigations above a garage on Woodward, and when he began to forget things and went to see a doctor he was told he'd been suffering from carbon monoxide poisoning for three years—hadn't he noticed the fumes? *Christ, Doc, this is Detroit. If I smelled petunias I'd of come to see you right away.* I wrapped the raincoat around the bundle and secured it with the belt. Hefted it. It still lacked weight.

Well, hell.

I must have caught some fumes of my own.

I tugged the .45 out from under my belt, kicked out the clip, and pocketed it. The clip was fully loaded. I hadn't bothered to pump one into the barrel when I dropped the hammer on North. I undid the bundle, put the pistol in the cigar box with the clippings, and did it back up again. Now it was heavy enough to anchor a small boat.

I cruised through the house one last time, but it was just for fun. I was satisfied I'd removed all physical traces of Dale Leopold from it and the office. I shut the bedroom window.

The drive to Jefferson Avenue was not without interest. The wet snow of the morning had frozen on the pavement, creating a hard slick base beneath the fresh powder, like glass under talcum. The Cutlass turned into a hydrofoil whenever I went around a curve or changed lanes. I snuck along at twelve miles per hour with the river on my right, gray as galvanized iron. The Windsor skyline looked like a matte painting in an old movie about King Arthur. The stuff was coming down in starched sheets.

The Belle Isle bridge was all mine. Farther down the river an ore carrier squatted low on the water, but it was something that didn't have anything to do with me or the century I was living in. The snow muffled my tires and the flakes coming down closed in around the car, flowing with it like a communion robe. They landed on the water without making a ripple, bobbed once, and dissolved. The temperature there was just above freezing. By nightfall it would drop and ice would form like candle wax along the banks.

I parked in the nearest lot, or what I assumed was one; the entire island was covered and I couldn't tell grass from asphalt, or for that matter the Scott Fountain from the Dossin Museum. Mine was the only car in sight. I felt like a French explorer.

Like a lot of Detroiters I almost never visit that oblong oasis on the watery border between the United States and the Dominion of Canada. When I do, it always seems to be winter. A few years back I had stood ankle-deep in snow on the softball field and watched three men die, their blood staining the white like that of a sacrificed lamb. It occurred to me that I had witnessed more than my share of that kind of thing, although probably not as much as Dale. No wonder he liked the comics.

I walked down to the beach. The cold was getting to me now through my thin shoes and saturated trousers. The fabric was frozen stiff as armor below the knees. The wind blew in gusts, kicking up pale clouds that settled into stationary waves in the intervals. The place didn't look anything like it had in summer, the one time Dale and I came to the island together.

People fish this river, kid. The sewers empty into it and so do the coke ovens at the plants. If you dip a toe in it the nail turns black and falls off in three days, but they eat the fish and somehow they live to come back and fish it again. I used to think they were too hungry to care. But it ain't the fish. The French paddled up that channel, the Indians too. Soldiers crossed it in bateaux and bootleggers in their big-ass black sedans when it froze solid. The whole history of the city's here, and will be long after they finish tearing down the best buildings and burning the rest. You can lay me down here too if you ever get a minute. Let the fish nibble my ears and swim up to the hooks and get themselves caught and bring back part of me with 'em. A hole in the ground's okay for some people. Not me. Nobody ever comes back from a hole in the ground.

Well, he wasn't in a hole in the ground. His ashes were in an overpriced urn in his sister's living room in Toledo and she and I weren't on speaking terms because she thought I was the reason he didn't throw over detective work and join her husband in the cement business. She may have been partly right, although Dale had told me the only thing that kept him from going into partnership with his brother-in-law was that he was the kind of twerp who would marry a woman like Dale's sister. Anyway he wasn't coming back from that urn either. I had all of his mortal baggage under my arm.

"Heads up, Dale."

I gave the bundle a football toss. I put teeth in it. It made a long loop, splashed, pitched twice, rolled over like a ship in a Viking funeral, and slid under the surface, as gone as virtue.